goodbye

Magnolia

a
CORNERSTONE
novel

KRISTA NOORMAN

BOOKS by KRISTA NOORMAN

Advance Praise
for *Goodbye, Magnolia*

"Brilliantly executed and kept me turning pages well into the night. Goodbye, Magnolia is a true gem in my book. I was hooked from the first page."

Laura Wilson, Blue Eye Books

"It was an emotional read ... laughter, sadness, happiness, and a lot of 'awww' moments. A wonderful story that will take readers on a journey of love, faith and perseverance."

Dianne Olczak, Launch Team member

"I couldn't help but think about Elizabeth and Darcy [from Jane Austen's Pride & Prejudice] ... I could see a picture of the classic here."

A.M. Heath, author of the *Ancient Words series*

"Anyone who has been through a tough breakup can relate to this story, but so can anyone who has found the love of their life. It truly is a beautifully written love story."

Heather Seifert, Launch Team member

"I feel like everyone can relate to someone in the book in some way. I am kind of sad I finished it in one day because I feel like the characters became people I knew and now they are gone."

Nicole Mantooth, Random Ramblings Blog

"Goodbye, Magnolia was such a fun book to read! I loved the flow and the sweet relationship between Maggie and Sarah. I felt like they were MY friends. The plot was engaging, and it was hard for me to put the book down!"

Carrie Orr, Launch Team member

For Jacob.
He knows why.

October 31, 1995
A Beginning

"Can I take your picture?"

They were the first words he ever spoke to her.

Maggie stared up into hazel eyes, clearly startled. "Excuse me?"

"For the assignment," he replied with a flirty grin.

The assignment given by Professor Wilkins, the instructor of their photography class, was to pair up and photograph each other using only natural light at a location around campus.

But *he* was the last person she wanted to partner with.

She glanced around the room and realized the other students had already chosen their partners.

"I guess," she reluctantly agreed.

Simon Walker was handsome and charming, immediately catching the eye of her roommate, Emma—the cute, petite one. His easygoing personality made him the friend of many, including her other roommate Michelle—the tall, athletic one. But there was something about him, an arrogance that was off-putting to Maggie. She often wondered if she was the only person on campus who disliked him, because it seemed every girl she knew was infatuated, and every guy wanted to be his best friend.

Maggie and Simon walked together from the Fine Arts building toward their assigned location—Miller Library. The air was brisk as they walked along the sidewalk lined with trees, half of which had already dropped their vibrant yellow and red leaves.

"You're Michelle's roommate," he stated. "Maggie, right?"

"Yeah. Maggie James." She had no idea he even knew who she was. They had been in class for two months, but he had never once acknowledged her existence.

"I'm Simon." He held his hand out to shake hers.

She hesitantly shook it. "I know who you are."

"What's with the Canon?" Simon asked.

"What do you mean?"

He pointed at the camera hanging around her neck. "Your camera."

She looked down at her Canon brand camera. It was new, purchased specifically for the class. Turning it over in her hands, she examined the lens and the camera body. Nothing appeared to be wrong with it.

"Huh?" She was confused.

"Why'd you go with a Canon?" he asked.

She noticed the shiny new Nikon camera with the expensive zoom lens in his hands. "What difference does it make? They both do the same thing, right?"

Simon shook his head, and his nut brown hair fell over his right eye. "Nikon is by far superior to Canon." He ran his fingers through his hair, smoothing it back into place.

Maggie was annoyed. "In what way?"

"Better lenses, faster focus—"

"Says who?" *Know-it-all.*

"My uncle's a photographer," he informed her. "He's done his research."

She rolled her eyes at his condescending tone. "Can we just get this over with?"

"OK." He seemed taken aback, as if no girl had ever been this cold to him before.

They walked into the library and found a bright spot near a wall of windows with light streaming in.

Simon slid a chair into position. "Sit here," he commanded.

She groaned inwardly as she put her camera on a nearby table and sat down in the chair. If she had known she would be the subject of a photograph, she might have worn something nicer than a hooded grey Cornerstone College sweatshirt.

He approached and smoothed a few of her sandy blonde hairs.

It was an awkward moment, and she wished she had chosen to wear her hair back in a clip rather than down.

He touched her chin and turned her head toward the window.

She pulled away from his touch. "What are you doing?"

"Don't move. The light is perfect on your face right now."

Maggie was completely uncomfortable. She hated being in front of the camera, but having Simon photograph her only made it worse. Every muscle in her body felt stiff and unnatural.

Simon crouched down and peeked through his camera. He shook his head, clearly exasperated, and looked up at her. "You need to relax."

"I hate having my picture taken."

"Why?" He looked puzzled.

She shrugged her shoulders. "I'm not very photogenic."

Simon let out a little laugh. "I don't believe that at all." He moved closer, still crouched, and examined her face.

Maggie could tell he wasn't really seeing her as a person, but as the subject of his photograph.

"You're not very good at this," she blurted.

He suddenly looked at Maggie the person. "Not good at what?"

"Making your subject feel comfortable in front of the camera."

His mouth fell open, and he stared at her in disbelief. "Maybe it's just you."

Maggie's eyes narrowed, and she crossed her arms. "Maybe I need a different partner."

He stood and lifted his arms in surrender. "Be my guest."

She shook her head. "It's too late now, and I'm not getting an incomplete on this."

"Fine," he grumbled. "Then relax."

She looked at him stone-faced, her arms still crossed, as he snapped a couple shots.

"Man, you're intense. Don't you ever smile?"

She refused to smile for him and kept her bright green eyes focused on his camera lens.

"I feel like you're about to melt me with laser beams from your eyes or something."

3

Maggie's face broke into a smile at his ridiculous comment.

Simon pressed the shutter release on the camera. "There it is." He looked over the camera and gave her a cocky grin.

She abruptly stood up. "OK, your turn."

They walked across the library to another wall of windows, and Maggie pointed to one of the large reading chairs.

Simon plopped down, leaned forward, and rested his elbows on his knees with hands clasped together. He was clearly as comfortable in front of the camera as he was behind it, which annoyed her immensely. It also bothered her how great he looked in a simple green henley and jeans. She shoved the thought from her mind. He looked at her with intense hazel eyes, brought out by the color of his shirt. She wished she could force away the warmth in her cheeks. She didn't want him to know he had any effect on her at all.

Maggie breathed in and out slowly as she looked through her camera's viewfinder. She begrudgingly took a few shots, but made a face, not satisfied with what she was seeing.

"What? Is this not intense enough for you?" he teased.

"Don't look at the camera."

He gave her a look of confusion. "Isn't that what we were assigned to do?"

"Yeah, but I like my pictures to be candid. More natural, like you don't know the camera's here."

"But I *do* know the camera's here." He looked thoughtful for a moment. "How do I do candid?"

"You need to relax." She gave him a sarcastic look as she echoed his earlier statement.

He grinned at her and nodded.

"I don't know. Pretend I'm not taking your picture or something." She lifted the camera again.

"Like how?" He shrugged his shoulders.

"Just look around."

"Can I still talk to you?"

"Whatever." She wished this was over already.

"OK." He sat up a little and looked directly at her. "Are you free tonight?"

She looked over the top of her camera in astonishment.

"What? I'm being candid." He had a little twinkle in his eye.

"That's a little *too* candid." She peeked through the viewfinder on her camera once more.

He stared directly into her lens. "We're having a costume party at the dorm. You should come."

Maggie glared up at him. "No, thanks."

All she could think about was Emma, who had been dating Simon since early in the semester. Sweet Emma, who had opened her heart to him. Yet here he was, very obviously flirting with her behind Emma's back. She didn't care if she *was* the only girl on campus who didn't like Simon. Her first impression of him had been dead on. Player, womanizer, heartbreaker—take your pick. They all described Simon Walker to a T.

"Michelle will be there." As if anything he said could convince her to come.

She took another look through the camera. "Well, good. Then you can hit on her instead."

Simon looked out the window as he laughed, a little glint in his eye.

Click!

"There it is," Maggie stated confidently.

He gave her a crooked, amused grin. Even his eyes seemed to smile. "You're good."

Maggie stood and gathered her things.

Simon stepped close and put his arm around her, pulling her against his side. "That was fun. We should do it again sometime."

She wiggled out from under his arm.

He took two steps away, then hesitated. "Hey."

Maggie looked over at him.

"It was nice meeting you, Maggie." That adorable grin of his was back again.

She didn't reply, just watched him stroll away, stopping to talk to—or rather flirt with—two girls before he walked out.

Her mind was made up.

Simon Walker wasn't worth her time—or anyone else's for that matter.

December 13, 2008

Katherine & Edward

$\mathcal{T}$he chapel lights were dim. Candle lanterns hung from hooks attached to every other pew, lighting the aisle. The stage was bright with candles, and strings of clear lights peeked through the white tulle draped along the walls. Clusters of poinsettias were arranged along the edge of the steps with one large arrangement center stage. And there, behind the flowers, flanked by their bridal party, stood the bride and groom. They faced each other, hands held, in the midst of their vows.

"I, Katherine, take you, Edward, to be my husband. For richer, for poorer, in sickness and in health." Katherine paused as she gazed at Edward with tear-filled eyes. "Until death do us part." A tear slipped down her cheek.

Edward reached up and tenderly brushed it away.

"By the power vested in me by the State of Michigan, I now pronounce you husband and wife."

They both just stood there smiling at each other.

"Ed," the pastor said with a wink. "You may now kiss the bride."

Crouched down at the front of the aisle, Maggie pressed the button on her camera and heard the familiar click as the shutter released, capturing forever in time the first kiss of Mr. and Mrs. Edward Williams.

The room suddenly filled with the applause of their guests.

Maggie softly sighed as she stood and quickly made her way to the back of the aisle to capture Katherine and Edward's recessional. The applause continued as the beaming couple departed, smiling from ear to ear. She followed them into the foyer and snapped a few pictures of their first moments as husband and wife.

"You are so beautiful," Edward whispered into his wife's ear just loud enough for Maggie to overhear him.

"I love you so much," replied Katherine.

They kissed, and Maggie sighed again as she took a few more photographs. *So sweet.* Her heart began to ache, but she pushed it down inside as she always did.

The bridal party filed into the room and spent the next few minutes hugging, congratulating, and organizing themselves for the receiving line.

Maggie glanced around the room. As a wedding photographer, she had learned the art of watching people and capturing moments when nobody noticed she was photographing them. This was her gift and one of the reasons couples sought her out for their weddings.

A little girl with blonde ringlets wearing a red velvet dress stood just inside the sanctuary doors waiting with her parents. Maggie watched as she peeked around her mother's leg and stared up at the bride. It was as if she couldn't take her eyes off of this beautiful woman in the flowing white gown. The girl snuck away from her mother's side, walked shyly over to Katherine, and tugged on the side of her dress.

"Hi, sweetie." Katherine bent down and gave the sweet child a kiss and a hug.

Click. Click. Click.

Maggie smiled to herself, proud of the moment she had captured.

"Hey, Mags." Sarah Scott, Maggie's assistant, approached carrying their coats in one hand, a backup camera in the other, and a camera bag with more equipment slung over her shoulder. She handed Maggie a business card. "The videographer gave me this right after he asked if I come here often." She shook her head in disbelief. "Who uses that line anymore?"

Maggie rolled her eyes and read his name from the card. "Apparently Rob does."

She glanced over at Sarah, admiring her long brown hair twisted neatly on the back of her head. She looked as perfect as she had that morning when they left for the wedding. Maggie, on the other hand, looked a mess. She had spent an hour with the bridal party before the ceremony to get all the posed pictures out of the way. Her creative style of shooting had her climbing on things and lying on the ground to get artistic angles and unique photos, which left her looking disheveled by the time the ceremony rolled around. She tucked a loose hair behind her ear, tightened her ponytail, and went back to scanning the crowd.

"Sarah, could you go outside and get a few shots of the guests waiting to throw the rice?"

"They don't throw rice anymore." Sarah laid everything on a nearby bench and slipped her coat on. "Birds eat it and it expands in their stomachs and makes them explode." She pulled her gloves from her coat pocket and put them on.

"Is that true?" Maggie looked horrified.

"I have no idea." Sarah laughed out loud.

Maggie glanced over just in time to catch a shot of Katherine's grandfather giving her a kiss.

"Aw, that was a good one." Sarah gathered their things and moved toward the exit.

The winter chill breezed into the foyer as Sarah opened the door.

With two weeks until Christmas, this wedding had Maggie in a festive holiday mood. The reception hall was filled with more poinsettias and twinkly white lights everywhere. A large, red stocking hung next to the gift table for guests to place cards. Christmas trees decorated with sparkly, white snowflake ornaments lined the walls, and packages wrapped in shiny red and gold were the centerpiece of each table. The wedding cake was frosted white and covered in snowflakes made of fondant. The sugar crystals sprinkled over each tier gave the look of glittery snow, and red roses were placed here and there for a touch of color.

A pianist sat at the large grand piano in one corner of the dance floor playing Christmas carols and taking holiday song requests. The bridal party was nearly finished singing their rendition of "Rudolph the Red-Nosed Reindeer" when the D.J. interrupted to announce that it was snowing. The beginning of December had been unusually warm, and this was the first real cold spell thus far. No snow had been in the forecast, so it was like a little wedding miracle.

Maggie bundled up and followed the bridal party outside. She photographed Katherine and Edward dancing on the terrace with the snow falling softly around them. It was a beautiful moment.

A sudden chill ran up her spine—one that had nothing to do with the cold outside—and she had the overwhelming feeling someone was watching her. Her eyes scanned the crowd outside, but no one appeared to be looking in her direction. She pushed the feeling aside and went back to shooting photos.

The groomsmen were having a snowball fight, though there wasn't much snow yet. A ball of slush abruptly hit her arm.

"Sorry," one of the guys called.

She waved her hand at him and took that as her cue to head inside so her equipment didn't get soaked. It was warm inside the reception hall, but she couldn't shake the chill.

After more pictures of guests dancing, the cake cutting, and the bouquet toss, Maggie and Sarah bid farewell to the couple and their families. While Sarah headed outside to warm up the car for their long ride home, Maggie went to the lobby to pack up the equipment.

"Canon? Really?"

A chill went up her spine again. It was a familiar voice, one she had not heard in a very long time.

She glanced over to see Simon Walker staring down at her. He was dressed in a dark suit with a festive red Christmas tie and carrying a camera bag of his own.

"This is my wedding, Walker. Are you stalking me?" She was annoyed to see him, especially so far from home. It was not uncommon to see him working around the Grand Rapids area, but they were all the way across the state near Detroit. *What are the odds?*

He put his arm around her shoulder and gave her a squeeze. "I missed you, too."

Maggie rolled her eyes as she shrugged away and went back to securing her camera in its place in her bag.

"It's been a while. How are you?" he asked warmly.

She could feel his eyes on her, and she was suddenly as uncomfortable as the day he photographed her in the library.

Maggie looked up and raised her eyebrow at him. "What are you doing here?"

"I was shooting a wedding in the other banquet room." He motioned toward the room at the end of the hallway.

"How was it?" she asked—not really interested, but making conversation until she could get the rest of her equipment packed up.

"I was amazing, as usual," he joked.

She zipped her bag and slipped her arm through the shoulder strap, lifting it from the table. "I meant the wedding." She glanced out the door and noticed Sarah sitting in the car waiting for her.

Simon shrugged. "Nice couple. Great party. Drunk bridesmaids. What could be better than that?" He laughed out loud, probably thinking he was amusing.

Maggie closed her eyes and shook her head. This conversation was over.

"We should get a drink sometime. I have something I'd like to talk to you about."

"Gotta go." She turned on her heel and walked away.

"See ya, Canon."

She groaned. When he called her that, it was like fingernails on a chalkboard. With a name like Margaret, she'd had no shortage of nicknames over the years—Maggie, Mags, Meg, Meggie, Magpie—but Canon was by far the most annoying nickname anyone had ever given her.

She pushed through the door, walked as fast as she could to the driver's side, and jerked the door open.

"Who was that you were talking to?" Sarah asked.

"The devil." She carefully dropped her bag onto the floor behind Sarah's seat.

"Oh, my." Sarah laughed. "Does the devil have a name?"

"Simon Walker," she grumbled as she climbed in and put her seatbelt on.

"So, that's Simon Walker."

Simon's name had been mentioned in their circle of wedding photographer friends many times before.

Sarah took another look inside, where he stood talking with a man in a tuxedo. "He's hot."

Maggie's head snapped in her direction. "Seriously?"

"Well, look at him." Sarah nodded toward the building.

"I've seen him." She shifted the car into gear and proceeded slowly into the slippery parking lot then onto the road for their two-hour journey home.

"So remind me again how you know him."

Maggie sighed. "Do I have to?"

Sarah raised an eyebrow at her.

"We went to college together, hung out with some of the same people, had a bunch of photography classes together."

"You were friends?" Sarah asked.

"Not even." She screwed up her face.

"Why not?"

"He's a jerk. Totally full of himself. And he won't hesitate to tell you all about his *amazing* business and his *awesome* clients and how *incredibly talented* he is."

"Tell me how you really feel." Sarah chuckled.

"When I started photographing weddings, he would call me up and try to give me advice, like he was the expert. We took the exact same classes." She shivered at the thought of those uncomfortable conversations. "And he would constantly tell me how superior his Nikon was."

"I used to have a Nikon," Sarah interjected. "They're really nice cameras."

Maggie gave her the evil eye.

"So that's it?" asked Sarah. "That's the reason he's the devil? Because he shoots with a Nikon?"

"Pretty much." She laughed.

Sarah stared at her, waiting for more.

"OK, that's not the only reason." Maggie confessed. "He dated my roommate, Emma, in college. She really liked him. A lot. And she thought they were getting serious, but she found out he was dating another girl in our dorm at the same time. He totally crushed her. I can't tell you how many nights I sat with her while she cried over him. And he never really apologized for it. He just kind of blew her off and stopped calling."

Sarah shook her head. "Wow!"

Maggie nodded. "And he had the nerve to ask me out the day we met, even though he was dating Emma at the time."

"He *is* a jerk."

"I know, right?"

December 15, 2008
The Proposal

*t*he warm glow of sunrise lit the streets of Hastings as Maggie drove into town. She traveled along State Street toward downtown, passing the big brick courthouse with its clock tower reading nearly eight o'clock. The old nativity scene was set up on the courthouse lawn as it had been every year for as long as she could remember, and the surrounding pine trees were decorated with colorful Christmas lights. She noticed the sign that read "Holly Trolley Rides Here". The red and green trolley came out every December for tours of the holiday light displays around town. The streets were all decked out for Christmas with holiday banners and wreaths hanging on all the light posts.

Maggie looked over at the movie theater to see what was playing in case Sarah wanted to see something later in the week. The marquee read: *Twilight*, *Four Christmases*, and *The Day the Earth Stood Still*.

The snow that had fallen overnight left the sidewalks blanketed. Only a few shops were open at this early hour, their owners outside shoveling, sweeping, and tossing salt.

As she braked for the stop sign at Church Street, she glanced over at Stevens Printing. The owner, Dave Stevens, was sweeping the snow off the stoop in front of his shop. Maggie tapped her horn, and he looked up with a smile and a wave. She waved back and drove on through town.

At Jefferson Street, she pulled into her usual parking space beside her office building and yanked on the emergency brake since it was a bit of an incline.

Maggie looked both ways, though the street was pretty much empty at this hour, and crossed over to the local coffee shop, State Grounds.

"Mornin', Maggie." Bill, the owner, handed her a warm cinnamon muffin and a newspaper.

She smiled at him. "You know me well."

Bill and his sister, Cindy, had opened the coffee shop right around the same time Maggie started her photography business. It had quickly become one of her favorite spots in town, not only for the tasty coffee, but because of the warm environment and friendship she had with Bill and Cindy. All of them had attended school in nearby Middleville. Cindy was a few years ahead of Maggie in school, while Bill graduated with her younger brother, Tom.

Maggie walked over to The Wall of Mugs—rows and rows of coffee mugs hung on pegs, all painted with the names of regular customers. She grabbed the one that read "Mags".

"How was your weekend?" She laid the muffin and paper on the counter and helped herself to a cup of the house blend.

"Very good," Bill replied. "We had a couple local singers perform on Saturday night." He leaned forward on his elbows, resting his goateed chin on one of his fists, giving her his full attention. "Thought you might stop by. It was quite the crowd in here."

"Oh, I'm so sad I missed it. It was a wedding weekend for me."

"I didn't think you did weddings in the winter."

"It's the off season, but I do shoot a few now and then. Gotta pay the bills."

Bill chuckled and his black-rimmed hipster glasses slipped down on his nose. He pushed them up as he took her money.

"Hi, Maggie." Cindy emerged from the back of the shop wearing hipster glasses of her own. Her short hair, identical in color to her brother's auburn curls, peeked out from under a black beret.

"Hey, Cindy."

"We missed you Saturday."

"I know. I had a wedding. It was a pretty Christmas theme."

"That sounds rad. We just finished decorating the other day." She made air quotes when she said *decorating*, nodding in the direction of the sparse silver garland and red bows around the window fronts.

Maggie laughed at the sight.

"Not really my forte," Cindy admitted with a wink.

The bells on the door jingled as Hank Sanders, the local sheriff, strode through the door.

"Mornin'," he said with a smile.

"Mornin', Hank," Bill greeted him.

Hank grabbed his mug and filled it up.

"Morning, Maggie." Hank handed Bill a buck and some change.

"How are you, Hank?" she asked.

"Can't complain. How's business goin'?"

"It's going very well, thanks. How's Janet? I haven't seen her in so long."

The tall, lanky man with the shiny bald head glanced down at her. "You'll just have to come back to church. We're there every Sunday. Everyone misses you."

Maggie nodded uncomfortably. "I work most Sundays," she mumbled.

He took a sip of his coffee.

After a few awkward moments, she glanced down at her watch. "Speaking of work, I guess I should get to it."

Maggie said her goodbyes and stepped out onto the sidewalk. She looked across the street at her cute storefront all decorated up for the holidays with twinkly lights and fluffy pine garland. The building was one of the older brick buildings in town, and she loved its small town charm. Above the door hung a large wooden sign, which read "Magnolia Photography", with a single white magnolia as her logo.

She walked to the shop, unlocked the front door, and let herself in. The main room was set up as a meeting space for potential clients to look at albums and talk about their weddings. Along the original exposed brick walls were large canvas prints of wedding couples, flowers, and wedding decorations. There were a few portraits of families, children, and babies, but the majority of Maggie's work was in weddings.

The room looked like a Pottery Barn ad with a heavy leather sofa and chair, pink and chocolate brown patterned pillows to match her business colors, wainscoting on the walls, and flower-filled vases scattered about the room. In the center of the meeting area was a large square coffee table with wedding albums, coffee table books, and a few popular bridal magazines spread across its surface.

Next to the sofa was an old wingback chair Maggie had found at an antique store and reupholstered in a pretty fabric that coordinated with the pillows. It was her favorite chair, and Sarah always teased that it was her throne since she sat there for almost every meeting.

Toward the back of the room was a solid wooden desk for Sarah, who also happened to be her office manager. Behind the desk, white french doors opened into Maggie's office, where she spent many hours at the computer working on photos. It was definitely an upgrade from the home office she used to have in her tiny apartment. Back then, she would meet people at the coffee shop because she didn't have a proper meeting space. Her shop wasn't set up as a traditional studio space with lighting and backdrops, because she mostly worked at weddings and her photo shoots were all done in natural light. It simply served as a workplace and the meeting space she had always wanted.

Maggie stepped through the french doors and set the coffee mug and muffin on her desk. She flipped on the light and powered up her iMac. It was just after eight o'clock, which meant she would have almost an hour of peace and quiet before Sarah arrived to take over the office.

Leaning back in her chair, she flipped through Sunday's Grand Rapids Press to find the wedding announcements. It made her happy to read each couple's story and imagine all the moments of their wedding day. On her way to the announcements, she came across a picture of David Hartman, the governor of Michigan, with his wife, Susan, and daughter, Lacey. The article was about a recent trip the governor took with his family, not something that usually interested her, but the picture caught her attention. Standing next to Lacey was a handsome young man. "George Summers" the caption read. She skimmed through the article and discovered that George was Lacey's beau and the son of Senator John Summers of Connecticut. They were a nice looking couple, and Maggie found herself wondering what it would be like to shoot the wedding of such a high profile couple.

She turned a few more pages and smiled when she saw Becky and John, one of her upcoming weddings, in the engagement section. They used one of the engagement photos Maggie had taken in their announcement. It always felt good to see her work in print. She found scissors in her desk drawer, snipped the announcement from the paper, and attached it to her bulletin board.

The wedding section had only one wedding featured. When she noticed it was photographed by Simon, she tossed the paper in the trash and got to work on the pictures from the weekend's wedding. She loaded the nearly two-thousand photos she had taken into her computer and went about backing them up on an external hard drive for safe keeping.

The familiar sound of a key in the door alerted her to Sarah's arrival. She heard the clicking of heels across the wood floor.

Sarah peeked her head into Maggie's office. "Working hard, as usual?" She grinned, then went about her business of tidying up the desk, checking messages, and answering general office emails, all to the tune of the local radio station, WBCH, which was now playing Christmas music 24/7.

At nine o'clock, she unlocked the front door and flipped on the lights.

"What's on the agenda for today?" Maggie stepped out of her office, knowing it was going to be a slow day.

Sarah jiggled her mouse and brought up the calendar program. "Lunch with DeDe at County Seat. Can I come?"

"Of course."

"I love that girl."

DeDe Rosenberg was a friend and wedding coordinator from Hastings with her office based in Grand Rapids. She was always in the know about everything going on in the wedding world as well as in their small town.

The phone rang then, and Sarah answered. "Magnolia Photography." She screwed up her face. "One moment please." She pressed the hold button and looked over at Maggie. "It's for you."

Maggie held out her hand to take the phone from Sarah.

Sarah clutched it tightly against her chest, refusing to give it up. "Who is it?"

"If I tell you, you probably won't want to take the call anyway."

Maggie raised her eyebrow. "Who?"

"The devil," Sarah revealed.

"What does *he* want?"

Sarah shrugged.

Maggie shook her head. "Tell him I'm unavailable and take a message."

"Seriously?"

"Yeah, I've gotta clean my lenses," she replied with a wink.

As lunchtime approached, Sarah taped a piece of paper in the window of the front door that read "OUT TO LUNCH. BE BACK SHORTLY."

Maggie locked up shop, and they headed out to County Seat for their lunch with DeDe.

County Seat was one of the oldest restaurants in town and had been named as such because Hastings was the county seat of Barry County. The restaurant had undergone an impressive remodel over the past few years with a newly added outdoor seating area, which Maggie and Sarah loved. They often ate on the patio in the summer months and people-watched.

DeDe was already waiting for them when they arrived. "Hey girls!" She greeted them with hugs. "I already got us a table."

Maggie slid into the booth on the opposite side from DeDe and Sarah. "I'm so glad we could have lunch today. You look great, De."

She dismissed Maggie with a wave of her hand as if it was the least important matter. But she did look great for her age. Her thick, black hair was styled in a professional looking bob and nobody would have guessed she was nearing the end of her forties.

"How's the Christmas shopping going?" Maggie asked.

DeDe's laugh was almost a cackle. "Haven't even started. My kids will wonder if Santa forgot about them this year."

They placed their drink orders with the waitress, and DeDe immediately began throwing out the gossip from around town. Maggie wasn't one to gossip, but she loved to hear her friend talk about what was going on around Hastings.

DeDe placed her well manicured hand flat on the table in front of Maggie. "Did you hear about Vi and Dave?"

She remembered seeing Dave on her drive in that morning. Viola and Dave owned the local professional print lab, where Maggie had her brochures and business cards printed. They also happened to be her parents' best friends. She looked at DeDe with curiosity and shook her head.

"They're getting a divorce. Probably have to sell the shop or decide which one gets to run it."

Sarah inhaled sharply and her jaw dropped open. "Are you serious?"

"That can't be true." Maggie could not believe it.

Dave and Vi had been married for thirty years and had been running that little print shop for almost as many. Last year, Maggie had photographed their anniversary vow renewal ceremony, and there weren't two people in the world who adored each other more than they did. She tried to remember if they had acted strangely the last time she had seen them together. But the only thing she could remember was everyone laughing and having a wonderful time, as usual.

The waitress interrupted when she arrived with the drinks and took their lunch order.

"What can I get you?" The waitress stared blankly at her.

The other girls had placed their orders, but she felt so flustered by the news of her friends that she could not remember what she had originally planned to order.

"I'll just have a Caesar Salad, I guess."

DeDe continued where she left off. "Apparently, Vi met someone else."

"What? No way!" Maggie felt nauseated.

Sarah leaned in closer. "Who is he?"

"Someone from her past," DeDe revealed. "I don't know his name, only that they were lovebirds in high school, and he recently moved back to town."

Maggie shook her head in disbelief.

"I'm sorry, Maggie. I know your family is close with them."

The girls grew quiet for a minute as they sipped their drinks. The waitress set a plate of bread in front of them.

"I think I've lost my appetite." She poked at a piece of bread with her fork.

Vi and Dave were like a second family to her. *How can this be?* She had always looked up to them and admired their marriage. Thirty years was rare these days, and she refused to believe Vi would run off with another man after all those years together.

DeDe seemed to sense Maggie's mood shift, so she moved on to another subject. "I saw Simon Walker at the coffee shop this morning."

Sarah and Maggie looked at each other.

"He told me he saw you at a wedding last weekend. Were you working together?"

Sarah couldn't contain her laughter.

"Hell will freeze over the day I work with Simon Walker." Maggie dropped her fork and leaned back against the padded seat. She really had no appetite now.

"Oh my!" DeDe replied. "Someone has a strong opinion of the gentleman."

Maggie snorted. "You can't possibly use the word *gentleman* to describe Simon Walker."

Sarah couldn't stop giggling.

"Then I guess you wouldn't be happy if I told you I invited him to join us for lunch."

Maggie's shoulders sank. She didn't think she could put up with him for five minutes, let alone an entire lunch.

A smile broke out on DeDe's face. "I'm kidding, sweetie."

"Not funny." She let out a sigh of relief and tossed a piece of bread at DeDe. "Why's he in town anyway? Not like he lives near here." Last she knew, he lived somewhere in East Grand Rapids, which was nearly an hour away.

"Visiting his uncle." DeDe started in on the main course the waitress had laid before her.

"Where does his uncle live?" Sarah asked curiously.

Maggie gave her a look, wanting to change the subject.

"He mentioned Algonquin Lake, so I'm sure that's where he was headed."

"So, De." She decided to change the subject herself. "What's new with you? Any fabulous weddings coming up?"

Dede's face lit up. "Of course!" She proceeded to share all the details of a wedding to be held at Frederik Meijer Gardens in Grand Rapids. It was an intimate affair with only fifty guests, and she assured them it would be amazing.

"Who's photographing that one?" Maggie asked. She knew quite a few of the area photographers and was continuously inspired by their work shared on websites and blogs.

"I've never worked with this one before." DeDe shrugged. "I dropped your name to them, but they had already chosen a photographer friend of theirs to shoot it. I don't think she has a business yet. She's just getting started. Her name is Anna Klein."

"Well, I hope she shares some of the pictures with you for your blog, so we can see some of this amazingness." Maggie knew whatever DeDe came up with for the wedding would be beautiful. She had a gift for taking a theme and making it more than the couple imagined.

As the meal continued, their conversation centered around weddings. Maggie was relieved there was no more mention of Simon Walker.

Maggie spent the entire afternoon working on pictures from Saturday's wedding. She scanned through the folder of images and chose a handful of favorites to post on her photography blog. The sooner she posted a few pictures online, the happier her brides were. They were always anxious to catch a glimpse of their wedding day.

As the end of the work day neared, she grew weary of looking at photos. Instead, she logged onto her Facebook account and commented on a few of her friends' pictures.

She stared at her Facebook wall. "Maggie is ..." the status line prompted. She typed "procrastinating."

Sarah poked her head in the office. "Hey, I'm headed out. You need anything else?"

She glanced over at the clock. "Is it really five already?"

"Time flies when you're having fun. See ya' tomorrow." Sarah departed with a wave.

Maggie sat still at her desk for a few minutes staring at her computer screen. Sarah had turned off the twinkly Christmas lights and the holiday tunes. Only the faint hum of her computer's fan and the low rumble of the building's heating system filled the room.

Maggie was no stranger to late nights alone in the quiet building, but for some reason this night seemed more silent than usual. She wasn't sure why, but she felt uneasy. Maybe it was all the talk of Dave and Vi at lunch or the mention of Simon after seeing him on Saturday night.

Whatever it was, she ignored it and returned to editing the pictures. The happy, smiling faces kept her company, which was more than she would find in her empty apartment. She clicked through picture after picture, touched them up, and adjusted the brightness and contrast levels as needed. Maggie was known for her colorful detail photos and bold black and whites. She spent extra time on each photo to give it "the Maggie touch".

Just as she was getting deep into her editing groove, an email alert sounded on her computer. She almost ignored it. When she saw who it was from, she wished she had.

```
From: Simon Walker Photography
Subject: Thirsty?
Date: Monday, December 15, 2008, 9:23 pm EST
To: Maggie James

Hey, Canon! Working late?
I'm in your neck of the woods tonight.
Wanna have a drink with me?
- S
```

Maggie groaned. Should she tell him she had other plans or just go and get it over with?

"Sorry, Simon! Maybe next time", she typed.

She almost hit "send", but pressed the backspace key and cleared the message. She typed again.

"Sorry, Simon! I'm tired and headed home."

I'm so boring. She stared at the screen and tapped her left leg up and down nervously. She *was* a little curious to know what he wanted.

One more reply.

"Sure. Where and when?"

She clicked "send" and listened to the familiar whooshing sound as her email went out. She immediately regretted it.

Ring!

The sound of her cell phone caused her to nearly jump out of her chair. She reached for the phone as it rang and knocked it off the desk onto the floor. As it rang a third time, she scrambled to retrieve it before it went to voicemail.

"Maggie James," she answered from under her desk on her hands and knees.

"Hey, Canon. I'm coming to pick you up right now."

"That's OK." She nearly choked on her words. "I ... I can meet you," she stuttered.

There was a sudden tapping on the front door.

She jerked her body upward and the back of her head connected with the underside of her desk.

"*Ow!*" she cried out.

"Everything OK?"

"Hold on." She crawled out carefully and pulled herself up with the help of her desk chair. Rubbing her head, she peeked hesitantly around her office door to see who it was.

Simon stood outside holding his cell phone to his ear. He raised a hand in greeting.

"Persistent, aren't you?" She ended the call and walked to the door to let him in. "What are you doing here?"

He wore a cocky grin. "I'm here to take you out for a drink. You've worked hard today. You deserve it."

"Whatever." Maggie walked back to her office. She grabbed her purse and coat, turned off the lights, and headed out the door with the most annoying man on the planet. "You want me to drive?" She offered knowing he wouldn't let her.

"It's not far." He pointed down the street. "We can walk."

She shook her head. "You want to go to Olde Towne Tavern?" She didn't think it was possible to be more annoyed than she already was. She was wrong.

"It's a nice establishment I like to frequent when I'm here."

"Why am I not surprised?" She followed along beside him leaving plenty of distance between them.

State Street was brightly lit with red and green lights on wreaths hung from the light posts. Christmas trees adorned every corner and the bare branches of the small maple trees along the sidewalk were draped with white lights. It looked festive and magical, especially with the recent snowfall.

The bitterly cold air had refrozen the snow that melted in the mid-day sun. As they crossed the street, Maggie slipped a bit on a patch of ice.

Simon held his arm out for support.

"I'm fine." She regained her balance and continued across the street.

Simon muttered something under his breath and quickened his pace. He reached the other side of the street before she was halfway across.

Maggie followed him half a block to the tavern and took a deep breath of fresh air before entering. It was dark and smoky, the kind of place you'd imagine a small town bar to be. The room was filled with locals playing pool, drinking beer, and watching sports on the TV attached to the wall in the corner. Country music played on the jukebox, and a cloud of smoke hung along the ceiling. Behind the bar, a heavy set bald man was mixing drinks.

"What can I get ya'?" the bartender asked.

"Two beers," Simon barked above the noise.

Maggie didn't even bother to tell him she didn't drink. She just wanted to get through this and go home. Her eyes were beginning to itch from the smoke, and she longed for the quiet of her office. This was not her kind of place.

Simon found them a table off in the corner as far from the noise of the jukebox and pool tables as they could get.

She was surprised when he pulled her chair out for her. It suddenly felt a little too much like a date. She took a seat and crossed her arms.

Simon sat back comfortably in his chair. He looked completely relaxed and in his element.

"So." Maggie spoke first. "What brings you to Hastings?"

He took a swig of his beer and stared at her with his cocky grin.

She was not amused. "Am I missing something here?"

Simon faced her square on. "I have a proposal for you."

The red flags instantly flew up. "What do you mean?" She was very nervous to hear what would come out of his mouth next.

"A partnership of sorts."

"Excuse me?" She stared at him, waiting for the bomb to drop.

He grinned. His hazel eyes could not conceal how brilliant he thought his plan was. "I'm opening a studio here in town ..."

"Why?" she blurted.

His brow furrowed a bit as he continued. "My uncle recently moved back here, and he asked if I would help him get his business started up again. He used to own a portrait studio here years ago."

Something clicked in Maggie's brain. "Oh, yeah, Walker's. I remember it, actually." She had gone there with her family when she was little to have some family pictures taken. It was a very traditional portrait studio with all the backdrops and lighting.

"We just found out the building where he originally had his studio is for rent again."

"Really? I thought there was a clothing store in there."

"Lucky us, it's going out of business." He took another drink of his beer.

She still didn't understand. "What does any of this have to do with me?"

"Well, I'll be handling the wedding part of the business, and he'll do all the portraits again."

The look on Maggie's face revealed her confusion.

He finally got to the point. "Our styles are different, yours and mine. I just think it would benefit both of us if we weren't competition in this small town."

"OK," she spoke cautiously. "What are you thinking?"

"I think we should promote each other's businesses. You can send me couples that want fashion formal photography, and I'll send you couples looking for that *candid* style of yours. Maybe we could even combine forces. Shoot some weddings together."

Maggie was sure her eyes were about to pop out of her head. She was in complete shock. There was no way she was going along with this.

"What do you think?"

She found her voice. "I'm not going out of my way to promote your business. Is that what you're asking me to do?" *The audacity!*

He nodded calmly. "I thought we could work together as a team to best serve the community's wedding needs."

Maggie's eyes narrowed. "How long have you been rehearsing *that* line?" Her tone gave away her annoyance.

He glared at her. "What's the big deal?"

"I see this benefitting *you* more than me."

"How?" His tone had a hint of anger behind it.

"For as long as I've known you, I've never seen you do an unselfish thing. Every move you make is to get you ahead in some way, and I won't be a part of it."

He could not conceal his sudden exasperation. "Are you kidding me right now?"

Maggie was furious that he had put her on the spot like this. "I won't fight you for clients, but I'm not going to send them to you either."

"Think about this, Maggie. It makes good business sense."

"For you!" Her volume grew as she spoke. "This new venture of yours is only gonna hurt my business. I can't believe you had the nerve to ask me this. Did you really think I'd agree?" Her voice squeaked a little on the *ee*.

Simon didn't speak. His expression was as cold as ice.

They stared at each other for several tense moments.

He finally stood, grabbed his coat, and walked out the door.

Maggie sat in absolute shock as she watched the door close behind him. *Did that really just happen?*

She pulled her cell phone from her purse and pressed "2".

Voicemail. "This is Sarah. I can't get to my phone right now. It's probably lost in the bottom of my purse somewhere. Leave it at the beep."

She pressed "end", then "3" to call her younger brother.

"You've reached the mailbox of Tom James. At the tone, please leave a message." *Beep!*

"Tommy, it's Maggie. Call me when you get this. I need to hear a friendly voice."

Maggie stepped out of the bar into the frigid night air, but she couldn't feel a thing. She was in utter disbelief. *The nerve!* Maybe in his warped little mind it made sense, but she knew too much about Simon to believe he was in it for anyone other than himself. This new studio was going to be a disaster for her.

She made her way back to Jefferson Street to her car and immediately cranked the heat up. As the engine hummed and the heater warmed, she thought more about Simon's proposal. Maybe it *was* a nice idea. And maybe if it had been anyone other than Simon, she would have agreed to it.

December 25, 2008

Christmas Dinner

*M*aggie opened the door to her parents' home and was instantly hit with the aroma of honey roasted ham and cinnamon candles. Mom had the place all decorated up for the holidays—pine garland and colorful lights wrapped around the banister of the stairway, "The Carpenters' Christmas" album played on the living room stereo, and white lights twinkled on the branches of the Christmas tree. Best of all was the sound of laughter floating in from the kitchen.

"Merry Christmas," she called out.

"Merry Christmas, Magpie." Her father, Ron, greeted her with outstretched arms and lifted her up in a big bear hug, his salt and pepper whiskers tickling her cheek.

"Dad, put me down!" She hugged him back and gave him a kiss on the cheek as he lowered her to the floor.

He took her coat and ushered her into the kitchen, where everyone was congregated.

"Maggie!" exclaimed Tom as he set his drink on the counter and practically jumped across the room to hug his sister.

"Hey, Tommy," she pulled away and gave him a look. "You didn't call me back."

"I'm so sorry. Work." He made a sad face as he put his arm around her. "Is everything OK?"

She nodded. "It was nothing." She missed her baby brother. He was constantly working, which seemed to run in the family. He looked tired, his green eyes sank in a little with dark circles beneath, and the whites of his eyes were bloodshot.

"How are *you*?" she asked.

Tom shrugged. "Same old, same old."

She reached up and playfully rubbed his strawberry blond hair. "You need a haircut."

"What for?" He grabbed her arm and twisted it around behind her back.

"*Ow!*" she cried out.

"Don't start, you two," their mother insisted.

Talking with Tom, she had not noticed Viola Stevens standing on the other side of their mother, helping with the dinner preparations.

"Vi." She scanned the kitchen to see if Dave was in attendance. *Nope.* "How are you?"

"I'm pretty good," Vi replied over her shoulder. "How are you, Maggie?" Her long brown hair, with the slightest hints of grey, was twisted neatly back into a bun. She was a thin, petite woman with the sweetest smile in the room.

"Is Dave coming?"

Vi looked at her uncomfortably. "Uh, he couldn't make it tonight."

There was a sadness in Vi's dark eyes. Maggie wanted to ask her what was going on, but she knew it wasn't the right time or place. Curiosity was killing her, but she bit her tongue and walked into the dining room instead.

The table was beautifully set as always. Her mother loved to do the holidays in style. The candles, table runner, and place mats all matched the holiday decor. Even the plates were festive, painted with old vintage Christmas trees in the center. Handmade candy cane napkin holders made each place setting complete.

She loved coming home, especially at the holidays. Though her parents only lived twenty minutes north of Hastings, Maggie didn't visit nearly as often as she knew she should. Work was her life. It was also her hiding place.

Maggie walked back to the kitchen and stood in the doorway listening to the happy chatter. Her mother, Patty, was laughing with Vi as they had for so many years. Dad sat at the table in the breakfast nook drinking coffee and playing solitaire—an all too familiar sight. Tom sat quietly across from Dad, seemingly deep in thought.

The doorbell rang.

"Ron, can you get that?" Patty asked her husband.

"I'll get it." Maggie turned toward the front door, wondering who else was joining them this year.

The door swung open, and Maggie froze where she stood. Before her, with casserole dish in hand, stood Simon Walker. He was accompanied by an older man, whom she could only assume was his uncle, wearing a long tweed overcoat and fedora.

"Merry Christmas," Simon's uncle spoke.

Maggie nearly laughed out loud. For some reason, based on his apparel, she expected him to speak with an English accent.

Vi emerged from the dining room then and took their coats and the casserole dish. She escorted the older man into the kitchen with her, leaving Maggie and Simon in the foyer alone.

She remained frozen in place as Simon approached.

"Merry Christmas." He held out his hand to shake hers.

She stared at him with disgust.

He lowered his hand and brushed coldly past her into the kitchen.

Maggie stood there for a moment listening to everyone happily greet them.

As her father walked past on his way to the dinner table, she signaled him over.

He stepped closer and leaned in with a puzzled expression.

"Why is Simon Walker at our family Christmas dinner?" She spoke quietly so no one else would hear her.

"Your mother invited him, sweetie." He shrugged and walked into the dining room.

Maggie waited until the others had moved toward the table and made a beeline for her mother in the kitchen.

"Mom!" She gave her mother a funny frown.

"What's that look for?" Patty asked.

"What is Simon doing here?"

"Oh, did I forget to mention he was coming?" Her mother had a little twinkle in her eye.

"Mom!" She tried to control her volume, but she wanted answers.

"Vi asked if I could invite Pete to join us, and I couldn't very well invite him without inviting his nephew, now could I?"

"Yes!" Maggie stared at her mother.

"Simon's parents live in California. Pete's the only family he has here."

"Wait. Pete?" The pieces were falling into place. "Is that who she left Dave for?"

"Margaret," her mother scolded. "It's not our place to judge."

"What about Dave?" She was disgusted that this Pete character had weaseled his way into their home.

"*Shhh!*" Mom slapped her hand on the counter. "Vi is my best friend and, though I may not always agree with her choices, I am here for her. And we *will* be civil to her special friend."

"Oh, God," Maggie cringed.

"Don't take the Lord's name in vain, Margaret," her mother scolded. "Anyway, why do you have a problem with Simon? He's a nice young man."

Maggie snorted and walked rudely out of the room leaving her mother to carry the last of the food to the table by herself.

She quickly scanned the seating arrangement. At the head of the dinner table was her father, of course. To his right was an open seat for her mother. Vi and Uncle Pete Walker sat next to her, while Simon sat on the opposite side of the table next to Tom. This left one seat open for Maggie, between Simon and Uncle Pete. *Oh, joy!*

She sat down as her mother joined them, and they all bowed their heads when her father began to bless the food.

"Dearest Heavenly Father, we thank you for this meal that you've provided for us and for the lovely ladies who have prepared it for us today. Thank you for this gathering of family and friends, our beautiful children, and dear friends—old and new—who have come to celebrate the birth of your Son with us. May we have a wonderful time together tonight. In Jesus name I pray all these things, Amen."

"Amen" was heard round the table.

Maggie heard Simon quietly say "Amen", and she almost snorted again. If he had any religion in him, maybe he wouldn't be such a self-centered jerk.

She was quiet throughout dinner, and Simon didn't try to converse with her, which made things much easier.

He did say, "Here you go," as he passed a basket full of biscuits her way, but neither said another word.

After dinner, the men gathered around the kitchen table to play cards, while the ladies remained at the dinner table, chatting and sipping coffee and tea.

Maggie was having such a nice time, she nearly forgot about Simon's presence in her childhood home. Until faintly, from the other room, she heard her name spoken.

"Are you talking about me?" she called across the house.

"Nothing bad, I promise," replied her dad.

"All bad!" cried Tom.

She took a deep breath as she left the safety of the ladies' table and headed into the kitchen. "What are you saying about me?"

"Peter here was telling me how you turned down his offer to help each other out in your businesses." Ron nodded toward Pete.

Her face turned red as a beet. Dumbfounded, she could not speak.

Ron looked up at her from his hand of cards. "I think it's a great idea to help promote each other, Maggie. Beats fighting over customers. It's such a small town."

Maggie straightened her back and went into business mode. "First of all, I was approached by Simon not Mr. Walker." She faced Pete. "I'm so sorry. I didn't know the offer was coming from you, too."

Pete nodded at her. "It's all right. No harm done."

"Secondly, Simon ..." She made the mistake of glancing in his direction, only to find him staring at her.

"Simon what?" He was grinning in that way of his again.

She didn't respond.

"Go on." Simon seemed to enjoy putting her on the spot.

"I just didn't think it was a good idea." She didn't say what she really wanted to.

Simon wouldn't look away, which turned into an impromptu staring contest.

Ron and Pete looked back and forth between the pair.

"We respect your decision," interrupted Pete. "Don't we, Simon?"

Maggie shook herself out of the stare down and turned to walk away.

"Just keep walkin'," Simon teased.

She spun around. "I'm not the one who walked out the other night."

"*Oooh*." Tom held his hands up. "Too much information, sis."

She gave him a dirty look. "It wasn't like that."

"OK." Simon's chair squeaked against the floor as he pushed it back and stood up. "Let's finish that conversation then."

Maggie swallowed hard. She hadn't meant to start something.

He stepped forward and took her by the arm, leading her through the foyer and out the front door.

"What are you doing? It's freezing out here."

He closed the door softly behind them. "Let's not spoil the holiday for everyone, Maggie."

"You've spoiled mine just by showing up." She crossed her arms over her chest. "I didn't invite you. I don't want you here, so I don't have to be nice to you."

"We need to finish our conversation."

She shook her head. "I will *never* promote you or your business. Conversation finished."

Simon stepped closer and stared into her eyes again. "Never say never."

She tried to ignore the chills that ran up her back, which had nothing to do with the air temperature.

"Maybe you don't like me, but we can help each other."

She glared up at him.

"Your dad's right," he continued. "This is a really small town, and I don't want to waste my energy fighting over who gets what wedding. I'd rather work with people who like my style and hire me for it. If someone comes in and tells me they want candid wedding pictures, I know I'm not the right fit for them. That's not my strength, it's yours. So I would send them to you. All I was asking was that you do the same for me."

Maggie stubbornly looked toward the barn.

"You don't want to spend the entire day posing couples for portraits. You want to focus on the moments, right? It's the tagline on your website, for heaven's sake." Simon made quotation marks in the air as he recited the words from her website, "Capturing the moments." He seemed frustrated and all worked up.

She glanced at him, but immediately looked away. She could not make eye contact.

"Just once …" He got in her face a little more and held up his index finger. "Once! I wish you'd give me the benefit of the doubt."

He didn't even bother to go back into the house. He walked off the porch, climbed into his car, and drove away. He was getting good at that.

Despite the cold, Maggie stood outside for a while longer, thinking about what he had said. She didn't trust him, but she was beginning to think he might be right.

January 29, 2009

Meetings, Meetings, Meetings

A s the weeks passed and turned into the new year, Maggie kept busy with photo editing, client meetings for upcoming weddings, and preparing for the annual photographer's convention in Las Vegas at the end of February. The days leading up to New Years had been spent obsessing over her conversation with Simon on Christmas night. Despite the fact he may or may not have been right, she decided to stand by her decision to decline his offer. She had built her business on her own, and she did not need his help. At least, that's what she told herself.

Walker's Photography was in full renovation mode down the street. Maggie couldn't help but notice as she passed by every morning on the way to work. Occasionally, she would see Simon or Pete or both through the window. This week, their new sign was hung above the door, and a large banner plastered across the front window read: MARCH GRAND OPENING!

So soon?

She wasn't sure what it was going to be like trying to run a photography business two blocks from another studio. She tried not to think too much about it and buried herself in her work instead.

This particular Thursday was a busy one for Maggie. She had a late morning meeting scheduled with two June brides anxious to talk about their upcoming weddings, a lunch meeting with DeDe about a wedding they were working together, then she was off to a meeting in Grand Rapids with a couple interested in hiring her for their

September wedding. She was already tired thinking about the day ahead, but she planned to stop by her parents' for a visit and looked forward to a home cooked meal.

When she arrived at the office, she found Sarah already there with a pot of coffee brewing.

"Morning, Mags," Sarah greeted her.

"Good morning." Maggie headed right into her office and got to work on an album design for Katherine and Edward's Christmas wedding.

She heard the phone ring a few times followed by the sound of the front door.

"Mags!" Sarah called for her. "You have a visitor."

Maggie emerged from her office and was greeted by her smiling brother.

"Tommy!" Maggie hugged him. "What are you doing here?"

He shrugged. "I stayed over at Mom and Dad's last night, and I wanted to stop in here real quick before I head back to Holland." Tom lived an hour away from Hastings and worked many long overtime hours at a factory job he hated. He rarely came to town anymore, so it was wonderful to see him again so soon.

"I'm glad you did."

"This place looks great." He glanced around the room. "Much different than the last time I was here."

"I think I can count on one hand the number of times you've been in here."

He gave her puppy dog eyes. "Sorry."

She punched him playfully on the arm.

Tom glanced over at Sarah. "Hi, I'm Maggie's brother, Tom." He held out his hand.

Sarah shook it. "I assumed so." She smiled at him.

"Oh my gosh. I'm so sorry." Maggie touched her brother's arm. "I completely forgot you guys have never met. It *has* been a while since you've been here. Tom, this is my assistant, Sarah Scott."

"It's very nice to finally meet you." Sarah grinned.

Tom nodded. "Likewise." Their eyes connected and held a little longer than was appropriate.

"So," Maggie interrupted. "Are you gonna hang out for a bit?"

He checked his watch and groaned. It looked like he was struggling to make a decision as he glanced over at Sarah again. "I wish I could stay longer, but I've gotta get back for work this afternoon."

Tom's factory job was killing him, completely sucking the life out of him. It had been a long time since she'd seen any real happiness behind his eyes.

"I'm sorry, Tom." Maggie gave him another hug.

"Hey, I might be back in town next week." He glanced in Sarah's direction once more. "I'll try to stop in again when I can stay longer."

Sarah gave him a shy smile.

"See ya, Tommy." Maggie waved as he headed toward the door.

He looked back one last time and gave Sarah a grin. "Nice meeting you, Sarah."

"You, too, Tom." She raised her hand in a little wave as he walked out.

Sarah floated into the office behind Maggie and sat on the edge of her desk. She flipped nonchalantly through the pile of mail on the corner. "Your brother's very nice."

"Yeah, he is." Maggie nodded and opened her email. She routinely got at least fifty emails every morning—some questions from aspiring photographers, several inquiries for weddings or photo sessions, and the rest spam.

"Does he have a girlfriend?" Sarah finally asked.

Maggie grinned up at her. "Not that I'm aware of." She was amused by her friend's dreamy expression.

"Just wondering." Sarah hopped off the desk and went back to work.

It suddenly occurred to her that her brother and Sarah were the same age—twenty-eight. In the four years Sarah had been working for her, she had never once thought of setting them up. Cupid wasn't a role she had ever played, but it appeared there was an attraction there, and she might have to intercede.

Maggie sifted through her inbox once more and noticed a new message from Walker's Photography. It was a mass email Simon had sent out announcing the new studio's March Grand Opening. She got a nervous feeling in the pit of her stomach at the sight of his name.

At a few minutes before ten o'clock, Maggie heard the door open and close. Giggly girl voices filled the other room, and she knew it was Angie and Dina, best friends she met last August, who had hired her on the spot. They were in each others' weddings and had scheduled them three weeks apart, so Angie, the first to marry, could return from her honeymoon in time to share in all the bridal shower and bachelorette party fun. They were both sweet girls, and Maggie was looking forward to their weddings.

Sarah had already taken their coats when Maggie emerged from her office.

"Hey, girls." She greeted them with a smile.

"Maggie!" They both screeched and quickly crossed the room.

She laughed as they simultaneously squeezed her.

"We are so excited." Angie's shoulder length blonde curls bobbed up and down as she spoke.

"This is going to be amazing having you at both our weddings." Dina took a seat on the leather sofa. "I can't believe we're down to like four months until Angie's wedding already."

Maggie took a seat on her throne.

Both girls had folders filled with information on locations, times, timelines of the day, seating charts—the works. Maggie was impressed by their thorough organization.

The three of them spent more than an hour going over all the details for both weddings. Angie and Dina were very much alike on the surface, but their wedding plans could not have been more different. Angie's church wedding would be pink with tons of pink roses everywhere followed by a country club reception. Dina had something different in mind—chocolate brown and ivory, with blue hydrangeas, white roses and lilies, with ceremony and reception to be held at the public museum in downtown Grand Rapids. Maggie was excited for both weddings. Client meetings always got her itching to get out there and shoot.

Dina turned to Maggie as they gathered their coats. "I saw there's a new photography studio opening up down the street. Will that hurt your business at all?"

"Nah." She shook her head and tried to sound confident. "They'll do a lot of in-studio portrait work."

"No weddings?" Dina asked.

"There will be a wedding photographer there, but he has a completely different style than mine. He does a lot of posed pictures in more of a fashion magazine style."

"Oh, really?" Angie was intrigued. "I've seen some weddings like that online. I love those."

Maggie pursed her lips and nodded. She glanced over at Sarah, who was watching and listening intently from her desk.

"*Oooh*, I would love to have that done," Angie continued. "Maggie, would you be offended if I hired him for a couple hours for my wedding?"

"Angie." Dina tapped her arm. "That's rude."

"No, it's fine." Maggie's throat felt tight as she spoke. "If that's something you're interested in, we can meet with him and talk about it. I can set it up if you want." She spoke before she even thought about what she was saying.

Angie replied with a hug. "Maggie, you are the best. I still want you to do your thing, and I wouldn't want this to get in the way of that. It would just be so cool to have some pictures like that, too."

"You should probably make sure something like that's in your budget before you get all excited about it, right?" Dina interjected.

"Yeah, you're right," Angie agreed.

The girls started laughing. Maggie faked a laugh and looked again at Sarah, who sadly stuck her bottom lip out.

Maggie wished the girls a nice afternoon as they headed out. The thought of calling Simon made her uneasy. She had a feeling he wasn't going to agree to the meeting until she admitted that he was right about everything. She grabbed her coat and headed next door to the Walldorff Brewpub & Bistro for her lunch meeting with DeDe.

"I feel like such an idiot." Maggie shared the entire story with DeDe, from the drink at the bar to their conversation at Christmas. "I know he's probably right, and I let how I feel about him cloud my judgment."

"How *do* you feel about him?" DeDe raised her eyebrow.

"Not like that," Maggie replied. "He's always been such an arrogant jerk, so the idea of promoting his business was the last thing I ever wanted to do. But just today, I had my June brides ask me about his studio, and when I told them about his fashion photos, they went crazy. Now one of them wants to hire him to do some couple shots at their wedding. *My* couple shots. I'm gonna be sick." She stirred the ice cubes in her drink with the straw. "I want my brides to be happy, though, so if this is what she wants then I'll make it happen. I just never thought I'd actually have to work a wedding with Simon."

"Maybe he won't be available on that date."

She got a huge smile on her face. "Oh my gosh, De! I hadn't even thought of that. I knew there was a reason you're my friend."

DeDe chuckled. "So, what else is new? Are you seeing anyone?"

Maggie laughed out loud at the absurdity of the question. She was far too busy for dating.

"You've gotta get back out there, Mags."

"Can't I just live vicariously through my brides?" She wished DeDe had never brought it up.

"For a while, maybe. But I know you. You'll want to be the bride someday."

She shook her head bitterly. "It didn't serve me well last time."

"And you're better off for not marrying Ben," DeDe reassured her.

Maggie winced at Ben's name.

"You should be thanking God every day that you didn't."

Maggie sighed. "It's been almost five years." She didn't want to think about Ben. She had gotten very good at pretending he had never existed in the first place.

DeDe rifled through her purse looking for her Blackberry. "Let's see. Who can I set you up with?" She clicked through her contact list.

"Put that thing away," Maggie insisted. She grabbed for the Blackberry, knocking it out of DeDe's hands. It flew up in the air and landed in DeDe's purse as if on target.

"I totally planned that," Maggie said with a laugh.

After lunch, Maggie drove north to Grand Rapids. She usually enjoyed driving to meetings. It was a peaceful time to listen to her favorite music, get out of the office for a while, and clear her head. But this drive was torture. One mention of Ben and she could not get him out of her mind. She wished DeDe had never spoken his name. The memories began to seep back in, and she did her best to stop them. But it was too late. He was there, riding shotgun, the radio cranked up, singing along, pretending the dashboard was a drum. She missed listening to him sing and singing along to their favorite songs.

She couldn't clearly remember his face anymore, and that brought her a strange kind of comfort. It had been so long since she'd last seen him that she could no longer recall the exact color of his eyes, the shape of his nose, or the way his mouth curved up at the corner when he smiled at her. It was there, buried deep down, but she preferred to leave it there indefinitely.

Maggie arrived at the Panera Bread on 28th Street ten minutes before her scheduled meeting. She scanned the room for couples, but none appeared to be waiting for her, so she went to the counter and ordered something to drink.

"Come here often?" A sudden tap on her shoulder startled her.

She turned around, and her shoulders sank at the sight of Simon's crooked grin. "What are you doing here?"

"I had a meeting," he replied. "What about you? Here for a late lunch?"

"Don't you usually meet people at your studio?" She was annoyed to see him.

"I do." He nodded. "But my couple had another meeting here, so I came to them."

She suddenly had a sick feeling in her stomach. "Another meeting?" She groaned. "I can't believe this."

"What?"

"I think I'm their other meeting."

His eyebrows raised in surprise. "Will and Jackie?"

She nodded sadly.

Simon laughed hysterically.

She crossed her arms and stared at him. "This is so not funny."

"It kind of is." He could not control his laughter.

"Stop laughing." Her eyes narrowed.

"Sorry." He patted her on the arm in mock comfort. "Want me to stick around for moral support?"

Maggie's eyes spoke for her.

"They're over there by the window. Good luck, Canon." He turned and walked out, laughing all the way.

Unbelievable.

It was dark by the time Maggie returned to Hastings. The meeting had gone well, but she felt unsure of herself the whole time, thinking Simon had probably wowed them. She also dreaded asking him for a meeting with Angie about her wedding. Her mood was too foul for dinner at her parents', so she returned to her shop to work on the album design instead.

When she arrived, the lights still shone through the front window. Sarah usually left by five and never forgot to turn off the lights, so this surprised her. She was even more surprised when she walked through the door and found Tom standing by Sarah's desk.

"What are you doing back here?" Maggie asked. "I thought you had to work."

He smiled at her and faked a cough. "I'm feeling a little under the weather."

"Nice." She grinned. "Have you been waiting long?"

"Oh, uh." He glanced over at Sarah, then looked at Maggie awkwardly. "I wasn't waiting for you."

Maggie smiled, knowing she wouldn't have to intercede after all. "OK. Well, I'm gonna get some work done then."

She disappeared into her office and closed the doors to give them privacy. Sarah's laugh occasionally echoed in the other room. Maggie was happy they had connected. Her brother had dated a few girls in the past, but never anyone really special. Sarah was an amazing person, and Maggie hoped this was the beginning of something wonderful for them.

There was a soft knock on the door, and Sarah peeked in. "I'm heading out."

"With my brother?" Maggie asked even though she already knew the answer.

Sarah blushed a little. "See you tomorrow."

She loved the thought of her brother and her best friend together. Her mind wandered to the two of them dating, falling in love, and getting engaged. But then her thoughts turned to the night Ben asked her to marry him. It was hard to think about those happy moments when they were so overshadowed by all that came after. She remembered their engagement picture in the newspaper announcing the wedding that would never be, the boxes and boxes of unused decorations, the pile of wedding invitations that, luckily, were never sent.

Her eyes burned and her chest tightened as the tears threatened to fall. "No!" Her voice echoed back at her in the empty office. "I will *not* cry over you again."

So she shoved the memories into a room in the deepest, darkest corner of her heart and locked it up with chains and the biggest padlock she could conjure. It was the way she had dealt with the breakup five years ago, *not* to deal with it at all. The pattern continued.

February 13, 2009

Friday the 13th

I booked your Vegas ticket today." Sarah handed Maggie a hot cup of coffee. "Wish I could go with you and escape this nasty winter."

"I know," she sadly replied. "I wish I could take you with me, too, but who would hold down the fort?"

"Things would crumble if I wasn't here to hold it all together," Sarah declared confidently.

"Are you and Tom going out again this weekend? Celebrating Valentine's Day maybe?" She winked.

"It's only been a couple weeks, Maggie." She blushed a little.

"But you're going out, right?"

Sarah smiled shyly. "Yeah."

Maggie chuckled, then almost spit her coffee out when she saw what was on her computer screen.

"Oh my gosh!" She erupted with laughter.

"What is it?" Sarah ran around the desk to get a better view.

On the screen was an email attachment with the famous Uncle Sam poster, except Simon's face was superimposed. Large red lettering across the top and bottom read, "SIMON WALKER WANTS YOU. IN VEGAS."

"Apparently, Simon has booked a big suite at the hotel in Vegas, and he's inviting people to come party with him the last night of the convention."

Sarah wiped the tears of laughter from her eyes. "Are you going?"

"As if." Maggie gave her best impression of Alicia Silverstone from the movie *Clueless*.

"Well, he did invite you even after everything that happened at Christmas."

"I'm sure he sent them to every photographer in his contact list."

Sarah nodded. "You're probably right." She paused to take another look at the invite, then giggled all the way back to her seat.

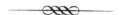

Friday the thirteenth was probably the worst day to set a meeting with Simon Walker, but nevertheless, it was the only date Angie had available to discuss Simon's fashion photos for her wedding. Instead of calling him to set it up, she had taken the coward's way and emailed. He replied immediately and was more than happy to oblige.

Maggie sat nervously in her office tapping her fingernails on the desk, bouncing her knee, clicking a pen. She was uncertain how this would go. Simon would soon arrive, and she had no control over how he would act or what he would say. This made her more than a little uneasy.

She could no longer sit still, so she made sure there were clean glasses on hand to offer drinks. She tidied up the meeting area, which was normally Sarah's job, but she had taken a long lunch to find a dress to wear for her Valentine's date with Tom.

The door opened fifteen minutes early. She was not surprised to see Dina tagging along with Angie.

"We're a little early." Angie removed her coat and placed it in Maggie's outstretched hand. She took the same seat on the sofa she had taken two weeks before. "I'm just so excited."

"That's OK. Mr. Walker should be here soon." She wasn't sure why she had referred to him as Mr. Walker. It sounded strange as the words rolled off her tongue, but it seemed like the professional thing to say.

The girls chatted until Simon strode in a few minutes later with portfolio in hand.

"Mr. Walker." Angie jumped up. "It's so nice to meet you."

"Oh, call me Simon," he stated with outstretched hand.

Angie shook his hand. "OK, Simon."

He glanced at Maggie, who was seated in her usual spot in the wingback chair.

Simon shook Dina's hand then took a seat on the ottoman next to Maggie. "Hey, Canon," he spoke quietly.

She held her hand out toward his portfolio, signaling him to proceed.

He opened the black leather case, and the girls *ooh'd* and *aah'd* over his fashion formals.

"So, which one of you lovely ladies is interested?" He gave them both a killer smile.

Maggie felt awkward sitting in her chair while Simon sold himself and his work to her clients. Part of her wished the girls had met with him alone at his studio, but she wanted to be there to make sure he didn't talk them into something crazy, like hiring him to work the entire wedding with her.

The phone suddenly rang. "Sorry." She excused herself for a moment to answer it.

"Magnolia Photography. This is Maggie."

"How's it going?" asked Sarah.

Maggie turned her body away from her guests. "It's weird," she whispered. "I don't like this at all."

"What's happening?"

"He's being all nice and charming, and they're eating it up. He's really good at this."

"So are you, Maggie," Sarah reminded her. "Don't let him steal the show."

"I know." She paused for a moment, thankful that Sarah was such an encouragement to her. "Where are you?"

"I found *the* dress for tomorrow night. I'm so excited. I hope Tom likes it."

"Awesome. Are you coming back now?" Maggie was excited for Sarah and Tom, but at the moment all she could focus on was what was happening across the room.

"I'll be there as soon as I can. Don't worry, OK?"

She turned in time to see Simon holding the door open for the girls. "Oh, this can't be good. I gotta go." She abruptly hung up.

"Done so soon?" she called after them. "What did we decide?"

"Simon's gonna show us his new studio." Angie wrapped a scarf around her neck as she walked out the door.

"You don't mind, do you, Maggie?" Dina's voice trailed off as she exited the building and hurried down the street behind Simon and Angie.

They left without another word or even an invitation to join them. Maggie sat in her chair and stared at the door. She was in shock. Simon had completely taken over the meeting and had them all to himself now. She knew this was a bad idea from the start, but she went along with it anyway. And now she was left feeling completely defeated and betrayed. It probably shouldn't have surprised her that he would do something so inconsiderate, but it did. The decent thing would have been to ask her. But Simon didn't have a decent bone in his body.

She sat and stared at the door until Sarah returned some time later.

Sarah slowly approached and waved her hand in front of Maggie's face. "Mags? What are you looking at?"

Her gaze shifted to Sarah. "He took them."

"What do you mean he took them? Where?"

"Away." She loosely waved her hand toward the street.

"They left with him?" Sarah's eyes widened.

"Yep." Maggie felt numb.

"Are you kidding me? And you didn't follow them?"

She shook her head. "I froze."

Sarah walked out the front door and looked toward Walker's studio. "Are they coming back?"

"I doubt it," she mumbled.

Sarah returned to Maggie's side and sat on the ottoman. "Don't worry. He can't steal those weddings from you. They both signed contracts."

Maggie nodded. "I know. I'm not worried about that. I just don't like this uneasy feeling I get when he's around. I don't trust him."

"It'll be fine. One wedding and then you never have to work with him again."

"Amen to that."

Sarah handed Maggie a stack of envelopes and magazines. "Here's your mail."

"Thanks."

Maggie flipped through the letters and tossed the junk mail into a pile on the floor. She placed the important stuff on the coffee table, climbed onto the sofa, and wrapped herself up in the throw blanket that was draped across the back. She laid down and glanced over at the mail on the table. Sticking out was an envelope with the Walker's Photography logo. She slid it from the pile and opened it. Inside was another copy of the "Simon Wants You" invitation with a hand written "Hope you can make it, Canon" in the bottom right corner. She tossed it at the pile on the floor and closed her eyes.

Through her sleepiness, Maggie dreamt that Sarah had locked up and gone home for the night. She dreamt that she was all alone at her shop, sleeping on the sofa as people stood outside watching her like they were window shopping.

Tap. Tap. Tap.

What was that noise?

Tap. Tap. Tap.

There it was again.

Maggie suddenly jumped awake when she realized someone was in fact outside the window, watching her, tapping on the glass. It was *him*. Of course.

She dragged herself to the door and unlocked it.

"Working late, Canon?"

She grunted as she folded the blanket and tossed it across the back of the sofa, where it belonged. Taking a seat on the edge of the chair, she smoothed her hair and stared up at him without a word.

"Looks like we'll be working together for Angie's wedding." He walked over and sat on the ottoman, a little too close for her comfort.

"Oh yeah?" Maggie tried to sound uninterested.

"You'll only have to put up with me for a couple hours."

"Sounds good," she blurted.

Simon looked like he wanted to say something, but he didn't respond.

"So, did they like your new studio?"

"They were thoroughly impressed."

She didn't reply to that.

"You wanna see it?" he asked.

"No, thanks." She looked down. "I need to get home."

"Just a quick tour," he offered.

"Maybe next time." She stood and walked over to open the door for him. "It's been a long day."

Simon looked at the floor and paused for a moment. Again, it seemed as if he might say something, but he stood instead and walked to the door. Pausing inches from her, he leaned in closer. "Thanks, Maggie."

The sound of her real name coming from his lips was strange. "For what?"

"For reconsidering."

Maggie gritted her teeth for a moment. "If you're talking about your proposal, I haven't reconsidered anything. Angie's the one who asked about your pictures, and I'll do anything to make sure my brides are happy. Even if that means working with *you*."

Simon stepped back from her with a look of disbelief.

"And I invited you into my space for this meeting today." Now that she had started, she couldn't stop. "You totally took those girls out of here without even considering how I would feel about it. These are my clients. My brides."

"Stop being so territorial." He stepped into her personal space.

Maggie pushed him out the door. "Goodnight, *Mr.* Walker."

He backed off, but continued to stare at her as she locked the door between them.

She made eye contact with him for a moment through the window and thought she saw a look of disappointment in his eyes as he turned and walked away.

Maggie wasn't sure whether to be furious or burst into tears, but she needed to get out of there. She glanced at the clock on the wall. 8:26.

Her computer was still on, so she plopped down in her office chair and clicked the mail icon one last time. There were emails from earlier in the day she had never gotten around to reading as well as twenty-three new messages. One stood out to her. It was from her bride, Angie.

Maggie!!!

You are the best photographer in the world! Thank you so much for setting up the meeting with Simon. His portraits are amazing, and I can't wait to see what he comes up with for our wedding. I saw some of his other wedding work, too, and he does a very nice job. I thought maybe two photographers would be better than one, but he said I already chose the best photographer for the job, and you wouldn't need the help of a hack like him. Simon is so funny!

Thanks again! Can't wait for the wedding!

Hugs!

Angie

Maggie suddenly felt very disappointed in herself.

February 14, 2009

Valentine's Day

State Grounds was surprisingly empty for a Saturday night, but then it was Valentine's Day after all. Maggie imagined most people were out to dinner celebrating their love. She sat just inside the front door on a comfy sofa, reading and drinking a mocha latte. There were several seating areas with mix-and-match furniture arranged around coffee tables of different shapes and sizes, as well as tall tables with bar stool seating toward the back of the shop. The place felt as cozy as home.

The bells on the door jingled to signal someone entering, and she looked up from her bridal magazine. A young couple holding hands talked happily all the way to the counter. She watched them for a moment as she took a sip of her coffee and felt a little twinge of jealousy. It had been a long time since she'd had someone to share Valentine's Day with. Five years, in fact. As much as she hated to think about Ben, she couldn't help it. He was in her thoughts on this most romantic evening of the year.

Maggie met Ben Leary the summer of 1991 before their freshman year of high school. His family had moved to Hastings and began attending her church, and they hit it off right away. He was charming and funny, not to mention dark-haired and handsome. Through high school, they developed a close friendship—one of the most important of her life—and as much as she hoped there would be something romantic between them, they were always just friends.

After high school, Ben went to Grand Valley State University in Allendale, while Maggie attended Cornerstone. Maggie could still remember how apprehensive she had been about college. It was supposed to be this exciting time with new friends and new experiences. She should have been happy about it, but her mood had been dismal the day she loaded her things into the family station wagon and left home. Not because she was afraid to move out, but because high school was over, and she feared Ben might forget about her in the next chapter of life. She liked the old chapter. She was happy there. Her heart was stuck in that chapter, and she didn't want to turn the page.

Cornerstone and Grand Valley were within twenty minutes of each other, and she and Ben kept in touch occasionally, but not as often as she would have liked. Sometimes they shared a ride back to Hastings to see family and attend their home church. But things were different. He had his own college experience going on, and she knew things would never be the same.

It wasn't until senior year of college that everything shifted. Ben began to look at her differently. Every conversation felt more important, every look gave her butterflies in her stomach, and they were soon spending all of their time together. It was a natural, gradual thing. He told her he always knew if they got together, that would be it for him. And it was. At least it seemed to be. They were serious right from the start and engaged six months later.

She glanced at the bridal magazine in her hand, remembering the days of planning their wedding, poring over the magazines, and browsing wedding photographer websites for hours to choose the perfect person to capture their special day—the wedding day that never was.

There were signs. Looking back, Maggie could see them now. But in the middle of it all … well, there's a reason people say "love is blind".

The first sign, the one that should have given Maggie more concern than she let it, was the constant string of other girls in his life—girls from high school, girls from college, girls from work. "Just friends," he claimed. If only that had been the truth.

The biggest sign was Ben's unwillingness to nail down a wedding date. After knowing each other for eight years, a quick engagement seemed like the next logical step, but he dragged his feet for another three years before committing to a date. Maggie chalked it up to their busy life—her opening her photography shop, him working long hours at a graphic design company. But it was more than that.

They had settled on June 26, 2004 for their wedding—five years to the day of their engagement. But a month before their wedding, Ben decided he wasn't ready for marriage after all. He gave no other explanation. And that was the end. The life they were building and planning together—the life Maggie had dreamed of for years—was over, and she was left devastated, broken, and alone.

Nearly fourteen years had passed from the moment they met to the moment he walked out of her life, and every second of that time felt like a complete lie. She wondered if she had ever really known him at all. And all those years she had been in love with him seemed like a total waste.

As Maggie let a few of the memories back in, she fought the tears. It had been nearly impossible for her to show up to work during those dark days. She remembered struggling to photograph a wedding the week after the breakup, barely able to contain her emotions. Between the bride getting ready and the start of the ceremony, she had escaped to the bathroom, hid in the stall farthest from the door, and let herself sob into a giant wad of toilet paper. When the ceremony prelude music played, she had shaken off the tears, emerged from the stall, and glanced at herself in the mirror. At the sight of her puffy, red eyes and smeared makeup, the tears had threatened to fall again. But she had slapped herself on the cheeks a couple of times, splashed some water on her face, and shoved her pain deep down inside.

She had mastered that over the years.

But on nights like this, watching couples parade their love in front of her, the sadness was nearly overwhelming. Funny how her life's work revolved around weddings, and it no longer phased her, but the sight of a couple holding hands made her nearly break down. Maybe it was because the everyday moments were what she missed the most. She missed having someone to share her days with—the good and the bad—someone to build a life with.

She hadn't been in a serious relationship since Ben. There had been the occasional date now and then, mostly guys her friends and family had set her up with. None ever made it past the first date.

The truth was Maggie's business had occupied so much of her

time over the past five years that she rarely stopped to think about how lonely she actually felt. She liked it that way. She would never have survived alone this long had it not been for her business to keep her company.

She took another sip of her mocha and returned her attention to the magazine, looking for photography inspiration in the "Real Weddings" section.

"Happy Valentine's Day, Maggie."

Maggie looked up as Bill set a muffin on the table in front of her with a little paper heart attached to a toothpick stuck in the top.

"*Aw*, that's so sweet. Thanks, Billy."

"You bet." He grinned sweetly and went back to work behind the counter.

The door jingled again. "Maggie-e-e!"

She was startled, but jumped up as soon as she saw who it was.

"Michelle?" Maggie hugged her former roommate. "Oh my goodness, what are you doing in Hastings?"

"Can't I just stop by and visit my roomie?"

The girls took a seat together on the sofa.

"Of course. It's been way too long." Maggie tucked her legs up under her.

"It's good to see you," Michelle said.

"You, too. You look great." She noticed Michelle's usually long brunette tresses had been trimmed just above her shoulders. It was a good look on her. "How's Jeremy? Any big plans tonight?"

Michelle shrugged her shoulders. "I have no idea how he is. We aren't seeing each other anymore."

"Oh, Chelle." She was sad for her friend. Michelle and Jeremy had been dating for a couple years. "I'm so sorry."

"It's no big deal, Mags." She dismissed it casually. "We've been broken up for a few months now."

Maggie was a little shocked that this was the first she had heard of their breakup. "I guess it's been longer than I thought since we last talked. Are you seeing anyone new?"

"Not really." Michelle paused. It seemed like she was going to say more, but she didn't. Instead, she dug into her purse for some money. "How 'bout you? Any big Valentine's plans?"

"Just me and Billy." She nodded toward Bill, who happened to look up at her at that moment and grin.

"Friend of yours?" Michelle asked.

"He and his sister own the place."

"Ah." Michelle laid her purse next to Maggie. "Be right back." She walked to the counter and ordered.

Maggie watched out the front window as more couples and groups of couples passed by on the sidewalk. It was a clear night, not a cloud in the sky, which made for bitter cold temperatures. She imagined all of the couples snuggling to keep each other warm and suddenly felt a little sick to her stomach.

Michelle returned to the sofa and turned to face Maggie. "So, what's it like having another studio right down the street from yours?" She took a sip of her coffee.

Maggie tensed up at the mention. "It's nice that he wants to help his uncle and everything, but what about his studio in Grand Rapids? Who's taking care of that?"

"Oh, he hired someone as his office manager," Michelle replied. "Some pretty young thing just out of college. And he travels back and forth. He works some days here, some days there."

She rolled her eyes. "Well, he should just stay out of Hastings and leave me alone."

"So you've seen him," Michelle remarked.

Maggie nodded.

"*Hmmm*, I'm sensing a little bitterness."

She didn't feel like rehashing their run-ins over the past couple months. "The thing is, he's everywhere in this little town. And I can't seem to get through an entire week without him bringing up his darn proposal."

"What proposal?" Michelle sounded concerned.

The door jingled again.

Maggie scrunched up her nose at Michelle. "Speak of the devil," she whispered.

"Oh, sorry," Michelle spoke quietly as she stood up. "Did I forget to mention that I asked him to meet me here? We're going to dinner."

Simon greeted Michelle with a bear hug and a quick kiss on the lips. "You ready to go?" he asked.

Michelle pointed in her friend's direction. "Coffee with Maggie."

Maggie held her hand up and shook her head. "Oh, no, that's OK. Don't let me keep you." As much as she liked catching up with Michelle, she hoped they would leave.

Simon glanced over at Maggie. "Coffee sounds great."

She suddenly felt like bolting as she watched Simon walk to the counter.

"I guess we'll have to finish our conversation later." Michelle nodded in Simon's direction. "You're welcome to come out with us tonight. It'll be like our old college days."

"Oh, please, no." Maggie had always hated being around Michelle and Simon when they were in college, and there was nothing that would convince her to go out with them now.

Michelle took another sip of her coffee.

Simon returned and took the seat closest to Michelle. He gave her knee a squeeze. "Long time no see."

Michelle grabbed his knee and squeezed back as tight as she could. This was a game they played in college. Who knew why they found this type of pain amusing. Michelle was never a match for Simon and always ended up screeching as he tightened his grip on her knee.

"*Ow!* Uncle! Uncle!" she cried.

"Well," Maggie spoke as she stood. "That's enough of a college flashback for me." She tucked her magazine in her bag and slid her coat on.

"Hot date tonight, Canon?" Simon's gaze was intense.

She gave him a sarcastic grin.

"Come with us, Maggie," Michelle begged her friend one last time. "Simon will pay."

"What am I paying for?" He grabbed her knee again.

"Our dinner." She smacked his hand off.

"You guys have a nice time." She leaned over and gave Michelle a hug. "We'll get together again soon and finish that conversation."

"You bet." Michelle kissed her on the cheek. "Call me."

Maggie was ten steps down the sidewalk when she realized she had forgotten her half finished coffee. She walked back to get it, but stopped when she spotted Simon watching her through the window. They held eye contact for a moment before he looked back at Michelle.

She decided to abandon her poor latte.

The bitter cold made the light dusting of snow on the sidewalk crunch underfoot. At first, she walked toward her car, but the thought of an empty apartment wasn't very appealing, especially on this night, so she headed to the office to get some work done instead.

How pathetic am I? Working on a non-wedding Saturday and on Valentine's Day.

Once inside, Maggie brewed a small pot of coffee and settled in for the night at the computer, her constant companion.

Her phone suddenly vibrated. One new text message.

"You work too much." It was from Michelle.

"Your point is?" she replied.

"Last chance for a free meal."

"I don't want to be a third wheel. Just you and me another time, OK?" Maggie sent the text and tossed her phone into her purse.

A few hours later, her eyelids began to droop while designing an album. She was determined to completely exhaust herself so she would fall fast asleep the second her head hit the pillow—no lying awake at night thinking about being all alone on this romantic holiday. The clock read 11:38 P.M., when she heard a knock at the front door.

She slowly peeked out of her office to find Simon standing outside, holding a small bag. She hesitantly unlocked the door for him. "Did you have a nice dinner?" She tried to sound polite.

"Yeah. Sorry to bother you." He held out the bag. "Michelle asked me to bring you some dessert."

"That was sweet of her. Thanks."

"You should've come out with us. She felt bad you were all alone tonight." He smiled sweetly at her.

"Well, I'm fine. I got a lot of work done."

Simon took a step back from the door and nodded politely. "Goodnight, Canon."

"Night."

Maggie locked the door and walked back into her office. It was a relief he hadn't hovered or tried to make conversation. She pulled a take-out container from the bag and discovered a mouthwatering piece of raspberry cheesecake within.

"*Oooh,*" she breathed.

She pulled her cell phone out and sent a quick text to Michelle.

"Thanks for the dessert."

A few seconds later came a reply. "Dessert?"

"The cheesecake," she replied.

She left her office for a moment to rifle through the drawer in the other room, where she and Sarah kept all their leftover take-out silverware. She grabbed a fork and knife wrapped in plastic and ripped open the package.

Her phone was buzzing across the desk when she returned. She sank the fork into the cheesecake and it practically melted in her mouth.

"Oh. My. Heaven."

She grabbed her phone to check the message, a response from Michelle.

"What cheesecake?"

February 23 - 27, 2009

Vegas, Baby

*T*he last full week of February, wedding photographers from around the country descended upon Las Vegas for the annual Professional Wedding Photographers Convention. Maggie stood next to her hotel room window with a view of the mountains. The sun was rising over the neon city and everything was covered in a warm glow. This was probably the only peace and quiet she would get the entire trip, and she soaked it in. The room was a little too quiet, though, and she wished she had brought Sarah along with her.

This was the second time she had gone in the past five years. Ben went with her the last three years they were together, when her business was starting to take off, so it was hard not to associate this convention with memories of him. But she knew it was important to connect with other wedding professionals and stay up to date on the latest technologies.

Inside the convention center were rows and rows of booths set up to display products for photographers—cameras, lenses, albums, editing software, and other equipment. Besides all of the booths at the trade show, there were great speakers and seminars given by top photographers in the industry. And the parties hosted by the big camera companies, bridal magazines, and online photography forums were always good for networking and just having a good time.

Maggie's days were filled with seminars on marketing, branding, and the power of social media, as well as time spent perusing the booths for all the latest products. Most nights she caught an early dinner and browsed through all the brochures and samples she had gathered during the day.

Late Wednesday morning, Maggie stood on the trade show floor near the Nikon booth of all places waiting to meet up with two fellow West Michigan photographers, who were only attending the last half of the convention. Back home, photographers from around the area got together for dinner and a little networking every few months. It was at one of those gatherings that she met Jamie and Shannon—both with wedding photography styles similar to her own—and they became instant friends.

"Maggie James!" cried Jamie. She and Shannon hurried across the room toward her.

Maggie greeted them both with hugs. "It's been way too long."

"I know. You are one busy girl." Jamie tucked her short auburn hair behind her ear.

"So are you. Kinda sad we had to travel all the way to Vegas to see each other."

Sweet, soft-spoken Shannon nodded in agreement. "I saw the last wedding you posted on your blog, Maggie. The bride was breathtaking."

"She looked so gorgeous, didn't she?" Maggie was very proud of her pictures from the Christmas wedding.

The girls chatted about recent and upcoming weddings as they walked the rows of booths together. After two days of walking the floor alone, she was happy to have friends there to keep her company.

When they could take no more of the product booths, the girls headed to Le Café at the Paris hotel for lunch.

A few minutes after they were seated, Shannon raised her hand and waved to someone across the room.

Maggie glanced over her shoulder to see who it was.

"It's Simon Walker," Jamie stated. "You know him, right?"

"Yeah." Maggie took a sip of her drink. She had been lucky enough not to run into Simon until now.

"Who's that with him?" asked Jamie.

Maggie looked again, but did not recognize the beautiful blonde girl following behind him in their direction. "I'm not sure."

"Oh, that's Anna," Shannon informed them. "His assistant."

Simon and Anna stopped at their table.

"Hello, ladies." His hands softly rested on Maggie's shoulders.

"Are you enjoying Vegas?"

"How could we not?" Jamie answered.

"Are you girls coming to my party on Friday? I got a suite at Bally's." He squeezed her shoulders lightly.

Maggie had forgotten about Simon's goofy party invitation. She smiled to herself. *I wish Sarah was here.*

"Yeah, we're planning on it," Shannon replied. "Hi, Anna. How are you?"

"I'm good." Anna spoke sweetly.

"What do you think of the convention?"

"It's incredible. There's so much to see and learn."

Shannon and Anna chatted back and forth about the convention, but Maggie could not concentrate on what they were saying. She could only focus on Simon's thumbs tracing small circles on the back of her shoulders.

"Well, we should get to our table. Enjoy your lunch." Simon let go of Maggie's shoulders. He moved to the other side of the table and their eyes met. "I expect to see you *all* on Friday."

She gave him a weak grin and let out a breath she didn't realize she'd been holding. Her cheeks were flushed and a few butterflies were flitting around in her stomach. Her shoulders missed the warmth of his hands, not because they were *his* hands, but because it had been a long time since any man had touched her like that.

Anna, with her perfect blonde hair and long legs, followed Simon across the room. Was this the girl Michelle had been talking about? Maggie grew curious.

"How do you know Anna?" she asked Shannon.

"Oh, a few of us had lunch downtown, and she was there."

"With Simon?"

"No, Simon wasn't there. One of the other girls invited her. She's new to wedding photography, a couple years out of college. She shot her first wedding for a friend last month at Meijer Gardens."

The pieces suddenly clicked into place. "Is her name Anna Klein?"

"Yeah, I think that's her last name."

"My friend, Dede, was the coordinator for that wedding. But I didn't know Anna was working with Simon."

"Oh, that's just recent," Shannon informed her. "She really wanted to work for a studio and learn everything she could about running a business. I heard he was looking for someone to help out, so I gave her his information."

"That was nice of you." *Not very nice for Anna, though. Poor girl.*

Jamie leaned forward and spoke quietly. "They make a cute couple, don't you think?"

Maggie tried to appear nonchalant as she glanced across the room to where Simon and Anna were seated. They were talking and laughing and seemed to enjoy each other's company.

Simon suddenly looked over at her, and she quickly looked away. "Yeah, they do."

When Friday evening arrived, Maggie found herself standing at the door to Simon's suite, wearing her cutest little black dress, poised to knock. She could hear music playing inside. The party was obviously underway. She wished she was anywhere else, but she had promised Jamie and Shannon she would make an appearance.

Just fifteen minutes.

She took a deep breath and noticed the door was propped open a couple inches, so she entered. The room was dark, with only a few lamps lit, where several small groups were gathered, talking and drinking. A couple photographer buddies of Simon's were playing music through a computer hooked up to a killer sound system. Off to one side was a lighting setup, complete with disco ball and colorful flashing lights, where people were dancing. Another photographer had set up a photo booth with fun hats, wigs, and other props, which some partygoers were already taking advantage of.

"Maggie!" exclaimed Jamie.

She joined her friends, who were standing with Anna by the bar just inside the room. "Hey! You girls look gorgeous."

"Thank you," Shannon replied. Her black hair was straightened, long and smooth, and she wore a low-cut dark blue number. "And look at you, gorgeous."

Maggie had taken extra time to curl her hair and apply a little extra makeup for the occasion. It wasn't often that she got to dress up. She attended weddings regularly, but she always wore her uniform—

black shirt, black pants, black shoes—to blend in and be invisible. It was definitely not a fashion show for her.

Jamie pointed across the room. "We have to go do the photo booth. So fun!"

Maggie scanned the room. There was no sign of the host, which was a relief.

"Hi, Anna. I'm Maggie." She extended her hand to Anna.

"I know. Simon told me." Anna stared at the cell phone in her hand as she spoke.

"Oh."

"I'm a huge fan of your work."

"Really?" Maggie watched Anna nod. She appeared to be texting someone and never noticed Maggie's outstretched hand.

"It looks like the booth is almost open," Jamie declared. "Come on!" She grabbed Shannon and Maggie's hands and pulled them across the room.

Maggie loved Jamie's enthusiasm. She was always fun to be around.

Anna followed along as they squeezed past the dancing guests, and they stood outside the booth to wait their turn. Some guys emerged then with no shirts on.

"*Woohoo!*" hollered Jamie at the sight of the shirtless males.

Maggie couldn't help but laugh. She wondered what *those* pictures would look like.

The girls filed into the booth. They wore silly hats and wigs, made crazy faces and model poses, and laughed the entire time. It felt good to laugh. Maggie needed more laughter in her life.

As they were finishing their turn, Simon peeked his head into the booth.

"Wait!" He squeezed in between them. "Another round."

Shannon, Jamie and Anna proceeded to hang all over him while he did some serious GQ poses. Maggie stood off to the side and let them have their fun. She wasn't sure where to stand or what to do, but she had no interest in making a spectacle of herself in front of the camera.

For the final shot, Simon grabbed Maggie's arm and pulled her center frame. He dipped her back with his face only inches from hers.

She was caught off guard, but she could not contain her laughter as the flash fired one last time.

He lifted her back up with a huge smile on his face.

Being so close to him, it occurred to her that he had a nice smile and very nice eyes. She mentally slapped herself.

The girls headed back over to the bar for drinks, except Anna. She and Simon hit the dance floor together. Maggie watched them laugh and dance—fast and fun at first, then slow and close. She wondered what kind of relationship they had. Was it strictly professional? Because it appeared to be much more than that.

She glanced around the crowded room at the other guests. Some were familiar faces in the wedding industry, others she had never seen before, but everyone seemed to be having a great time. Simon sure knew how to throw a party.

A few songs later, Simon dragged the West Michigan girls out to dance with him.

"Come on." He took Maggie's hand and tugged her across the room.

The other girls surrounded him like they had in the photo booth and danced to the beat, but Maggie held back.

Simon faced her and raised an eyebrow. "Get over here, Canon."

When she moved closer to the group, Simon lunged forward and wrapped his arms around all four of the girls, turning them around in a strange, clumsy, group hug sort of dance.

Maggie's laughter earned a smile from Simon.

He has the best smile.

She blushed at the thought, but grinned when she realized she was actually having fun with him. It was the first time that had ever happened. Ever since the day they met, she had steered clear of him and his womanizing ways, but something felt different. She couldn't put her finger on it, and she didn't know exactly when it had happened, but she no longer found him intolerable.

When the music changed to something slower, the group dance broke up, and Simon held his hand out to Maggie. Normally, she would have declined in an instant, but she moved without resistance into his arms. He wrapped one arm around her waist and pulled her a little closer. Taking her hand in his other, he moved slowly to the music.

64

It felt strange to be so close to Simon. Strange, yet nice. Again, not because it was Simon, but because it was nice to be held.

"I like this song." Maggie tried to make conversation. It was Michael Bublé's version of the song "You Don't Know Me".

"It's nice," Simon agreed.

"Michael Bublé is my favorite." She couldn't think of anything else to say. She felt suddenly nervous, so she stared at one of the buttons on the front of his shirt.

"Canon," he spoke softly as they swayed.

She refused to make eye contact.

He leaned closer and whispered, "Maggie."

She gave in and looked up at him, which was a big mistake.

Their eyes locked for what seemed like forever, and she could feel him slowly moving in.

Simon's lips touched hers once, ever so lightly. She didn't move a muscle. His breath was warm against her mouth as he leaned in again, brushing his lower lip gently against her top lip, urging her to respond.

Maggie's pulse quickened. Her eyelids slid shut as her lips began to move against his, against her will.

The swaying stopped. They stood motionless under the disco ball, but their lips continued the dance.

His kisses were sweet and gentle, his lips so soft against hers. He pulled her closer, and a warmth started in her heart and spread throughout her body. She slid her hands up his chest, her fingers finding their way into the back of his hair, and the kiss deepened. She couldn't seem to form a coherent thought. Her brain was fuzzy, and a sudden panic seized her. *I'm kissing Simon Walker!*

She abruptly pulled away, which left her a little dizzy.

He looked at her, dazed, as if the kiss had surprised him, too.

She tried to walk away, but his arm remained around her back, pinning her tightly against him. He reached up with his other hand and brushed a hair out of her face. His touch against her cheek made her stomach flip.

"I have to go." She wiggled out of his grasp.

She heard him call her name as she bolted out the door as fast as her legs would take her.

"Maggie!" He chased her into the hallway and took hold of her arm.

She turned to face him and pulled her arm from his grip, not quite knowing what to say. "I ... that was ..."

They spoke simultaneously.

"A mistake."

"I like you, Maggie."

"What?" Her eyes revealed the shock of his confession.

His eyes showed only disappointment.

Maggie's expression was a mixture of shock and disbelief. "You like me?"

He smiled so sweetly, it was almost enough to melt down a few of the steel bars that guarded her heart.

"I like you," he repeated. "I want us to spend some time together. See where things go."

She continued to search for the right words. "But ... this ... it was just a kiss. That's all."

"And a darn good one, if I do say so." His signature cockiness was back again.

If Maggie wasn't so confused, she might have found him charming. But his comment only reminded her of the kind of guy he was—the kind she could not afford to get involved with. "I shouldn't have come tonight. I have to go."

He caught her hand to stop her. "Maggie, please."

She looked him straight in the eye. "Let me go, Simon."

He released his grasp, and she walked away. One quick step after another, she moved toward the elevator at the end of the hall. There was no sound of footsteps behind her, and she was relieved that he wasn't following.

She pressed the down button. It seemed a century passed while she waited for the doors to open. She pushed the button three more times hoping it would speed things up. All the while, she could feel his eyes boring a hole in her back.

When the doors finally opened, she felt his stare follow her in. She turned around to press the lobby button and, although she tried not to look at him, curiosity got the best of her. She glanced down the hallway, but immediately regretted it when she saw the wounded expression on his face.

What have I done?

"You kissed him?" Sarah nearly choked on her oatmeal cookie.

Maggie buried her face in her hands. She and Sarah sat at the kitchen table with Patty and Vi having tea and cookies on the Sunday afternoon following the convention.

Sarah spoke through her laughter. "How did this happen?" She didn't let Maggie answer, her expression suddenly turning serious. "How was it?"

"Those Walker men do know how to kiss," Vi revealed with a wink.

"Um, overshare." Sarah screwed up her face.

Maggie looked up at Vi. "Can I ask you something without you being offended?"

Vi nodded. "Of course, dear."

"Are you and Pete really together now?"

Vi and Patty exchanged knowing glances.

"I mean, you and Dave had your vow renewal and everything. Thirty years and it's over, just like that?"

"Maggie," her mother scolded.

"It's OK." Vi touched the table in front of Patty.

The room was silent for a few long moments.

"I'm not with Pete," Vi admitted. "People took that story and ran with it."

Maggie looked at her with concern. "Really?"

"We spend time together. He's a nice man. An old sweetheart of mine from high school. But we're friends now. Nothing more," Vi assured Maggie.

She didn't look convinced.

"He wasn't right for me back then, and he's still not the one I love." Vi gave her a comforting grin.

"But you're not with Dave now? I don't get it. You two were so happy."

Vi nodded her head in agreement. "Looks can be deceiving sometimes, sweetie."

"Yeah, I know that." She knew first hand what it was like to put on a happy face and act like things were fine, when in reality they were falling apart.

"I'd like to work on the marriage, but he's going to have to be the one to make the first move. I've held us together all these years. It's up to him now." Vi gave a determined nod of her head and reached for another cookie.

Sarah set her tea cup on the saucer with a clink. "I like how you cleverly changed the subject, Maggie."

Everyone laughed, except Maggie.

"Spill." Sarah elbowed her friend.

"I don't know where to start." Maggie tilted her head slightly to the right, remembering the moment Simon's lips had touched hers. She felt flushed.

"Do you like the boy?" her mother asked.

"No," she answered without hesitation.

"Right," Sarah mumbled through a bite of cookie.

"I don't," Maggie insisted. "It was just a moment of weakness. We were having fun dancing with some of the other photographers. Next thing I know we're slow dancing, and he's kissing me." She covered her face with her hands again.

"The next thing you know?" Her mother chuckled. "Were you forced to dance with him?"

"No, Mother." She emphasized *mother* the way she had when she was a young girl fighting for her independence.

"You gonna let him kiss you again?" teased Sarah.

Maggie narrowed her eyes at her friend.

"You know I'm not gonna be able to look at him now without thinking that's the guy that kissed my boss."

"Stop!" Maggie elbowed her this time.

"How does he feel about you, Maggie?" asked Vi seriously.

"He told me he likes me."

"He likes you?" Sarah grinned. "Aw, that's sweet."

"No, it is *not* sweet." Maggie shook her head.

"Maggie, is he really such a horrible guy?" her mother asked.

"Yes! ... No. I don't know."

She had been thinking about him ever since she stepped out of the elevator that night in Vegas. No matter how nice he seemed or how good it felt to kiss him, she knew the real Simon—the guy who came off as charming and funny, when in reality he was unfaithful, flirtatious, and a total player. She couldn't be with someone like that again. Her heart couldn't take it. She was determined not to make the same mistake twice.

"We just don't get along," she continued. "Not since college. And I told you about our conversations since he came to town." She shook her head. "I don't know what I was thinking."

"You weren't," remarked Vi. "Sometimes things happen that we don't plan."

"It's gonna be weird the next time I see him." Suddenly Maggie remembered Angie's wedding. She groaned. "And we have to work together at a wedding in June."

"Awk-ward." Sarah giggled, which got her another elbow in the ribs from Maggie.

May 7, 2009

Revelations at Rose's

Maggie's first wedding of the season in March had come and gone, as had the Grand Opening of Walker's Photography. Things were in full swing down there, but she tried not to dwell on it. Instead, she focused on editing wedding pictures and updating her website with fresh new images.

Before she knew it, the trees around town had sprouted buds, the tulips bloomed, and the magnolia trees blossomed. The winter-themed "Welcome to Hastings" banners on the light posts were replaced with bright, flowery ones. Spring had arrived and everything felt new again.

On the first Thursday evening in May, Maggie and Sarah drove to Rose's, a restaurant in East Grand Rapids, for the quarterly gathering of area wedding photographers. She wondered if Simon would be there. She hadn't seen or heard anything from him since Vegas, not that she was surprised after their last encounter. Through the grapevine—better known as DeDe—she heard that he was only coming to town for meetings or if his uncle needed something, but he was mostly staying in GR now that wedding season was underway. Maggie couldn't help but wonder if it was partly because of her.

East Grand Rapids was one of Maggie's favorite spots. The history fascinated her. She liked to imagine all the people who used to frequent Ramona Park, an amusement park that once stood on the shores of Reeds Lake in the early 1900's, with its roller coasters, lovely pavilions, and boat docks. Rose's was a bathing beach and swimming school at that time. Sadly, the amusement park was demolished in 1955, and a decade later, the bathing beach and its facilities met the same fate. But one building was left standing—Rose's, which had become a beloved restaurant over the years.

Maggie admired the old black and white photos displayed in the entryway of the restaurant—the original owners and building, the roller coaster, people swimming in the lake, boats at the dock. It looked magical. She thought about a simpler time, a quieter way of life, without the internet or cell phones or computers. *What would that be like?*

Most of the photographers were already there, seated together at a few tables by the expanse of windows overlooking the lake. They maneuvered their way across the room, and Maggie recognized the back of Simon's head. Her stomach flipped quite unexpectedly. Shannon sat to one side of him, and his arm was draped around a brunette on the other.

As they neared, she realized the brunette was Michelle, which was surprising. It was hard to miss the way she was looking at Simon, how she leaned into him, her hand resting on his atop the table. Michelle had never been interested in photography, but she was obviously interested in a certain photographer.

"Hey, Chelle."

Michelle's face lit up. She stood and greeted her friend with a hug.

"How are you?" Maggie asked.

"Really good." She smiled and raised her eyebrows up and down.

"You and Simon?" Maggie whispered, hoping her tone sounded more curious than concerned. She glanced over at Simon, who avoided eye contact.

Michelle smiled happily as she took her seat next to Simon again and kissed him on the cheek.

He leaned in and gave her a soft kiss on the lips, then looked straight at Maggie.

Maggie looked over at Sarah, who was also witness to this exchange.

"We're gonna go get a drink." Sarah nudged Maggie toward some seats a couple tables away.

Maggie took the chair facing away from the happy couple. All these years, Michelle and Simon had been just friends and *now* they were a couple? The timing seemed like more than a coincidence, and that felt very unsettling.

"He's looking over here," Sarah whispered.

Maggie shrugged. "Who cares."

"You do." Sarah tilted her head and raised her eyebrows.

"No, I really don't."

"I saw the look on your face when you saw them together."

"I was just … surprised, that's all."

"You broke his heart, Mags. He's rebounding."

She shook her head. "It's not a rebound. It's Michelle. They've known each other forever. And we weren't together, so there's nothing to rebound from."

"He kissed you, Maggie. He likes you."

She glanced over her shoulder and spotted Simon plant a kiss on Michelle's neck.

"Liked. Past tense."

Sarah rolled her eyes. "Whatever."

A few hours had passed when the group finally started to break up. Jamie and Shannon caught up with Maggie and Sarah as they walked along the hall leading out of the restaurant.

Shannon linked arms with Maggie. "You going to the park?"

"Yep," Maggie replied.

It was the perfect evening for a stroll through the park next to Rose's.

"Girl!" exclaimed Jamie. "I have not seen you in months. You need to fill us in on what happened in Vegas."

Maggie pretended to be clueless. "What do you mean?"

"We saw you and Simon kissing at the party, then you just took off," declared Jamie with girlish excitement. "We need details!"

Maggie heard a gasp. She glanced back and discovered Michelle and Simon following close behind them—obviously close enough to overhear Jamie's comment.

Michelle stopped in her tracks and looked up at Simon, shock and betrayal written all over her face. "You kissed Maggie?"

"Keep walking," Maggie whispered to her friends, and they quickened their pace.

The girls sat in the park talking about their recent weddings as the sun went down. Simon and Michelle had not joined the group in the park for obvious reasons. Maggie didn't blame Michelle for being upset. They hadn't spoken since Valentine's Day, so there had been no chance for them to talk about Vegas or this new development in Michelle's relationship with Simon.

When they were in college, Maggie often came home to their apartment to find Michelle and Simon snuggled up on the couch watching a movie together. The two of them were close from the start. Lots of people assumed they were dating because they spent so much time together and were always flirting, but they never were. Maggie had always wondered if Michelle had romantic feelings for Simon, but she would never admit it. The chemistry was undoubtedly there, though, and it made total sense that they would end up together.

Maggie felt a sudden unexpected twinge of disappointment. She dismissed it as quickly as it came and looked out at the lake. She was only half listening to what the girls were saying.

"Maggie?" Sarah interrupted her thoughts.

"Sorry, what?"

"Are you up for some Starbucks before we head home?"

"Always."

The four girls walked out of the park toward Gaslight Village.

"Hey! Wait up!"

They all turned at once to see Simon jogging to catch up.

"Can I talk to you?" he asked Maggie, slightly out of breath.

"I guess." She glanced over at Sarah, who gave her a nod, and headed back toward the park with Simon.

They walked in silence at first, then he motioned to a bench that faced the lake, and they took a seat.

"Haven't seen you around town lately," she stated.

He raised an eyebrow. "Miss me?"

Her only reply was a look of sarcasm.

He grinned. "Too many weddings, too little time."

"Avoiding me?" she asked point blank.

He feigned shock. "Would I do that?"

She shrugged her shoulders. "I think you would."

He chuckled. "Well, can you blame me?"

She knew he was referring to what happened in Vegas.

"The thing is ..." He paused as if searching for his words. "Well, I wanted to make sure we're OK, because we have that wedding coming up, and I didn't want things to be ... awkward between us."

"We're fine," she stated confidently. "We're both professionals. We have a job to do, even if we feel uncomfortable around each other."

Simon leaned forward with his elbows resting on his knees and looked over at Maggie. "Do I make you uncomfortable?" He smirked.

Sunset had passed, and they were losing the light. Simon's face was barely lit, his dark hair tousled, and those hazel eyes reflected the subtle glow remaining in the sky. The butterflies floated around in her stomach again, and suddenly she *was* feeling uncomfortable. She glanced at his mouth and remembered what it felt like to kiss him that night in Vegas.

He gazed seriously into her eyes.

Maggie looked away, out across the water at the glowing windows of the lake houses.

"I'm sorry about Vegas." She couldn't look at him.

"I'm not." The corner of his mouth turned up a little. "I'm only sorry we didn't get to finish that dance."

"Yeah, well, it's your fault our dance was cut short."

He laughed a little. "I'll gladly take the blame."

It was difficult for her to look at him. He was being all flirty and charming, and she didn't want to fall for it.

He checked his watch. "Listen, I've gotta get back to Michelle. I told her I was making a quick coffee run."

Reality check. She remembered being *that* girl, the one who never knew if what was coming out of his mouth was the truth or a lie.

"So, we're good?" He was already standing, barely giving her time to respond.

Heck, no! That's what she wanted to say, but instead she forced a grin. "Goodnight, Simon."

"See ya', Canon," he called back as he walked away.

Jerk!

June 6, 2009

Angie & Steve

$\mathcal{T}$he air outside the church was filled with bubbles—bubbles meant to be blown when the newly married couple exited the church, but the children were anxious and could wait no longer. The wedding ceremony of Angie and Steve had gone off without a hitch, and their guests were gathered around the door of the church waiting for them to emerge.

Maggie observed the crowd. Some people waited quietly, others talked and laughed, and some headed right to their vehicles to depart for the reception. She looked through the viewfinder on her camera and snapped a few pictures as one group erupted in laughter. She glanced over the camera looking for her next shot.

Just as she trained her camera on a group of little kids with bubbles, she spotted Simon in the background walking across the parking lot toward her. It was no surprise that she would see him at some point during the day, but the plan was for him to meet them at the country club before the reception began.

He gave her a friendly wave.

She ignored him and continued shooting.

Two seconds later, he walked directly into her line of sight, completely blocking her shot.

"Simon!" Her head whipped up from behind her camera.

He glanced back to see an adorable little boy and girl giggling and blowing bubbles at each other. They abruptly stopped and ran off.

"Aw, that would've been a good picture."

"I know." Maggie gritted her teeth. She hoped this wasn't how the next couple of hours would be.

Sarah, who had been inside while the couple dismissed their guests, came scurrying out of the church to join them. "They're coming!" There was sudden applause and cheering behind her.

Maggie moved quickly around Simon so she wouldn't miss it.

Angie and Steve walked blissfully hand in hand as thousands of bubbles drifted around them. They hopped into their getaway car and waved to the guests, both with the biggest smiles they'd ever worn. One quick pause for a photo, and they drove away.

Once the car was out of sight, she turned her attention to Simon. "I thought you were meeting us at the country club."

"Well, I knew they were coming back here first for pictures in the church, so I thought I'd come watch you work."

Great. She glanced over at Sarah who was trying to suppress a smile.

On the drive to the country club, Maggie and Sarah guzzled bottles of water and munched on granola bars. Early on in Maggie's wedding photography career, she learned that without proper sustenance it *is* possible to pass out in the middle of photographing the ceremony. She never made that mistake again.

"Simon was totally watching you at the church." Sarah spoke between bites.

Maggie shook her head. "Let's just get through the next couple hours. Then we can enjoy the reception without him."

"If I knew something about a certain photographer and a certain girlfriend of his, would you want to know?" Sarah gave her a questioning look.

Maggie was curious. "I guess so."

"Remember what I said at Rose's about him rebounding? Pete said Simon and Michelle only got together because someone else rejected him."

She placed her fingertips to her left temple like a sudden headache was coming on. "He told you that?"

"Oh, Tom told me. He overheard Pete and Vi talking at your parents' house one night."

Maggie chewed on her bottom lip. "This is not good." She did not want to be the reason he had chosen Michelle and, if this was true, she was very worried for her friend.

Sarah shrugged. "Maybe they'll be happy together."

"Or maybe she'll get hurt, because he's not being honest with her."

"Have you talked to her lately?"

Maggie frowned and shook her head. "She won't return my calls."

"I'm sure she'll get over it. Eventually," Sarah replied.

"Not while she's with Simon, she won't."

Sarah took a swig of water, and all was quiet for a few minutes.

"Is Simon really all that bad?"

Maggie was dumbfounded.

"He might be a little conceited, but he's a decent guy. I don't think he'd jerk Michelle around."

"You don't know him." Maggie could name several girls at college whose hearts had been broken by Simon Walker. They were girls like Michelle and Emma, who thought he was all in, when he wasn't so truthful about his real feelings or intentions.

"He's a nice guy, Mags. He and Tom have become good friends." She paused for a couple beats. "I like him."

"If you like him so much, *you* date him."

Sarah laughed aloud at that. "I can't. I'm in love with your brother."

Maggie's head jerked to the side and her mouth dropped open a little. "What? You love Tommy?"

"I love him. I have since I met him."

"Sarah."

"And he told me he loves me, too." Sarah's smile lit up the car.

"Well, I'm not surprised. You're very lovable." Maggie grinned at her friend.

She could not possibly be upset with Sarah over her opinion of Simon after hearing that.

Love was in the air. If only for some.

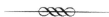

When they arrived at the country club, Maggie climbed out of the car and took a few external shots of the clubhouse. She and Sarah

77

then headed inside to scope out the reception hall before the bridal party limo arrived. There were still group photos to be taken and a few pictures of the couple before she turned them over to Simon.

The tables were decorated with candles and various shades of pink roses in short and tall vases. The wedding cake was a simple, white, three-tiered beauty, with light pink roses on top. Some of the guests had already arrived and were finding their seats. The D.J. was set up and playing instrumental music, while the caterers prepared the buffet dinner.

Maggie and Sarah split up, taking pictures of the flowers, the cake, the place cards, every detail they could find. Maggie recognized the little favor boxes that Angie and Dina had told her about at one of their meetings. The two friends had spent hours putting them together, cutting ribbon and attaching the label with Angie and Steve's monogram. Inside were white chocolate coated almonds. She snapped a few close up pictures of the boxes and a few shots of the entire table.

When the girls felt they had captured all the details, they headed outside to meet up with the bridal party. They were nowhere in sight. Maggie glanced at her watch and wondered why it was taking them so long. It had been over an hour since they left the church, and the limo should have already arrived.

A few guests stood on the front steps smoking cigarettes.

"Did you see the bridal party arrive yet?" asked Maggie.

One of them pointed at a golf cart. "They took off in those."

"With a photographer," another man informed them.

"What?" Her heart dropped and panic set in.

"Did you see which way they went?" asked Sarah.

Both men pointed out toward the line of pine trees in the distance.

"Thank you," the girls both replied.

They hopped in one of the other golf carts and took off. Maggie had not worked at this country club before, so she wasn't familiar with the course. She remembered Angie mentioning a pond toward the back, but she wasn't sure how far back it was. They followed the trail that led from hole to hole, but when they reached the pond, there was no one there.

Maggie stopped the golf cart. She was livid. "I can't believe he did this to me. After all his talk about helping each other out."

"Don't worry, Mags."

"And we discussed this with Angie. I was supposed to shoot some pictures *before* he took over." Her hands tightened into fists. "Oh, I could kill him right now," she spoke through gritted teeth.

"We'll find them," Sarah assured her.

They followed the trail around the rest of the holes, hoping to come upon them. No such luck.

As the clubhouse came back into view, Maggie spotted Simon and the bridal party. He was taking pictures as Steve helped Angie out of the golf cart and led her by the hand into the building.

She sped across the yard as fast as the golf cart would allow and aimed straight for Simon.

"*Whoa!*" He dodged the cart at the last second. "What are you doing?"

Maggie jumped out of the cart, her fists clenched again. It was all she could do to keep from exploding.

"Where were you?" Simon asked.

"You knew we were here waiting. Why didn't you come get us?"

"I didn't know where you were," he replied innocently. "I thought you were running late or something."

She glared at him. "I'm *NEVER* late for a job."

He held his hand up. "It's OK, Maggie. I—"

"It is most certainly *NOT* OK!" She walked toward the clubhouse, with Sarah quietly following behind.

Simon followed them up the steps and reached out to open the door for her.

"Stop!" Maggie exclaimed.

"Listen, I covered for you. I did all the bridal party pictures while we were out there."

"You covered for me?" Her voice squeaked. She wanted to scream, and if there had not been guests all around them, she might have. "I can't believe you did this to me."

Sarah slipped past them and entered the building.

"What's the big deal?" Simon was oblivious.

"I didn't need you to cover for me, Simon. I was here and ready to do my job. This is completely your fault." She walked back down the steps, trying to avoid a scene.

Simon followed her into the parking lot.

She spun around and poked him in the chest. "This was *MY* wedding. I told you that." She was physically shaking now. "I didn't want you here at all, but I wanted Angie to be happy, so I went along with it. I knew this was a mistake."

He took a step closer to her. "Maggie, calm down."

She shoved against his chest causing him to stumble backwards.

"*Whoa!*" Simon's eyes were wide with shock. "Why are you so upset?"

"You made me look bad in front of my clients today, Simon." Her eyes began to well up. "I looked totally irresponsible and unprofessional, and now I won't have all those pictures to give them as promised." Her chin quivered as she fought back the tears.

"Maggie, I didn't ..." He looked genuinely saddened by her words.

She glared at him. "I have to go back in there now and finish my job. *Don't* follow me."

She pushed past him and ran up the steps, disappearing inside the building.

Maggie received numerous emails and voicemails from Simon over the next week apologizing and asking her to come look at the pictures he had taken at the wedding. When she didn't reply to any of them, the messages finally stopped.

On the following Monday, she arrived at the office two hours late after a morning dentist appointment. Sarah and Tom were seated on the sofa, holding hands, and looking contentedly at each other.

Maggie grinned at the sight. Even after four months, it was wonderfully refreshing to see them together. She almost couldn't remember a time when they weren't a couple. Theirs was the love at first sight story Maggie had once dreamed of for herself, but she didn't begrudge them that. It was the opposite, in fact. She was ecstatic that it had happened for two people she loved so much.

"Good morning," Tom greeted her.

"It is," she announced. "I'm cavity free." She flashed them a smile and headed for her office.

Sarah entered the room a few moments later.

"Any messages?" asked Maggie.

"Just this." Sarah hesitantly held out an envelope.

"What's that?"

Sarah pursed her lips. "Simon was here."

Maggie looked at the envelope, then back at Sarah.

"He seemed really torn up about things."

"As he should." Maggie sat down and stared at Sarah's outstretched hand for a moment. She reached over and snatched the envelope.

Sarah slowly closed the door behind her when she walked out.

She stared at the envelope. Her name was written on the front and underlined three times. She slid her finger under the flap and ripped it open revealing a CD in a clear slip case. Sticking to the front of the disc was a Post-It note that read:

> Maggie,
>
> I feel absolutely horrible about the wedding. There is no excuse for it, but please let me try to make things right. Please use these pictures.
>
> I'm more sorry than you could ever know.
>
> - Simon

Curious, she popped the disc into her computer. There before her were beautiful photos of the bridal party in several poses as well as some candids of the group laughing. He had taken the time to touch them up, and the files were ready to show the couple.

Maggie ejected the disc and tossed it to the side of her desk. She wasn't finished being angry with Simon.

The night of the wedding, she had apologized to Angie and Steve for what had happened on the golf course. They were quick to dismiss her apologies and express how grateful they were that Simon had taken the bridal party photos for them, even though it wasn't what he was paid to do.

She had barely spoken on the drive home that night. Sarah asked several times if she wanted to talk about it, but she shook her head and tried unsuccessfully to hide her tears. Never had she felt so uneasy, so vulnerable in her work. She was used to being in complete control, but Simon had thrown everything for a loop. Never would she let him or anyone make her feel that way again.

June 27, 2009

Dina & Alex

$\mathcal{M}$ aggie couldn't shake the feeling she had forgotten something. As she stood at the end of the aisle waiting for the bride's entrance, she felt uneasy, antsy.

What am I missing?

She glanced over at the groom, who winked at her. Her parents were sitting in the front row, which seemed out of place. Her eyes scanned the crowd and locked on Sarah and Tom. She wondered why Sarah wasn't in the back taking pictures of the bride.

The doors suddenly opened, and the bride stepped through on her father's arm. She reached for her camera and panic gripped her. *Where is my camera?* She searched behind her on the floor for her bag. Nothing. She couldn't very well walk down the aisle to go find her camera bag with the bride walking toward her. Maybe she could sneak out the side. But she could not move. Her feet were as heavy as lead, holding her frozen in place.

Then, she heard the click of a shutter, again and again. Crouched in front of her was Simon, taking the pictures she was supposed to be taking.

A loud beeping sound interrupted the bridal march. Maggie glanced over at the pastor. She hadn't noticed before that it was Pastor Jon, the youth pastor from her church youth group. The beeping didn't seem to bother him. In fact, nobody else seemed to notice. Her heart raced faster with every beep. With every step the bride took, the beeping grew louder and louder.

Maggie suddenly jerked awake.

She groaned as she rolled over and hit snooze on her alarm clock. It had been a long time since she'd had a wedding nightmare. They used to come more often in the early days of her business, when she was establishing herself. She would dream that she forgot equipment or lost the directions to the ceremony, but she never dreamt another photographer had taken over her job.

Her cell phone suddenly rang causing her to jump. In her haste to grab it, she reached too quickly and rolled onto the floor with a loud thud.

"*Ow!* This is Maggie."

"Hey, Mags, it's Tom. Are you hurt?"

"*Mhmm.* What's up?" she mumbled as she rubbed her now sore hip.

"Sarah's sick," he revealed. "She'll be spending the day bowing to the porcelain throne."

"Gross."

"She feels really bad she can't help with the wedding today."

"It's not her fault. Tell her to take it easy and get well soon."

"I will."

Maggie rolled onto her back and stared up at the ceiling. She had no idea how she was going to find someone to replace Sarah on such short notice.

The next two hours were spent pacing and calling all the names on her backup photographer list to see if anyone was available. But everyone had their own weddings to shoot. It was June, after all.

She plopped onto her bed, racking her brain for anyone she could call. Only one other person came to mind, and she really didn't want to call him.

Maggie stood just outside the entrance to Grand Rapids Public Museum waiting for Simon to arrive. Their phone conversation had been the most uncomfortable of her life.

"Simon, this is Maggie," she had said.

"Wow! I thought you were never gonna speak to me again. To what do I owe this honor?"

"Do you have a wedding today?"

"Nope. It's a rare Saturday off for me. How 'bout you?"

Maggie dug down deep for the courage to say, "I need your help."

"You need *my* help?"

She could tell from the tone in his voice that he was shocked and amused at the same time.

"Well, what can *I* do for *you*?" he asked.

She knew he was enjoying this, and she paused a little longer than necessary.

"Canon?" he broke the silence.

She spoke quickly. "Sarah's sick, and I need someone to assist."

He chuckled. "You need an assistant?"

"Yes."

"Well, I don't know. I had a lot of important stuff to do today," he teased. "Aren't you afraid I'll try to take over the whole wedding?"

"Knock it off, Walker. Can you help me or not?"

"This is hard for you, isn't it?" he asked with a hint of amusement.

"No comment."

There was a pause on Simon's end. "Where should I meet you?"

She was grateful he had agreed to help, but as she stood waiting for him, she wondered if she should have tried to go it alone. This might have been the worst decision she could have made.

It was too late to turn back, though, as Simon rounded the corner from the nearby parking garage.

She took a deep breath in and let it out as he strolled up to her. "Thanks for coming."

He took the backup camera bag from her shoulder and draped it over his own. "It's the least I could do."

Maggie didn't respond to that. She wasn't sure what to say.

"Shall we?" He opened the door for her.

They walked into the museum, and she led him to the room where Alex waited with his groomsmen.

"I'll meet you before the ceremony." She walked away nervously, part of her afraid to leave him alone, and headed upstairs to the room where the girls were getting ready.

Maggie opened the door to an absolutely stunning Dina. She was a pretty girl, but on this day, she was glowing. Her dark hair cascaded over her shoulders in loose curls and a tiara was pinned neatly to the top of her head.

Dina and Angie greeted her with big hugs, as did Dina's mother, grandmothers, and cousins. They were a very loving family, and she was welcomed in with open arms. Literally.

The wedding dress was soon brought out, and the bridesmaids helped pull it over Dina's head, careful not to mess her hair. Maggie stood on a chair to capture Dina climbing through. The girls talked and laughed as they zipped and buttoned her up.

When the bridal party lined up for the ceremony, she positioned herself near the back of the aisle to get the best shot of both Dina's entrance and Alex's expression when he saw her for the first time.

She glanced around the room. Simon was nowhere to be found. *Figures.* Her first instinct was to chew him out, but she couldn't think about that now. She had a wedding to photograph.

The museum's first floor had been set up for the ceremony with rows of white chairs leading to an arch set up under the huge whale skeleton—the centerpiece of the museum—suspended overhead.

As Dina's father walked her down the long staircase and toward the aisle, Maggie pressed the shutter release on her camera, then rotated on her heel to get a shot of Alex seeing his beautiful bride for the first time. The look on the groom's face was always her favorite moment of a wedding.

Just as she was about to capture Alex wiping a tear from his eye, a large man with a camera of his own stood from his seat and stepped into the aisle in her line of sight. Her shot was completely blocked, and by the time he moved, Dina and her dad had passed by and were at the front of the aisle. The moment was lost. Maggie was beyond disappointed, but she continued on through the ceremony with no other hindrances.

The guests filtered out after the ceremony for a cocktail hour in the lobby, while the first floor was cleared and set up for the reception. Maggie and the bridal party worked their way through the unique museum displays, taking photos as they went. After finishing up in the *Streets of Grand Rapids* exhibit, they made their way outside to the Blue Bridge, a pedestrian bridge over the Grand River and a popular spot for wedding photos.

Simon was still nowhere to be found, which infuriated her. He was carrying her other camera bag, and in the front pocket was her list of specific posed pictures requested by the couple. She had no choice but to go on without it and hope she didn't miss anything.

The sky had grown dark as the day progressed and storm clouds threatened, but Dina was insistent on getting some pictures on the bridge before the rain came. The breeze picked up, and rumbles could be heard in the distance. The bridal party walked further down the bridge, some of the guys were goofing off, and the girls complained about the wind messing up their hair. Maggie wished she had her assistant there to help keep them all organized. She tried to work quickly and creatively, but the weather was a distraction to everyone. Losing patience and time, she hollered at them to line up and walk toward her. They did as she asked, talking and laughing as they walked in her direction. She then posed the bridesmaids, followed by the groomsmen, then the whole group together. A couple rain drops hit her cheek, and she knew they didn't have much time left.

Dina and Alex posed together, just the two of them, with the museum in the background. They leaned in for a kiss, and a strong wind gusted. A sudden bolt of lightning struck across the river with an instantaneous clap of thunder, and the skies opened up.

The girls screamed and ran for cover. The guys laughed hysterically. Maggie tried to tuck her camera under her shirt to keep it from getting water damage. *Why didn't I bring an umbrella?*

When they were all back inside, the girls scurried off to get dry and reapply Dina's makeup for the reception, while the guys shook the rain off and went to mingle with the guests. Maggie escaped to the restroom. She shook her head at her appearance in the mirror. The phrase *drowned rat* came to mind.

Once she had used all the paper towel she could find and was as presentable as she could get, she went looking for Simon. She found him in the reception area taking photos of the decorations.

"Where have you been?" she snapped.

"Right here." He was taking a picture of the centerpiece. "I've been getting shots of the guests at cocktail hour." He leaned down and took a picture of the menu cards. "I also got some pictures of the tables before all these people sat down. And right now, I'm getting detail shots for you, boss." He looked over at her. "What happened to you?"

She ignored his question. "You have my list."

"Your list?" He gave her a confused look.

"For the posed pictures."

"Real pros don't need lists." He turned back to the table and looked through his camera again.

She wanted to slap him across the face.

"I got some good ones during the ceremony," he bragged.

Maggie remembered the moment she had missed. "I got a nice shot of a big bald man's head."

Simon chuckled at that.

"I was trying to get the groom's expression when he saw the bride for the first time. Big guy got right in my way."

"I got it," Simon stated.

"You got what?"

"The groom seeing the bride for the first time," he replied.

"You did?" She was shocked. "I didn't see you anywhere."

Simon gave her a sly smile. "I tricked them into seating me up front as a guest."

"Are you serious?" She couldn't help but laugh. It was so typical of Simon.

Once the introductions had been made at the reception, Maggie and Simon found their assigned seating at a table with some of the couple's friends.

"How did you swing this?" Simon asked.

"What?"

"The prime seating." He pointed at the main table just feet away from theirs.

Maggie's photographer friends often talked about vendor meals in a room separate from the reception or in a back corner away from the guests, but she had never experienced that. She had always been given a seat close enough to the bride and groom to capture all the kisses and special moments during the dinner hour.

"They love me," she replied with a smile.

Simon pulled Maggie's chair out for her. "What's not to love?"

His comment brought color to her cheeks. She glanced up at Dina and Alex, who were taking their seats. Dina saw Simon pull out her chair and gave Maggie a thumbs up.

She shook her head.

Simon tapped his elbow against Maggie's arm as he took his seat.

She thought maybe he had noticed their exchange, but instead he was holding his knife in the air.

Maggie grinned, as he tapped it gently against the side of his glass. The room suddenly filled with the clinking of glasses.

She lifted her camera and pointed it at Dina and Alex, poised to capture their kiss.

They gazed into each other's eyes as they stood for the first of many such kisses throughout the night. Alex dipped her back and kissed her sweetly to the sound of loud cheers and applause.

Click. Click. Click. Maggie loved capturing these moments.

Simon leaned closer. "You're welcome." He spoke softly, his breath tickling her ear.

A little chill came over her.

As the night went on, Maggie realized she no longer regretted her decision to ask Simon for help. She hadn't forgotten the debacle at Angie's wedding, but they seemed to work well together, and she was actually enjoying it. It wasn't the same without Sarah, but she had a new appreciation for Simon and the way he worked. He was good at his job, thorough in his coverage, and she was glad to have his help.

After the first dance, she noticed Simon standing off to the side of the dance floor talking with a couple of older ladies. They were very chatty, and he seemed to be charming them in that way of his. She grinned as she watched these adorable ladies fawning all over him.

But then Simon reached into his pocket and handed them his business card.

Her mouth fell open. She couldn't believe what she was seeing. *How could he?*

When the ladies walked away, she marched straight over to him. "No!" she scolded.

"No what?"

"You can't pass out your business cards here." She shook her head in disgust.

"What are you talking about?"

She pointed in the direction of the ladies. "I saw you. You've got some nerve."

Just then, one of the ladies approached him again. "Excuse me. Can I get another one of those for my friend?"

Simon pulled out another card and handed it to her.

Maggie's stomach dropped. It was her own business card.

"Thank you, dear." The woman gently squeezed his hand.

Maggie looked up at him and saw the disappointment on his face. She hung her head a little.

He shook his head as he tossed the remainder of her business cards on the nearest table and walked away.

Dina and Alex's friends were a riot on the dance floor. They spent hours dancing and having the time of their lives to all the usual party songs—the Chicken Dance, YMCA, the Hokey Pokey. Maggie had witnessed these at dozens of weddings before, but she always found them entertaining. She moved around the edge of the dance floor, photographing it all.

Simon kept to himself for the rest of the night. Every time she spotted him, he was photographing guests or little details. And when she asked him to go upstairs and take some photos from above, he went without a reply. He was all business—no more charming, flirtatious Simon—and she didn't like it one bit. It served her right for accusing him of something he didn't do.

The D.J.'s voice cut through the beat. "It's time to slow things down."

The first notes of the next song paralyzed Maggie where she stood. It wasn't a song she expected to hear. It wasn't on the list of popular songs usually played at weddings, but it was well known to her. Her camera slipped from her fingers, the strap jerking her neck as it pulled taut. She tried to will herself to lift the camera and take pictures, but she couldn't. How long had it been since she'd last heard this song?

Her eyes stung as she watched the dancing couples, the tears so close to falling.

Her mind returned to another time and place, when this song had meant so much to her—to a beach at sunset, dancing in the arms of the man who had just become her fiancé. It was *their* song, the one they loved, the one he played when he asked her to marry him, the one they had chosen for the first dance at their wedding. Hearing it now made her heart ache in places deep down inside, places that had not seen the light of day in many years.

She closed her eyes for a few moments, attempting to compose herself, but the memories could not be shaken. The sadness washed over her until the final notes faded into the next song.

In a glass pavilion off the main floor of the museum stood a beautiful old carousel with its hand-carved chariots, wooden horses, and other animals. It was one of the highlights of the museum and Maggie's favorite.

As the guests took rides, Maggie stood to the side and watched the carousel turn round and round. It felt a little like her life—spinning and spinning, never moving forward, stuck in the same place.

The bridal party soon hopped on the carousel, and Maggie joined them for some photographs. She chose a spot ahead of Dina and Alex, between two of the wooden horses, and leaned against one for balance as the carousel began to move.

Simon stood by the ticket booth watching and taking pictures. She didn't blame him for being upset with her after the way she'd spoken to him. She was still pretty upset with herself.

Taking photos while riding the carousel was not an easy task, especially for someone with a tendency for clumsiness. The centrifugal force and the movement of the horses going up and down made it nearly impossible for her to shoot. She felt unsteady and more than a little dizzy. Stumbling forward, she grabbed onto a stationary bar behind one of the horses. It was difficult to take pictures and retain any kind of balance. She lifted the camera to her eye and attempted to steady herself against the bar, but instead she missed the bar and stumbled to the left. Her camera, which had unfortunately not been secured around her neck, flew from her hand and bounced off the edge of the carousel. The loud crack of the camera landing on the cement floor by the wall made her cringe.

Simon suddenly jumped the gate and hopped onto the carousel behind her.

"Hey!" the operator hollered.

Grabbing onto the bar she had been holding, he moved behind her until she was leaning back into him. It felt a little too close for comfort, but she couldn't escape until the carousel slowed down, so she used him for balance.

He took the camera from over his shoulder and placed the strap around her neck. "Use mine."

"Thanks." She was dizzy again, but not so much from the motion of the carousel.

He moved his hand down the bar until it was resting on hers and placed his other hand on her hip. "For support," he explained.

A shiver went through her at his touch, and she found herself leaning back into him more. His breath was warm against the back of her neck, and she was having a hard time focusing.

Maggie took a few photos of Dina and Alex laughing, then scanned the carousel for the others. She noticed Angie and Steve riding two horses just past a lion and a giraffe. She let go of the bar and turned swiftly to the right. The quick motion of the turn and the feel of Simon's hand sliding across her stomach and around her waist made her head spin, and she gripped his arm. "*Whoa!*"

"You OK?" he asked.

"Yeah." She kept hold of his arm, and he squeezed her tighter against him, her camera arm pressed into his chest. "Just hold me steady."

He grinned. "Will do."

She lifted the camera to her eye and rested her arm against Simon's to get as steady a shot as she could. Angie and Steve were talking and laughing, no idea Maggie was about to take their picture.

Simon looked over his shoulder.

Steve leaned in toward Angie, and she joined him halfway in a kiss.

Click. Click. Click.

"Nice." Simon smiled down at her.

As the carousel began to slow, she finally regained her balance, but Simon's arm lingered.

Maggie looked up at him uncomfortably.

He chuckled and shifted away from her.

When the carousel came to a complete stop, the bridal party posed for one last group photo of the night.

Dina approached and gave Maggie a hug. "Thank you guys so much."

"You're welcome. It was ... a day to remember."

"That's for sure." Dina laughed. "It was great seeing you again, Simon."

"Nice seeing you, too. Congratulations!"

"You two make a great team." She winked at Maggie.

Maggie grinned at her.

She and Simon watched as the happy couple walked away hand in hand behind their bridal party to enjoy the rest of their reception.

"We do make a great team, Canon."

She glanced up at him, but didn't respond. She was too exhausted to disagree.

Simon reached out and slid his fingers under the camera strap around her neck and tugged her closer.

A quick breath escaped her lips.

"Let me help you with that." He lifted the camera up and over her head, relieving her of its weight.

She squeezed her sore shoulders, and let him take care of everything. He packed up all the equipment, then retrieved her broken camera. The camera body was banged up, but looked relatively unharmed. The lens, however, was shattered. Replacing camera equipment was not exactly in the budget.

The walk to the parking garage was a wet one. The thunderstorm had passed, but the rain continued in a steady drizzle. They walked quickly down the street, avoiding the huge puddles as best they could.

Maggie pressed the unlock button on her key fob when she spotted her car.

"Did Sarah give you my disc?" Simon asked, once they had dumped her bags in the back seat.

"She did."

"I'm really sorry. I didn't mean for any of that to happen. I hope you'll give Angie and Steve those pictures."

She could see the sincerity in his eyes.

"I will," she admitted.

"So you looked at them then?"

"Yeah. They're really good."

Simon took a step back. "*Whoa!* Was that a compliment?"

She shrugged and fiddled with her keys. "Sorry about before ... the business cards." She felt embarrassed for jumping to conclusions.

He took a step closer. "Don't worry about it. Let's just call it even?" He raised his eyebrows.

She nodded. "Thanks for all your help today. You weren't completely useless."

"Now *there's* the Canon I know so well." He grinned at her.

She grinned back, then looked nervously at the ground.

He took another step closer, very clearly invading her personal space, and spoke in an intimate whisper. "It was a joy to watch you work."

As much as she wanted to, she would not look up at him. He was still the same Simon. And he was still dating Michelle.

He leaned in close enough for Maggie to feel his breath against her cheek. "Goodnight, Maggie." He turned and walked away.

Maggie got in her car and hit the lock button on her door. She drew in a deep breath and let it out. *What a day!*

June 29, 2009
The Big Picture

*E*veryone had a case of the Mondays. Sarah was recuperating from her weekend of sickness, and Maggie was recovering from a wedding hangover—their term for what consisted of a killer migraine headache from squinting through the camera viewfinder, agonizing muscle and back pain from carrying camera gear around, and sore feet from standing most of the day.

Coffee was always the best medicine, so they closed up shop and headed across the street to State Grounds. From their seats toward the front of the coffee shop, they could keep an eye on Magnolia while they took turns grumbling about the aches and pains they were feeling.

"I'm so sorry I had to bail on you Saturday." Sarah set her cup on the table in front of them.

"I'm glad you had Tom there to take care of you."

"Yeah," Sarah replied. "He even held my hair back while I puked."

Maggie laughed at the thought of it. "That's true love for ya'."

"Did you find anyone to take my place?"

"No one can take your place." Maggie grinned sweetly.

"*Aww.*" Sarah tilted her head and grinned. "So you had to shoot it alone? I feel even worse now."

Maggie shook her head. "I didn't shoot alone."

"Oh, good, who helped you?"

"Simon," she stated very matter-of-factly.

Sarah inhaled sharply at Maggie's news, and the coffee she was drinking flooded her windpipe. She coughed and hacked until she could manage a reply. "How did that happen?"

"Nobody else was available. Are you all right?"

She coughed and nodded.

"We actually worked surprisingly well together. He kinda saved my butt."

"Is this going to become a regular thing? Am I out of a job?" Sarah looked worried.

Maggie shook her head. "It was an emergency situation, Sarah."

Sarah searched Maggie's face for more.

"What?" She tried to hold back her smile.

Sarah laughed a little. "I thought you weren't on speaking terms with Simon."

"I wasn't."

"OK."

The girls sat in silence for several minutes, and Sarah didn't press her for more.

Maggie stared across the street at her shop. She took in the sign with its magnolia logo, which had been designed for her by Ben. They had been together for two years when she decided to start her photography business, and he had been there every step of the way. He was there when she chose a business name and launched her website, when she got her first call, and when she booked her first client. He had truly been her support system during that time—the early years, when things were so good between them. Even after all this time, she felt sad that he wasn't there to help celebrate her successes.

"Are you thinking about Simon?" Sarah teased.

She grinned weakly. "I was actually thinking about Ben."

"Your ex, Ben?" asked Sarah.

"Yeah, he's been on my mind lately. You know, this was the same weekend Ben and I would have been married five years ago."

"No! Maggie, I'm so sorry."

"I'm fine."

"Are you sure?" Sarah looked very concerned.

"Yeah."

If *their* song hadn't played at the reception, Maggie might not have remembered what weekend it was. She wished she could forget.

<hr />

The afternoon dragged by as slowly as the morning had. After Sarah left for the day, she decided to load the pictures Simon had taken at the wedding on Saturday. She opened the folder on her computer's hard drive and clicked through them. Maggie was very impressed with Simon's candid skills. He claimed his strength was the fashion shoots, but clearly he had an eye for capturing the moments as well.

As she came to the ceremony pictures, she searched for the shot of the groom she had missed. There it was. Maggie stared at the photo. Simon had completely nailed it. The groom's eyes glistened a bit from the tears that had formed at the sight of his bride. She clicked forward to the next photo of him wiping his tears away. *Amazing!* She was suddenly overwhelmed with gratitude to Simon for catching this priceless moment for her and for the couple. And again, she wanted to kick herself for treating him so horribly.

She moved on through the folder and came across a photo of herself shooting. She smiled. Sarah sometimes took pictures of her working, too—action shots for the website.

A few shots later, there was another one of her working. And another. And another. She came upon several shots of her laughing with Dina and Angie, then another series of her wiping her own tears during the father-daughter dance. She was very impressed with the pictures, but she also realized he had been watching her work far more than she knew.

She blushed a little at the thought. These photos felt different than the ones Sarah usually took of her. More personal, more intimate somehow.

After a couple dozen dance pictures, there were a few of her standing alone near the dance floor. Her shoulders were slumped, hands hanging at her sides. She looked sad. In the next, her eyes were closed, and she knew exactly what she was looking at. *The song.* And she realized then why Simon had warmed up to her again after her reprimand over the business cards. He felt sorry for her.

The melody of the song from that dance returned to Maggie again, and she let the memories of Ben wash over her. Her throat grew tight at the thought of them dancing in the sand. Tears burned behind her eyes as she remembered his kisses, and she fought hard to keep from breaking down at the memory of him slipping the engagement ring on her finger. *Lies. All lies.*

On Wednesday evening, Maggie packed a bag with albums and price lists and drove to East Lansing for a meeting with potential wedding clients. After seeing the Magnolia website and falling in love with Maggie's work, the bride immediately set up a meeting to see album samples and go over pricing.

She pulled into the Starbucks and went inside. There was one other person there—a middle-aged man in a suit reading a newspaper—so she ordered a coffee and sat down at a table to wait.

Fifteen minutes later, a lovely blonde girl breezed through the door and approached her table.

"Are you Maggie?" she asked.

"Yes, I am." She extended her hand.

The girl shook Maggie's hand. "I'm Beth. It's so nice to meet you." Beth took a seat across the table from her. "My fiancé's parking the car. I'm so sorry we're late."

"That's fine. Not a problem." Maggie retrieved a couple albums from her bag.

"Thank you so much for meeting us. I know it was a little far for you to come."

Maggie shook her head. "Oh, I meet people here all the time. It's a good halfway point between Hastings and Detroit."

"Well," Beth began. "I'm so excited to get going on our plans. We met with two other photographers and weren't thrilled with either of them. Then I found your site online, and the second I saw your work, I knew it had to be you. "

She was so flattered by Beth's kind words. "Oh, thank you. That's very sweet of you to say."

"Your pictures are incredible and exactly the style we're looking for."

"I'd love to hear more about you and your fiancé and what you have in mind for your wedding. Will you be getting married in the Detroit area then?"

"My fiancé actually has family near Hastings, so we're getting married on Gun Lake."

"Oh, really? I spent lots of summers swimming in Gun Lake when

I was growing up. What's your fiancé's last name? Maybe I know his family."

"Maggie?"

The sound of a familiar voice startled her. Her heart sank when she looked up. "Ben?" She couldn't believe he was actually standing before her. It had been so many years since she last saw him. Her heart began to beat rapidly, and a large lump formed in her throat.

Ben glanced over at Beth and then back at Maggie. "Oh, no."

Beth turned to look at Ben. "What's the matter?"

He let out a nervous laugh, and Maggie's heart ached as she remembered that familiar sound.

"*This* is the wedding photographer we're meeting with?" he asked.

Maggie thought she might have a heart attack right then and there. She couldn't speak, and her eyes stung from the tears that threatened to surface. She could hear the loud beat of her heart in her ears and feel the blood pumping hard through her veins.

"You know each other?" asked Beth, totally clueless.

Maggie's hands shook as she slowly slid the albums from the table and tucked them back into her bag. She had to force herself to breathe in and out. Everything felt like it was moving in slow motion.

Beth looked concerned. "Are you OK, Maggie? You don't look so good."

Maggie clutched her bag and attempted to stand, but she suddenly felt weak in the knees and collapsed forward.

Ben reached out and caught her as she went down. With his arms wrapped around her back and his face inches from hers, he looked into her eyes. "You OK, Magnolia?"

She winced at the nickname he had given her back in their high school days. "Please don't call me that," she responded quietly through her tears.

He hung his head a little, then helped her back up to her chair.

"What's going on?" Beth looked utterly confused.

Ben took a deep breath and looked at his new fiancée. "Maggie and I used to date."

Her mouth dropped open. "You two dated?"

"Yeah." He was clearly uncomfortable.

Beth couldn't hide her shock. "When?"

"In college."

"For how long?"

Maggie grabbed her napkin and blotted the tears away, trying to get a hold on her emotions so she could get out of there.

"Five years," he confessed.

"*FIVE* YEARS?" Beth's voice grew louder.

Maggie gathered her bag and made another attempt to stand. This time she was more steady.

"I'm really sorry, Mag—" Ben caught himself this time. "I'm just sorry."

She paused and looked him straight in the eyes. "Don't forget to tell her that we were engaged, and that you dumped me a month before our wedding." She pushed past him and shoved through the door, the tears freely falling.

"Engaged?" Beth's voice slipped through before the door closed. "Why didn't you ever tell me about her?"

Maggie sobbed her way back to Hastings. The floodgates had been opened, and there was no way for her to stop the tears now. Seeing Ben was the last thing in the world she expected, and she wasn't sure what to do or how to feel about him getting married.

She drove straight to her parents house and discovered a couple extra cars in the driveway.

"Mom!" She stumbled inside with puffy red eyes, sniffling loudly.

Her mother emerged from the kitchen. "Maggie? What's the matter?" She scooped her daughter up in a hug and let her cry into her shoulder.

Maggie sobbed. She tried to speak, but she couldn't get a word out. She was shaking as the tears left her body.

Vi and Sarah came when they heard the commotion.

"Maggie." Sarah stroked her hair gently. "What's wrong?"

Vi rubbed her back as she let it all out.

Many minutes passed before she faced her mom. "Ben was the groom at my meeting tonight."

A loud gasp escaped Sarah. "Are you serious?"

"Yeah. It gets better. I pretty much fainted into his arms."

"Oh, sweetie." Her mother squeezed her tight and gave her a kiss on the cheek.

The ladies guided Maggie into the kitchen. Sarah grabbed a tissue and wiped the tears away. Vi put on a pot of coffee, and Mom set out a plate of chocolate chip cookies.

Maggie was happily surprised to see Dave, Vi's husband, sitting with her Dad and Tom playing cards. She glanced curiously at Vi, who gave her a knowing smile.

Tom noticed the condition his sister was in. "Hey, are you OK?"

She nodded. "I will be."

With coffee mugs in hand, they moved into the dining room so they could talk without the listening ears of the men. Vi carried the cookies, and Sarah grabbed the whole box of tissue.

Maggie took one of each.

"I'm so sorry you had to go through that tonight, sweetie," her mother said.

"The worst thing was being completely blindsided. It felt like a dream, like it wasn't really happening, but it was." The tears started to well up again. "And he looks good. He really does."

Sarah put her arm around Maggie.

"I miss him. I know I shouldn't after everything that happened, but I do. He was my best friend. We were going to spend our life together. And now he's all happy and getting married to someone else."

"No way," Sarah interjected. "Can you imagine being that girl and finding out your fiancé was engaged before and never told you? There is no communication going on there. Not gonna happen."

"It really doesn't matter what Ben does now or who he's with or the state of their relationship," her mother said. "What matters is you, sweet girl. We love you, and we want you to be happy, Maggie. We want you to find someone who will love you and only you, and we believe you will. We believe God's preparing that man for you right now. If you will open yourself up to God again and pray and trust Him, he will show you just who that man is."

Sarah and Vi shook their heads in agreement.

Tears slipped down Maggie's cheeks. "I want to believe that. I do. I just don't understand why this had to happen. Things were fine. I had my life and he had his, and there was no reason for them to ever intersect again. Why did I have to see him? And why like this?"

Mom squeezed her hand. "Do you remember your favorite Bible verse back in high school? 'For I know the plans I have for you, declares the Lord, plans to prosper you and not to harm you, ...'"

"I know, I know," Maggie interrupted. "Plans to give you hope and a future."

Her mother raised an eyebrow. "You're awfully flippant about the Word of God, Maggie."

"I'm sorry. I don't mean to be. It just doesn't seem like there's much hope for a great future for me right now."

"God's word is truth. Trust in it."

Tears filled her eyes again. "I don't know if I can anymore." She sniffled.

Vi passed Maggie another tissue. "It's hard to understand why things happen the way they do, but God does have a plan, Maggie. We can't see the big picture when we're in the moment, but God's got a much better view than we do, and He's working everything together to give you that future He's got planned for you."

Maggie went through another round of tears.

"God loves you." Mom squeezed her hand. "He hates it when you're hurting, just like I do. I wish I could take it away for you. Please talk to Him. Make things right. Let Him help you heal."

The doorbell rang.

Sarah gasped. "Maggie, you might want to go freshen up a bit."

"What for?" She blew her nose loudly into a tissue.

"It's Pete ... and Simon."

"Great. Just what I need."

Maggie quickly left the room and ran up to the bathroom at the top of the stairs. She splashed water on her face, dabbed it dry with a towel, and pulled her hair into a messy bun on the top of her head. *Sigh.* There wasn't much she could do to correct the red blotches around her eyes.

She heard the happy greetings and laughter downstairs.

As she left the bathroom, her gaze landed on the door to her old room, and she stopped. She slowly moved to the end of the hallway and pushed the door open. It was now a completely redecorated guest bedroom, with purple floral bedspread and lavender striped wallpaper. Nothing looked as it had when she lived there, but she still felt comforted being in her childhood room.

Maggie sat on the end of the bed and took a deep breath. She stared straight ahead at the closet doors for a while, wondering if her mom had left any of her old clothes in there. When curiosity got the best of her, she crossed the room and opened the doors. There were a bunch of her old sweaters from high school and a few college sweatshirts hanging there along with the overflow from her mother's own closet.

She took another deep breath and suddenly grabbed the clothes in the middle, pushing them to the left as hard as she could. She shoved another handful of shirts to the side and yet another until she found what she was looking for.

There—tucked away in the back of her closet—was her wedding dress.

She reached for it slowly, almost afraid to touch it.

The zipper of the garment bag stuck at first, giving her second thoughts. *Maybe I shouldn't do this. Maybe it's too much.* But she couldn't help herself. She unzipped the garment bag and pulled the dress from the closet.

Her fingers traced the neckline of the gown as she remembered the day she first tried it on. Simple yet elegant, she knew instantly this was *the* dress. She held it in front of herself and glanced into the full length mirror by the window. The pain and grief washed over her, and she slumped to the floor, her tears wetting the soft lace around the bodice. She cried until she could cry no more, but then remembered the humiliation of seeing Ben and his fiancée, and the tears began all over again.

"Maggie?" Simon was suddenly there in the doorway. He glanced at the dress then back at her face.

She wasn't sure how long he'd been there or how long she had been sitting there on the floor crying into her wedding dress.

"Are you all right?" He stepped hesitantly into the room.

Maggie shook her head and mumbled, "I just need to be alone right now."

His expression was filled with concern.

"Please, Simon." She sniffled.

He nodded and quietly left the room.

She buried her face in the dress, her shoulders shaking from the sobs. After all this time, it still felt like someone had reached in and grabbed hold of her heart, squeezing it so tightly that it physically hurt. It was almost too much to bear. She lay on the floor for a long time clinging to the dress as the tears flowed steadily.

Oh, Lord, I'm so sorry I haven't talked to you for a while. Please forgive me. You know how hard the breakup was for me, how devastated I was. I felt like nothing mattered anymore—my relationship with Ben, my hopes, my dreams, my faith. It all felt pointless. And it hurt. So bad.

It still hurts. After all this time, why does it still hurt so much? Please, God, please let this be the last time I cry over Ben. Please heal my heart once and for all.

When Maggie finally descended, the group was in the middle of their euchre game, laughing and enjoying their time together.

"Come join us, Magpie," her father insisted.

She shuffled across the kitchen floor, her eyes puffy from crying.

Simon jumped up. "Here." He offered her his seat next to Sarah.

She grinned weakly and took the empty seat.

He walked over to the kitchen counter and returned with a cup of coffee, as well as the cream and sugar.

"Thank you," she spoke quietly.

Sarah put her arm around Maggie and gave her a squeeze.

"Will you all be joining us on Saturday then?" asked Pete.

Maggie saw Dave look over at Vi with a questioning glance. She returned his glance with a nod.

"We'll be there," replied Dave.

"What's Saturday?" asked Maggie as she propped her elbow up on the table and rested her chin on her hand.

"Pete invited us over for a Fourth of July bonfire." Her mother filled her in.

"Sounds like fun." She couldn't muster much enthusiasm.

Simon leaned against her shoulder. "You should come, Canon."

"Canon?" Dave asked curiously.

"It's Simon's little pet name for Maggie," answered Tom.

Sarah smacked him on the arm.

"*Ow!*"

Maggie and Simon smiled at each other.

His eyes dropped to her mouth for a moment.

"Will Michelle be coming then?" Maggie asked.

His eyes returned to hers. "Oh, yeah, of course." He stuttered a bit with his answer.

"Good. I haven't seen her since that night at Rose's, and we didn't really get to talk."

"She'd like to catch up with you, too."

Maggie had a feeling that wasn't the truth. "Was she very upset about Vegas?" She winced a little, waiting to hear how Michelle had taken it.

Simon shrugged his shoulders. "I told her we were drunk."

She covered her face with her hands and groaned. "You didn't."

"I did." He scrunched up his nose, realizing his mistake. "I thought it would hurt her less that way."

"Well, it's not like you two were together then."

He pressed his lips together and didn't respond.

"You were?" Maggie let out a breath. "Oh, now I feel even worse."

"What are you two talking about?" asked Ron.

She looked over at Simon. "Can we go out there?" She nodded her head in the direction of the front door.

"Here." Simon handed his cards to Sarah, who up until then had been a spectator, and left the table with Maggie.

They walked outside and took a seat on the porch swing.

Maggie got right to the point. "You told me in Vegas that you liked me, that you wanted to spend time together and see where things would go."

Simon nodded. "Yes. Yes, I did." He laughed nervously.

"And you already had a girlfriend?" She raised an eyebrow at him.

"Well, technically, I wasn't dating her until *after* Vegas, but we did talk about it before then. So it was kind of in the works, if you will."

Maggie was through playing games. After the night she'd had, all she wanted was complete honesty. "So, why did you kiss me then?"

Simon cleared his throat. "You walked into the party in that little black dress. What did you expect?" He had a sly grin on his face.

She glared. "I expected you to be faithful to your girlfriend, who is also my very good friend."

"I know, but technically—" He held up his index finger.

She held up her hand and stopped him right there. "*Blah, blah, blah*. Technically she wasn't your girlfriend. Whatever." She looked him in the eye. "You were about to start something with her, and you tried to start something with me. So, what did you really want?"

"I wanted you," he answered firmly.

She shook her head in doubt. "*And* Michelle," she added.

"Just you."

She glanced over at him again. He was staring straight ahead, nervously avoiding eye contact with her. This was not the usually confident Simon she knew. There was no way she would ever understand the male psyche.

"Look, I get it," he finally spoke. "I'm not exactly at the top of your list of favorite people. You weren't interested, so I moved on."

Maggie laughed at that. "No, you didn't." The honesty was spewing out of her faster than she could stop it.

"What do you mean?"

"I saw those pictures you took of me at the wedding. You were watching me."

He looked at her then. "You were amazing."

"Those *pictures* are amazing."

"Yeah, well, a few nice pictures don't prove anything."

Maggie pushed back on the swing to get it rocking. "Yes, they do," she replied confidently.

"Man, you're in a feisty mood." They settled into a rocking rhythm.

"I've had a horrible night. I think I deserve to be a little feisty."

Simon looked at her seriously. "Do you want to talk about it?"

She was touched by his genuine concern for her. The tears began to sting her eyes again, but she pushed them back. "Let's just say I came face to face with my past and leave it at that." She didn't want to think about the disastrous meeting anymore.

"I never liked him," Simon declared. "He didn't appreciate you. Anyone could see that."

She glanced over at him. "Well, I couldn't."

"Love is blind, right?" he said with a shrug.

Maggie nodded.

"He didn't deserve you, Maggie."

She wiped a rogue tear from her cheek.

Simon looked concerned and wrapped his arm around her shoulder. "I'm sorry. I didn't mean to upset you."

"It's OK. It was a long time ago. I really need to get over it already." Maggie sniffled.

He pulled her closer. "Healing takes time."

"Five years?"

"However long it takes," he assured her.

Maggie stared at the damp spots on the front of her shirt left by the tears. "I'm so sick of crying over him."

"Maybe you need to. Maybe you need to talk about it."

She shook her head sadly. "I was so happy. At least I thought I was." She thought back to the night of the engagement. "We went to the beach at Gun Lake. He made us a picnic, and he asked me to marry him at sunset. It was so perfect. He told me I was his best friend, and he couldn't imagine life without me."

Simon kept his arm around her and listened as she shared.

Her tears were falling steadily again.

"I didn't even have to think about my answer. I knew him for so long, and I always knew I wanted to marry him."

She looked at the empty ring finger on her left hand.

"And now he's found someone new. And they're getting married. And she wanted me to be their wedding photographer." She said it with a bit of a laugh, then broke down crying as she remembered the utter humiliation.

Simon pulled her toward him, and she wrapped her arms around him, burying her face in his shirt. He stroked her hair as she sobbed softly against his chest.

"I'm just so tired of being alone," she cried the words. "But I'm afraid Ben ruined my heart forever, and I'm never gonna be able to love again."

When she finally got control of herself, she sat up and wiped her eyes with the back of her hands.

He gently took her hands in his. "Maggie, you are amazing and intelligent and warm and—"

"Simon," she interrupted, feeling shy and embarrassed.

"And beautiful." He spoke softly and looked deep into her eyes. "And you are not going to end up alone. You're gonna find love again. I promise you that."

The tears filled her eyes as she moved into his arms again. He planted a kiss on the top of her head and rubbed his hand up and down her back until her tears subsided. She relaxed into him. With her head resting against his chest and her arm draped across his stomach, she gave in to the emotional exhaustion and drifted off to sleep.

July 4, 2009
Independence Day

Confused emerald eyes stared at Maggie from the other side of the mirror. Though she looked perfectly presentable for Pete's Fourth of July party, she removed the clip from the back of her head and flipped her head upside down, combing her fingers through her tresses. She liked the look of the curls. They made her feel pretty. She turned her head slowly side to side, not sure why she cared so much about her appearance tonight. It was the same group of people who had seen her at her worst only days before. But something had shifted, and things seemed different somehow.

Though it was a little awkward crying all over and then falling asleep on Simon, she felt like the air had been cleared with him. A part of her thought they might actually be friends now, and she was surprised to find she wanted that.

She drove slowly down the winding road that wrapped around Algonquin Lake, following the house numbers until she spotted a few familiar cars—Simon's, her parents' and Tom's. She pulled in behind them, checked her reflection in the mirror once more, applied a little extra lip gloss, and hopped out of the car.

The sound of laughter led her around the side of the house to the backyard. As she rounded the corner, she spotted Simon and Michelle sitting atop a picnic table. He whispered something into her ear, which caused her to smile. She playfully squeezed his knee in that annoying way of theirs, then leaned in and kissed him.

A nagging feeling hit Maggie in the gut.

"Mags!" exclaimed Sarah, running toward her with sparklers in hand.

Simon abruptly turned from Michelle and his gaze followed Sarah's.

A weak grin was all Maggie could manage, especially when she saw the look of disbelief on Michelle's face at Simon's sudden distraction.

Sarah handed her a sparkler, and they walked across the yard to Tom, who was seated near the dock.

"Mags, we need you," Tom cried.

"For what?"

Sarah giggled a little and held her left hand in front of Maggie's face.

She shrieked at the sight of the diamond on her friend's ring finger. "Oh my gosh! Are you serious?" She hugged Sarah tightly. "I can't believe it!"

"Is it so hard to believe that I actually found someone?" Tom asked. "Or that she actually said yes?"

"You said it, not me," teased Maggie, leaning over the back of the chair and wrapping her arms around her brother's neck.

Sarah was beaming brighter than the rock on her hand.

Maggie's head suddenly jerked toward Sarah and her mouth dropped open.

"A mosquito's gonna get in there," Tom warned.

"We're gonna be sisters!" Maggie declared.

There was more shrieking and hugging and congratulating.

When they finally settled down, Tom looked seriously at his sister. "What we need to know is would you rather be maid of honor or photograph the wedding?"

Maggie bit her lip for a second. "Oh my goodness."

Sarah reached over and squeezed her hand. "There's nobody in the world I would rather have photograph my wedding than you, but I really want you to stand next to me when I marry your brother."

So much happiness and joy filled her heart as she squeezed back. "And I want to be your maid of honor."

"Really?" Sarah hugged her once more. "Thank you, sis."

"This is the best news I've heard in ages." Maggie took a deep breath of fresh air and sighed. "The night can't get much better than this."

Sarah was the missing piece in Tom's life, and Maggie was overjoyed to have her join their family. It had been hard to see Tom down in the dumps so often because of his job, but since Sarah, it was like none of that mattered anymore. He had found the one who made his life complete.

To see her brother so happily matched made Maggie feel hopeful about love. She even started to entertain the thought that she might find it again.

Simon's words came back to her then. *You are not going to end up alone. You're gonna find love again. I promise you that.*

And then she remembered him calling her beautiful, and her heart skipped a beat. She glanced across the yard at Simon. *Maybe I've been wrong about him all this time.*

Sarah grabbed hold of her arm and pulled her from her thoughts. "So, don't freak out, but we set the date."

"Why would I freak out?"

"It's December nineteenth," Sarah joyfully proclaimed.

Maggie's eyes grew wide. Had she heard Sarah correctly? "December? Of this year?"

Sarah nodded.

"That only leaves us five months!" Maggie held her hand up in the air, five fingers spread. "Five!"

Sarah laughed at her. "It's fine, Maggie. I hired DeDe to coordinate everything."

A wave of relief washed over her. "Oh, good."

"We can make this happen," Sarah assured her.

"If anyone can do it, DeDe can."

When darkness came, a loud thud from across the lake signaled the launch of the fireworks. Brilliant reds and blues sparkled against the starry night sky. Maggie sat on a blanket on the lawn with Sarah and Tom, who were all snuggled up despite the summer heat. The darkness of evening had done nothing to diminish the sultry daytime temperatures. Stretching her legs out in front of her, Maggie leaned back on her elbows. She glanced around the yard.

Her parents were seated on a blanket just behind them with Vi and Dave. It appeared Dave was attempting to make the marriage work. The two of them looked rather cozy, which made Maggie happy. Across the lawn, Uncle Pete and a couple of his neighbor buddies sat in lawn chairs, talking and smoking cigars, not paying much attention to the fireworks.

Maggie's glance fell on Simon and Michelle, who were lying on a blanket watching the fireworks display. Maggie should have been watching, too, but she couldn't tear her eyes from them. There was no logical explanation for her reaction earlier when Simon and Michelle had kissed. She was his girlfriend after all. Michelle rolled over against Simon, draped her leg over his, and leaned her head against his arm. *She looks happy.*

Just then, Simon shifted Michelle off of his arm and propped himself up on his elbows. He gazed at Maggie.

Busted.

She gave him a friendly smile, to which he nodded in an almost polite manner.

She turned to watch the fireworks, but she could feel his stare. She ran her fingers through her hair and fluffed it up. When she glanced back at him again, he was still watching her. He gave her that crooked grin he got when he was amused, then laid back down next to Michelle.

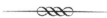

When the fireworks ended, Pete started the bonfire with the help of Tom and Simon. The ladies sat at the picnic table near the house and watched the men rearrange the wood to get the best flames.

"Good job, honey," called Sarah.

Tom gave her a thumbs up and jumped back suddenly when a large flame licked up at him. "*Ah!*"

The girls laughed.

"Aren't they so strong and manly?" teased Maggie. "We made fire," she mocked in her manliest voice.

"Let us see you do it better, Canon," Simon called across the yard. He peeled the gloves he was wearing from his hands and held them out to her.

Maggie grinned at Sarah and strolled across the lawn. She glanced back at the ladies and flexed her muscles to show how tough she was.

"Here," Simon slipped the gloves on her hands and gave her a pat on the back. "Go for it."

She looked over at the girls again and caught Michelle's eye for a second. She wasn't smiling at all. Maggie felt a little twinge of guilt.

The fire was burning pretty well already, but Maggie helped Pete stoke it until it was burning steady and strong. She glanced over at Simon, who was holding a long branch and attempting to burn pieces of mulch, which had found their way out of the nearby flower beds.

"What is it with guys and fire?" she asked. "Pyro."

"It's a bonfire. You're supposed to burn stuff." His attention returned to the fire, and he pushed on a log, sparks floating up into the black night.

Maggie nodded toward the cooler sitting next to her mother's lawn chair. "Go roast a wiener or something. Make yourself useful."

Simon laughed aloud at that.

This friendly banter was new for them. She liked it. A lot.

He walked to the cooler and returned with a hot dog, stabbed through it with a stick, and stood next to Maggie while he held it over the hot coals.

She glanced up at him, and he wore that amused grin again. He looked good in the firelight, comfy and casual in his khaki shorts and blue t-shirt, which perfectly accented his broad chest and muscular arms.

"Simon," Michelle walked up beside him and wrapped her hands around one of those muscles. "Can you take me home now?" Michelle was very obviously unhappy. Her voice was unsteady, pouty lips turned down in a frown, and her forehead was tight, leaving an unmistakable crease between her eyes.

When the girls had gathered at the picnic table earlier in the night, Maggie had attempted a conversation with Michelle, but she had not been a willing participant.

"How are you, Chelle?" she had asked.

"Fine," was her reply.

She tried again. "How's it going with you and Simon?"

"Great."

Conversation over.

Ever since that night at Rose's, the communication lines between them had been closed. Despite Maggie's many attempts to reach out to her in emails, phone calls and texts, Michelle never responded to one. She knew now that their friendship was probably damaged beyond repair.

Still, Maggie tried.

"We should have coffee next week."

Michelle clung tighter to Simon and said nothing more.

He finished roasting the hot dog and walked over to the table to grab a bun.

Michelle glared at her for a moment, then turned and walked across the lawn toward the driveway.

Maggie could tell from her bitter expression that they would never have coffee or anything together again. All she could do was watch one of her closest friends walk out of her life for good.

Simon handed the hot dog to Maggie as he passed by. "For you, Canon. Enjoy."

She took it from him and grinned. "I'm a vegetarian." She tossed the dog into the fire.

He shook his head in amusement and followed Michelle across the lawn.

"Margaret," her mother scolded. "You are *not* a vegetarian. And you just wasted perfectly good food."

Maggie couldn't stop laughing. She returned the gloves to Pete and sat down next to Sarah.

"Wow!" Sarah spoke once Simon and Michelle were out of earshot. "Could that have been any more obvious?"

"What?" Maggie asked.

"You and Simon."

Maggie looked at her searchingly. "What do you mean?"

"The flirting."

She gasped. "We weren't flirting."

"You most certainly were," Vi piped in.

Maggie shook her head. They had not been flirting. They were two friends joking around. *Friends.* Surprisingly, she no longer cringed at the thought.

"How do you explain yourself?" her mother asked.

"There's nothing to explain," she answered. "There was no flirting."

Sarah elbowed Maggie. "I don't think Michelle would agree."

"Well, it was unintentional," she insisted.

"It looked intentional." Her mother gave her the look only a mother gets when she knows exactly what her child is trying to get away with. "He's no longer available, young lady."

"I'm *not* after Simon, Mom."

Nobody seemed to buy it.

Maggie's feet dangled from Uncle Pete's dock, and her toes made circles on the surface of the water. Her mother's laugh floated across the yard, and she smiled to herself. Moments like these didn't come along often. She was beginning to realize with each passing day how important her family and friends were and how precious time with them was. Her constant work schedule and busyness had caused her to lose focus on what was most important. Their love and support the other night had shown her that.

She glanced out at the dark lake in front of her. The lights from the houses reflected across the rippling water, the crickets chirped, and a soft, warm breeze blew in from the lake. A few boats were out motoring about, and she could hear the sound of happy people enjoying their Independence Day.

The wooden planks of the dock felt cool as she laid back and looked up at the perfectly clear night sky. The stars twinkled just for her. It had been a long time since she laid out under the stars. The last time had been with Ben a month before they were to be married. She closed her eyes and listened to the sounds of the night, trying to shake off the memory of them lying in the backyard at Maggie's parents house, kissing and talking about their future. It was only days later that the dream of their future together was shattered.

Footsteps on the dock conveniently interrupted her thoughts, and she sat up to see who it was.

"Can I sit?" Simon approached and sat down without waiting for her answer.

"I didn't know you were coming back." She laid down again.

He kicked his flip flops off and dropped his feet into the water. His eyes met hers.

"So how is it that you don't have a wedding tonight? I thought you were the most sought after photographer in town," he teased.

"How is that *you* don't have a wedding?" She threw back at him. "I thought *you* were the most sought after ..." She stopped. "Nah. I can't finish that sentence. I don't like to lie."

"Funny." He laid back next to her. "Wow! The stars are really bright tonight."

Maggie could feel the heat from his arm resting next to hers. If she moved an inch to the left, their arms would touch.

Oh my gosh! Mom was right. It was intentional. I'm so pathetic. This is Simon we're talking about. Simon! Come on, Maggie!

She sat up.

Simon sat up, too, his arm now touching hers.

She wanted to move, but she couldn't. His arm was so warm against hers, and it felt really good. She missed being close to someone—the snuggling, the hand-holding, the kissing, all of it.

It had been three days since their conversation on the porch swing, but she could still feel his strong arms wrapped around her, his lips touching the top of her head. That night had been completely innocent. He had been there for her and made her feel safe.

But tonight, a strange electricity hung in the air between them, and something was drawing them together. This was the first time since she had known Simon that she actually wanted to be close to him—like wrapped up in his arms, making out under the stars kind of close.

She looked over at him at the same time he turned to look at her.

"How are you doing? Feeling any better about things?" he asked.

"Better now." She didn't even try to veil her meaning.

They didn't say anything. They looked at each other for what seemed like an eternity.

Simon was the first to move. He brushed her hair back off of her shoulder, his fingers grazing her skin ever so softly.

Maggie's eyes closed at the sensation, and she let out a slow breath, bracing for something more to happen. But when she opened her eyes again, he was getting up.

Disappointment overcame her. "Leaving so soon?" she managed.

"I think I should," he replied, not very convincingly, his voice shaky.

She stood then.

He took a few steps away from her.

"See ya', Nikon," she teased.

He spun around and gave her the Simon grin once more. "Oh, you did *not*." He was clearly amused by his new nickname.

She shrugged. "I did." She'd been waiting months for just the right moment to call him that. "I think it's only fair."

He lunged forward, grabbed her arms, and held her back over the edge of the dock.

"*Ah!*" she cried. "Simon, don't you dare."

He leaned her back a little further.

Maggie tried to wiggle out of his grip, which caused him to lose his balance, and sent them both splashing down into the lake.

Their laughter traveled across the water.

"I can't believe you did that." She splashed at him.

"That was all you, Canon." He splashed back.

They circled each other in the water, splashing back and forth.

"Maggie?" her mother called from the yard.

"Yeah, Mom!"

"We heard a splash, are you all right?"

"Just going for a swim." She laughed at Simon, who had hidden himself under the dock.

"I'll go get you a towel," Patty called back at her.

Simon grabbed her arm and pulled her weightlessly through the water and under the dock with him. He held his finger up to his lips, as if they were little kids about to get in trouble. "*Shhhh!*"

Maggie started to giggle.

It was so dark under the dock, they could barely see each other. She hoped he couldn't see how big her smile was.

He suddenly reached for her, and the smile faded from her face as things took an unexpected but not completely unwelcome turn. Strong hands held her hips and pulled her closer to him. The water slipped like silk around and between them, and in an instant everything became very fuzzy.

116

She immediately thought of Michelle's reaction earlier. Michelle had always been a faithful friend to her and here she was with Michelle's boyfriend about to do God knows what. *No! No! No! I can't do this.*

But she was lonely, and it felt good to be held. It had been such a long time since any man wanted to be this close to her. So when Simon's hands glided smoothly around her waist, she ignored her thoughts, and slipped her arms around his neck.

Simon pulled her into a hug and rested his chin on her shoulder. His breathing was unsteady, coming in quick bursts now.

They floated there motionless for a minute before he rotated his head away from her face. His wet hair tickled her cheek, and she reached up and touched it.

Simon breathed out and turned so his lips were pressed against the spot where shoulder met neck. He remained very still while she played with his hair. It wasn't until Maggie raked her fingertips against his scalp, that he began to move. His lips slid excruciatingly slow up the side of her neck until he stopped at the spot just below her ear.

As if to prod him on, Maggie hugged him tighter to her. She felt his lips part and his breath escape hot against her throat as he kissed her neck.

Patty's footsteps on the dock above brought them back to reality, and they froze where they floated.

"Maggie, I'm leaving a towel here for you," Patty informed her. "There's one for Simon, too. You two better come in now." Her mother wasn't born yesterday.

Simon let out a slow breath against Maggie's neck and lifted his head away. His hands moved swiftly up her back, over her shoulders and down her arms, leaving little goosebumps in their wake. When he reached her wrists, he pried her arms from around his neck and they separated. The water felt much colder than it had just moments before.

Never had Maggie felt such a mix of emotions. On the one hand, she felt horribly guilty for what had just happened. She had betrayed her friend and let herself be more influenced by her hormones than her morals. And Simon had basically cheated on his girlfriend ... with her. What kind of a person was she to let that happen? She had been in Michelle's shoes and knew the pain of being cheated on all too well.

There was another part of her, though—the lonely part that longed to find someone, to be loved and wanted again—that was feeling pretty good.

Simon turned his back on her to climb up onto the dock. Floating alone in the water, her heart still raced as she watched him. He grabbed her wrists and lifted her up. She fell forward a bit, gripping his forearms for support. His hands held her waist to steady her.

They stood for several long moments, fighting the pull between them. But it only took one look into Simon's eyes to realize this had been a mistake. He looked guiltier than she felt, and she knew he regretted it.

Maggie swallowed hard.

Finally, he let go and reached for one of the towels Patty had left for them. He wrapped it around her shoulders and rubbed up and down on her arms.

"I can do it," she spoke quietly.

He grabbed the other towel, tossed it over his shoulder, and walked quickly across the yard, disappearing into his uncle's house.

Maggie felt like a complete idiot.

July 6, 2009
An Unexpected Meeting

I practically threw myself at him." Maggie buried her head in her arms.

"I'm sure it's not as bad as you're making it sound." Sarah tried to comfort her.

She lifted her head from the desk and looked up at Sarah. "Yes it is. I made a complete fool of myself. He had to pretty much pull me off of him." She dropped her head again.

Sarah started laughing.

"Not funny." Her voice was muffled by her arms.

The phone rang, and Sarah leaned over to answer it. "Magnolia Photography. This is Sarah."

Maggie sat back in her chair and moved the mouse to wake the computer from screensaver mode.

"Yes, she is. Hold one moment, please." Sarah pressed the hold button and handed the phone to Maggie. "It's Becky Bristol wanting to talk to you about her wedding."

"Oh, great. That's next month. Thanks." She grabbed the phone from Sarah and pressed "line one". "Hi, Becky. How are you? I was going to call you next week to go over last minute details."

"John and I are calling off the wedding," Becky blurted.

"Oh, no," Maggie replied. "Are you OK?"

Sarah was perched on the edge of Maggie's desk looking through some mail. She gazed curiously at Maggie.

"Not really," Becky admitted. "John cheated on me."

Maggie's heart sank. "Oh, Becky, I'm so sorry." She heard Becky sniffle.

"I'm so sorry about this, Maggie. I feel so bad cancelling on you so last minute."

"Don't worry about me. How are you doing?" She knew exactly what Becky was going through and wished there was something she could say to help.

"Well, obviously, I've been better. My mom keeps saying it's a good thing I found out who he really is before we got married."

"Your mom is a very smart woman."

"I know she's right, but a part of me still wants to marry him."

She shook her head in agreement, though Becky couldn't see her. "That will pass. You'll get through this in time. Trust me." *In about five years.*

"Thank you, Maggie," Becky spoke quietly. "Someday when I do find the right guy, you're the first person I'm calling."

"Take care of yourself, Becky."

When Maggie hung up, she couldn't shake the surge of depression that suddenly gripped her. Why did things keep happening that brought Ben to the forefront of her mind? The emotions she had dealt with surrounding her own breakup came rushing back. Getting through those days had been excruciating, not to mention humiliating. There were so many phone calls to make—the photographer, the hall, the church, the caterer, the florist, the list went on and on. Becky would have to deal with all of those things now.

"The wedding's off," she announced to Sarah. "He cheated on her."

"Oh, no." Sarah shook her head.

Maggie put a large X over their names on her calendar and groaned when she realized it was too close to their date to book another wedding. She worried about the lost income.

Just then, the front door opened, and Sarah flew from her perch to see who it was.

"Hi, Sarah," DeDe greeted her.

Maggie came out of the office when she heard DeDe's voice.

"Hey, Maggie. Do you want to go to lunch?"

"Of course," she replied.

"Do you have time for a lunch meeting?" DeDe gave Maggie a big grin.

She almost laughed out loud at how big DeDe was smiling at her. "What's up, De?"

"Do you have time to go to Grand Rapids with me?"

The girls looked at each other and back at DeDe, who was acting very strangely.

"I can make time."

"Good. You'll need your sample albums and price lists." She gave Maggie a once over. "And maybe give your hair a brush and touch up your makeup."

Maggie raised an eyebrow at DeDe.

"Come on, Maggie," DeDe ordered. "Chop chop."

She rushed around the office, grabbing everything she needed for this impromptu meeting. This wasn't the first time DeDe had dragged her somewhere at the last minute to meet with wedding couples. She ducked into the bathroom and ran a brush through her hair.

"De, you have to tell me what's going on." Maggie could barely stand the suspense.

"I'll tell you on the way."

"No fair," Sarah cried. "Tell me, too."

"All in good time." DeDe grabbed Maggie's bag and headed out the door.

Maggie shrugged her shoulders at Sarah and gave her a frightened look as she followed DeDe. "I'll call you later."

They hopped in DeDe's minivan and drove west following State Street out of town past all the banks, fast food restaurants, and gas stations. After they passed Bob's Gun and Tackle Shop on the outskirts of town, DeDe headed north toward Grand Rapids.

"Are you gonna tell me before we get there?" asked Maggie impatiently.

DeDe glanced over at her with that huge grin again. "The governor's daughter is getting married."

"*Whoa!*" Maggie exclaimed.

"I've been hired to coordinate." DeDe was bubbling with excitement.

"Are you serious?" Maggie was so happy for her friend. "That's huge."

"Yes, thanks to my wonderful connections."

"Congratulations! That's amazing, De."

"This bring me to why I kidnapped you today." DeDe smiled deviously. "Photographers from all over the state are vying for this job, but they've asked me to compile a list to help them in their decision. This is going to be a huge event on Mackinac Island next summer."

Maggie's eyes widened. "Am I on your list?" She didn't need to ask.

"You know you are." DeDe smiled.

The idea of photographing the wedding of the governor's daughter was exciting and intimidating at the same time. She suddenly developed a queasy sensation in the pit of her stomach. "Wait! Are we meeting them right now?"

DeDe nodded. "They're in town for the day and will be meeting us at my office to talk with you about their vision for the wedding and, of course, let you wow them."

She took a deep breath in. "Oh, I think I'm hyperventilating." She breathed out slowly. "This would totally make up for the cancelled wedding this morning and then some."

"Oh no, who cancelled?" asked DeDe.

"Becky and John."

"What happened?"

"John cheated." Maggie suddenly had a flash of her and Simon under the dock on Saturday. Thinking about the situation from the other perspective made her feel even more guilty about it. *I'm a horrible person.*

"That's awful." DeDe looked at her searchingly. "How are you doing? I know that must remind you of things."

"I'm fine. Just sad for her." Maggie shook off the feeling again. She couldn't possibly be depressed after the news of the governor's daughter. "So, who else will they be meeting with?"

DeDe reached into her bag and handed Maggie the list of vendors. There were florists and cake companies as well as a few other photographers on the list. Simon was among them. She felt more nervous knowing that fact. Not only did she have to impress them, she had to compete against Simon for this one.

When they reached DeDe's office, Lacey Hartman and her fiancé, George Summers, were already waiting. Maggie remembered them both from the newspaper article she had seen months ago. DeDe made the introductions, and the four of them sat together to talk wedding.

"Maggie, we were so impressed with the work we saw on your website. You have such a gift for capturing the moments, and that's something we're really interested in." Lacey flipped her perfect shoulder-length blonde hair over her shoulder. It was a seemingly common thing for a girl to do, but her movement seemed much more graceful. She was as tall and beautiful as any supermodel, but she exuded such sophistication and class.

"Oh, thank you," Maggie replied. "That's definitely my strength and what I focus on the most in my work."

"Have you ever shot a wedding on Mackinac Island before?" asked Lacey.

"Yours would be my first, but I've been to the island several times. I love it there."

"We do, too. I go there often with my family. It's always been a special place for me. George actually proposed to me there on the porch at the Grand Hotel, so there was really no question as to where we would have our wedding." She glanced over at her fiancé, and he squeezed her hand.

"Lacey and I are looking for someone who can capture the beauty of our day and showcase not only our ceremony and the details of the wedding, but also the unique atmosphere of the island." George Summers was a handsome man. At first glance, one might have mistaken him for John F. Kennedy, Jr. The son of a senator, he was proper and well-spoken, but not in a condescending way. He had a certain charisma that made people instantly comfortable around him.

"Absolutely. There's so much charm to the island." Just thinking about the island made Maggie want to go for a visit. There was something so magical about it. "One of the reasons I love my job is that each wedding is different. Every couple has a different story—how they met and fell in love, when they knew that they were meant to spend the rest of their lives together. It's those stories that I'm drawn to. The weddings, these celebrations of love, all the little details—the dress, the shoes, the flowers, the decorations, the food—well, that's all beautiful. But it's the moments that make it what it is. It's the looks, the touches, the kisses. It's about your story, and that's what I want to capture."

George smiled at Lacey, and she squeezed his hand this time.

They spent over an hour looking through albums, discussing the details of Maggie's coverage, and going over the special requirements for their wedding. She was already looking forward to it, and they hadn't even hired her yet.

After Lacey and George said farewell, Maggie collapsed into one of DeDe's chairs. She felt confident that the meeting had gone well.

"You were perfect," DeDe praised her. "Now, we wait."

"When will we know?" Maggie was already anxious.

"As soon as they decide, good or bad, I'll let you know."

July 24, 2009

Surprises

*H*appy Birthday, Maggie." Tom hugged her tight. "I'm sorry I'm a couple days late."

"Oh, that's OK." She waved it off. "Just another year older, right?" As the years passed by, birthdays didn't seem to hold as much meaning to her anymore. And thirty-two was certainly nothing special at all.

"I want to make it up to you," he replied. "Can Sarah and I take you across the street for some coffee?"

"Sure. I could use a break." She was presently working on pictures from the two weddings she had photographed in July and had been glued to her office chair all week. On her birthday, she had worked the day away, despite Sarah's attempts to get her to take the day off.

The three of them wandered across the street to State Grounds.

Maggie opened the door. The coffee shop was strangely quiet, and the lights were off in the back, which she found rather odd.

Suddenly, the lights flipped on. "SURPRISE!" cried the waiting crowd.

She jumped and nearly knocked Tom and Sarah over backwards. Laughter overtook her.

"You guys!" She gave Tom and Sarah a dirty look. "I can't believe you did this."

"Well, we had help." Sarah hugged her.

DeDe approached and gave her a hug.

"I suspect you had something to do with this, De."

"Guilty."

Maggie was beaming. This was completely unexpected. No one had thrown her a surprise party since she was in high school. She glanced around the room. Her parents were there, as well as Vi and Dave. Pete had stopped by, and there were a slew of her wedding friends, including Jamie and Shannon. She scanned the faces. No Simon. No Michelle. She was disappointed, but pushed the feeling aside.

Suddenly, a pair of hands covered her eyes from behind and a horribly camouflaged voice said, "Happy birthday, Magnet."

Maggie screeched and pulled the hands away. "Kay?" She whipped around and threw her arms around her high school best friend. Standing next to her was their other partner in crime. "Brooke? I can't believe you guys are here!" It had been several years since they last saw each other and even longer since they were all together.

"Tommy called us," Brooke replied as she took her turn hugging the birthday girl.

After high school, the friends had gone their separate ways. Kay moved to Virginia to attend Liberty University on a basketball scholarship, while Brooke went to the University of Michigan in Ann Arbor. Both were married with small children now, which made it more difficult to get together.

The girls found a table in the corner, where they could chat.

"How are you, Magnet?" Kay asked.

Maggie grinned. "I love that you still call me that." Magnet was the nickname she'd been given by P.J., otherwise known as Pastor Jon. He liked to say Maggie, Kay and Brooke were together so much that they were attached magnetically at the hip. The nickname stuck and it's what everyone in the youth group called her. Well, all but one.

"How's business?" asked Brooke.

"Oh my gosh, I'm more interested in what's happening with you two."

"Well," Brooke patted her belly. "Baby number two is on the way."

"Really? Brooke, that's so wonderful." Maggie was happy for her friend, but felt a sadness deep down inside. Her best friends were married with families of their own. She wanted that so much it made her heart ache. "What's new with you, Kay?"

Kay ignored Maggie's question. "So, this might not be the perfect time to bring this up, but Tom told us you've been having kind of a rough time lately."

Maggie rolled her eyes. "I'm gonna kill him."

"Do you wanna talk about it?" Kay asked.

"There's nothing to talk about."

Kay looked at her in disbelief. "This is us you're talking to. We know you. Tell us."

Maggie relayed the humiliating story of her discovery of Ben's engagement.

"I can't believe him." Brooke shook her head. "This girl, Beth, he's engaged to, he's known her for like six months."

"How do you know that?" asked Maggie.

"His mom and mine are still really good friends."

She had forgotten. This information did not make her feel any better about the situation, but it sort of explained why Beth didn't know he was previously engaged. They barely knew each other. At least not compared to how long she and Ben had known each other before they got together.

Sarah joined them at the table, and Maggie made introductions. It felt wonderful to be surrounded by all of the most important people in her life. She was in a happy little bubble all night long.

Maggie walked through the crowd to Bill and Cindy, who were standing by the counter talking with a couple of their employees.

"You guys!" She hugged them both at the same time. "Thank you so much for having my party here."

Cindy returned her hug. "We know how hard you're always working and we wanted to help do something special for you."

"Happy Birthday, Maggie." Bill squeezed her a little too tightly. "Promise me you'll relax and have fun tonight."

"I will."

"Because you really do work too hard and you need to take care of yourself."

"I know."

"I hate to see you looking so tired." He seemed overly concerned about her.

Maggie knew he didn't mean it as an insult, but she was suddenly self-conscious. Did she have dark circles or bags under her eyes? Was it really so easy to tell how exhausted she was?

She was about to excuse herself to check her reflection in the bathroom mirror, when she heard music from the back of the room. A band had taken the stage and was now playing just for her. It was a group she'd heard at the coffee shop before and had enjoyed. She moved closer and took a seat at one of the tables.

Sarah, Tom, Kay and Brooke joined her.

She pointed at the band. "This is too much."

"We didn't hire them." Tom revealed.

Sarah shrugged her shoulders.

"You didn't?"

Cindy overheard them and piped in. "Oh, they showed up earlier and said they were here for the party. I assumed one of you had called them."

"Wasn't us." Sarah replied.

Tom shrugged his shoulders this time.

"Well, it's great." Maggie turned to Kay and Brooke. "I heard these guys play here last year, and they were amazing."

Everyone enjoyed the live music and plenty of coffee as the night went on.

Maggie knew she should mingle more, but all she wanted was to be with Kay and Brooke. She had missed them so much, and longed for those youth group days when they were attached at the hip. Things were so much simpler then.

"Hey, birthday girl." DeDe walked over to the table and tapped her coffee cup against Maggie's mug.

"Any news on the big event?" Maggie asked.

DeDe shook her head as she took an open seat. "They've got a couple more vendors to meet with, then they'll make their final decisions."

"I'm dying here." Maggie had never been very good at the whole patience thing.

"I know." DeDe replied.

"What's this big event?" Brooke asked.

Maggie's face lit up. "The governor's daughter is getting married, and I'm up for the photographer job."

"Wow!" Brooke exclaimed.

"That's so great," said Kay. "Are you all booked up this year?"

Maggie hesitated. "My calendar's pretty full this year and about half what I'd like to shoot for next year."

"Don't worry. The weddings will come. People are always getting married," DeDe replied with a smile.

She hadn't been completely honest. There had been another cancellation, this time one of her September weddings. Truthfully, she was growing worried. The timing was horrible with the cancellations being so close to the end of her wedding season. And her calendar for next year wasn't even close to half booked. She had a few weddings on the books, but nowhere near as many as she needed to stay afloat— nowhere near as many as she had booked by the same time last year. She wasn't sure if Walker's new studio was to blame or not. What she did know was that her finances were going to be extremely tight, and without new bookings, she would have to come up with new ways to cover her losses.

Maggie heard the door jingle. Her heart leapt a bit, thinking perhaps it was Simon making a late appearance, but it was someone who didn't see the sign on the door that read: CLOSED FOR PRIVATE PARTY.

She took a sip of her mocha and stared out at the street. Simon had surely been invited, and she knew why he hadn't come. Since the Fourth, there had been no sign of him in town. Maggie was a little sad about it. He was a busy guy, but she knew he was probably staying away to avoid any more ... under the dock moments. She wondered how his meeting with the governor's daughter had gone. DeDe would tell her nothing, and she felt too unsure of where their friendship stood to call him and ask.

Bill stopped by the table with a fresh mocha for Maggie without being asked.

Suddenly, the notes of a familiar song came from the band. A smile spread across her face. It was "You Don't Know Me", the song she and Simon had danced to in Vegas, and she had a sudden realization.

"I bet Simon hired the band," Maggie stated.

A little snort escaped from Bill.

Tom made a face at him.

Sarah raised her eyebrows. "Really? Why?"

Maggie grinned. "Just a hunch." She looked over at her brother, whose curious gaze followed Bill all the way to the counter.

"Tommy? Do you know something."

"What? No."

Sarah leaned forward and looked him in the eye. "To-o-om?"

"No, I don't."

Maggie stared him down.

"Honestly. I don't know who hired them. But I'm pretty sure it wasn't Simon."

"I'm so right." Maggie felt proud of herself, so sure she had figured it out.

"Who's Simon?" Kay asked. "Do you mean Simon from college? Your roommate's friend?"

"Roommate's boyfriend now," Maggie stated.

"*Oh*." Kay nodded.

Bill approached their table again with a small plate of muffins. "I forgot to tell you. Cindy saw your friend, Michelle, in here with her boyfriend the other day."

"Oh, yeah?" Maggie managed.

"Tell them congratulations for me."

"What does that mean?" Sarah asked as she grabbed one of the muffins.

"On their engagement," he replied.

Maggie's mouth went dry.

"They're engaged?" Sarah's eyes grew wide.

Bill looked nervous. "Oh, I thought you all knew."

"No, we hadn't heard that." Sarah looked at Maggie.

"Sorry to ruin the surprise." Bill sheepishly returned to his post.

"I can't believe they're engaged." Maggie tried to feel happy for Michelle, but all she could think about was being under the dock with Simon.

Tom was watching Bill again.

Maggie followed his eye line and received a grin and a nod from Bill.

"What are you looking at?" Maggie asked her brother.

He was wearing his usual deep in thought expression, but came out of it at Maggie's question. "I'm just surprised Simon didn't tell me himself, that's all."

At the end of the night, after all the hugs and thanks and sad farewells to Kay and Brooke, Maggie walked across the street to her office. Tom and Sarah had rushed her out of there so quickly that she had no time to finish answering emails or power down her computer.

Her inbox remained open on the computer desktop, and there were a few new messages. The last one caught her eye.

Simon. She couldn't stop herself from grinning.

```
Happy Birthday, Canon!
Click this link for your gift.
- S
```

She clicked the link, which took her to a webpage with the photo booth pictures from Vegas. Her face broke into a huge smile. There on the screen were all the silly photos of her and the girls as well as the round of photos when Simon had joined in. She looked ridiculous just standing to the side while the girls hung all over Simon. She rolled her eyes.

But the very last picture caught her attention and brought her the biggest smile of all. Simon was dipping her back. His nose was nearly touching hers, their faces so close, both of them smiling, and the girls were laughing in the background. She stared at the photo for a few minutes, remembering what had happened not long after it was taken, and she got butterflies in her stomach thinking about his lips touching hers.

This was the best gift she'd received all night. She clicked to reply and paused, unsure of what to say.

```
Simon,
Thank you for the pictures. Best gift ever!
You were missed tonight.
Maggie
```

She paused again and considered congratulating him on his engagement, but she couldn't bring herself to mention it. She clicked "send" before she had a chance to change her mind.

By Monday, Maggie was extremely anxious about the Hartman wedding. She was dying to know their decision. Ever since the meeting, she had been praying daily that they would choose her, that this whole thing was meant to be. Deep down in her heart, she had always believed every client she worked with was chosen for her by God. Other photographers she knew would complain about bride-zillas, horrible family situations, and overall nightmare weddings, but Maggie had never experienced that. And she had to believe all of the cancelled weddings weren't by accident, that there was a reason she wasn't supposed to photograph those weddings. She had to believe that or she might lose faith in everything.

Sarah was already at her desk when Maggie arrived, which meant she was ducking out early to do something with Tom.

"Hey, sis," Maggie winked at her.

Sarah didn't respond right away. She wore a look of concern.

"What is it?"

Sarah walked over and gave her a hug.

"What's the matter?" She was acting so strangely that Maggie was overcome with panic. "Is everyone OK?"

"Yeah. Sorry. Everyone's fine." She handed Maggie a piece of paper with a message on it. "Megan called this morning."

"Megan?" Her brain wasn't registering the name.

"Your August fifteenth bride Megan."

"August fifteenth Megan called? Oh, this doesn't sound good." She backed up and grabbed onto her wingback chair.

"She and Chris broke up." Sarah winced as she spoke. "The wedding's off."

The paper slipped from Maggie's fingers and floated to the floor. "What is happening? Doesn't anyone stay together anymore? Why don't we just call up the rest of the weddings and tell them we're cancelling them, too."

"Maggie, it's gonna be fine." Sarah tried to comfort her. "You'll book more."

The phone rang, and she jumped. "I've gotta get out of here." She bolted out the door as fast as a spooked horse.

Maggie didn't know where she was going, but she climbed into her car and turned the ignition. She drove around town for a while, taking State Road out toward Algonquin Lake. As she neared Algonquin, she thought of the Fourth of July, which caused her to suddenly turn left on Airport Road to get away from there, too. She kept driving, turning randomly at every stop sign. Before she knew it, she was at Gun Lake. She stopped at the gas station across from the Curly Cone ice cream stand to fill up, then drove to the little park on the west edge of the lake. It was the place she always went when she needed to think things through.

She parked her car and walked across the street toward the water. There were several children running around the playground and some families having picnics together. Maggie found an empty picnic table under the shade trees and sat facing the lake.

She wasn't aware of the time passing, she just sat for hours, letting the thoughts freely flow—first the cancelled weddings, then her own broken relationship, then Ben's engagement, and now Simon and Michelle's engagement. It all felt like too much.

Each cancelled wedding was like salt on an open wound. Seeing Ben again had been excruciating, worse than she ever thought it would be. But knowing he had moved on *had* given her some sense of closure—if only a little. There was even that part of her that thought she might finally be ready to move on. But all of these breakups reminded her that there was no such thing as a secure relationship. Not even Dave and Vi were safe and stable after thirty years. Things never worked out like they were supposed to. Happily ever after wasn't a reality.

She felt like a fool for believing it could ever happen for her again and for letting Simon into her thoughts so much after the dock incident. He was with Michelle, and they were engaged now.

The more she thought about their time under the dock, the more it infuriated her. How could he show her so much attention one minute, then go and propose to Michelle the next?

And what about Michelle? Part of her thought she should be honest and let Michelle know what had happened under that dock. Could she really let Michelle marry someone who was so capable of infidelity? Shouldn't Michelle have all the facts before she made such an important decision?

She felt nauseated. It didn't help that she hadn't eaten all day.

Her cell phone buzzed. It had been buzzing all day, but she ignored it again.

She walked closer to the water. The breeze off the lake caressed her face, and she closed her eyes and took a deep breath. It was peaceful there, and she hated to leave, but when her stomach growled for the tenth time, she decided to drive to her parents house to bum a free meal.

Her mother greeted her with a big hug when she arrived.

"Sarah called. Are you OK?"

"No." Maggie was so numb that she couldn't cry. "I've lost so much business in the last month, Mom. I feel totally helpless."

"Hello, Magpie." Ron was playing cards with Dave, Vi and Pete, as had become the usual.

"Hi, Daddy."

"Here." Patty pointed to the mug on the counter. "I made you some coffee."

"How did you know I'd come?"

"You're my daughter. I know you."

Maggie was glad for that. She slid the mug closer and added some sugar and creamer.

"I'm scared, Mom. Business has been going along really well for the last few years. I've had cancellations before, but never three in one month. And I'm just not booking weddings right now. I'm taking a huge hit."

"There's a reason for everything, Maggie," her father piped in.

Pete was listening intently. "Everything will work out," he encouraged. "You've gotta have faith."

She grinned at Pete. He really was a kind man. "I know. I'm hoping to get this big wedding for next year." She faced her mom. "The governor's daughter is getting married, and I met with them a few weeks ago."

"Wow!" her mother replied. "That would be great for your business."

"I know. They're getting married on Mackinac Island next summer. It's going to be a huge affair."

"Simon mentioned that wedding, too," Pete blurted.

"Yeah, they met with several photographers from around the state."

"Maybe I shouldn't have said anything," Pete spoke hesitantly.

"Why not?" Vi asked.

Pete didn't speak. His eyes shifted from Vi to his cards, and he looked very uncomfortable.

"Pete?" Vi spoke again.

"Well, Simon got a call from them today." He paused. "They hired him for the wedding."

The look of shock on Maggie's face made Pete cringe.

"I'm so sorry, Maggie. I'm sure everything will work out. Hang in there."

Her eyes began to sting. "Excuse me."

She hurried out the front door before Pete could see her cry and dropped onto the porch swing. She had been praying about this for weeks. Not only would this help her financial situation, but it would be a stepping stone for her business. It would lead to bigger and better things for her. She wondered why good things never seemed to happen to her. After all the talk about God having a plan, she really wanted to believe it, but so far, all she'd gotten out of that plan was a broken heart and a failing business.

Please help me, God. Why aren't you helping me?

Tuesday dragged on endlessly. Maggie shut herself in her office and worked all day, barely speaking to Sarah at all. She felt bitter and resentful toward Simon and angry at everything.

Things seemed to go wrong all day. Her computer locked up while editing a batch of photos, she had trouble uploading some files to the internet, and her website server was down all afternoon.

By the time she got home, she was emotionally exhausted and more angry than ever, which made it impossible for her to fall asleep. She tossed and turned, a bundle of worry and frustration.

When she walked through the door on Wednesday morning, Simon and DeDe were waiting for her in the meeting area.

"Good morning, Canon." Simon gave her a dazzling smile.

Maggie grunted and walked past them to the office. She threw her purse on the desk and fired up her computer before emerging again.

"What brings *you* here?" She directed her rudeness at Simon.

"We bring good news," announced DeDe.

"Yeah, I already know. Simon got the wedding." She gave him a dirty look. "Your uncle spilled the beans the other day." She didn't even try to hide her bitterness.

"Maggie, sit," he commanded her.

"I'm not a dog," she snapped at him.

He crossed the room and gently took her arm, leading her to sit next to him. "Please."

"Did you come to gloat?" She threw herself onto the sofa.

"Maggie." He sat down next to her.

"What?"

"We got the gig."

She was confused. "What do you mean *we*?"

"You *and* I." Simon's eyes searched hers, eagerly awaiting her reaction.

"What?" Her expression suddenly changed from anger to astonishment.

"Lacey called me last night," replied DeDe. "They want to hire both of you. I guess they thought two was better than one."

"Oh my gosh. Really?" The tears filled Maggie's eyes.

Simon's face lit up. "Really." He put his arm around her and gave her a squeeze.

She turned into him, wrapped her arms around his neck in a full blown hug, and started laughing from pure happiness.

He held her tightly until she loosened her grip.

"Sorry." She let go with an embarrassed smile. "This is amazing news. You don't even know how much I needed to hear this today." She brushed a few tears from her cheeks.

Simon relaxed back into the sofa, his eyes remaining on Maggie. "So, we're off to the island next summer."

She leaned back next to him. "I'm so excited. This is gonna be so incredible." Her head fell back against a pillow, and she closed her eyes. She could feel him watching her.

"I'm so happy for you both." DeDe gathered her purse to leave.

"Maggie, let's have lunch tomorrow, and we'll get things finalized with the contracts and such."

"Yes!" she replied, still leaning back against the pillow with her eyes open now.

A huge burden had been lifted off of her, making her feel so light she thought she might float right off of the sofa.

When she glanced over at Simon, he had laid his head back, too, and continued to stare at her with a contented smile.

She grabbed his arm and shook him back and forth. "We got the wedding!"

He laughed at her crazy burst of energy.

Their eyes met, her hands still gripping his arm.

"Congratulations." He spoke almost in a whisper.

She never thought that word could sound so intimate.

"You, too," she quietly replied.

Sarah, who had been sitting at her desk across the room the entire time, cleared her throat.

They broke eye contact, and Maggie let her hands fall folded into her lap.

"I better go." He sat up. "I'll see ya'."

She watched him walk out the door and sighed as she looked over at Sarah.

Sarah shook her head and smiled. "Oh, man. You two have got it bad."

"Whatever." Maggie rolled her eyes. "He's engaged."

The door opened again, and Simon leaned inside. "Almost forgot. Do you have a wedding on the fifteenth of August?"

She shook her head sadly. "I used to."

"Oh, sorry," he replied. "Well, I need an extra shooter. I know it's last minute, but I could really use your help."

"Sure." Maggie shrugged. "Why not?"

"It's an out of town wedding." He looked at her questioningly.

"How far out of town?"

"Petoskey."

Maggie's eyes brightened, and her mouth formed into a giant smile. "I love Petoskey."

"Great." He smiled at her and left again.

Sarah laughed to herself.

"What's funny?"

"Oh, you are in so much trouble."

Maggie stood and smoothed her shirt. "It's work. It'll be completely professional."

"You just keep telling yourself that."

August 14, 2009

Petoskey

*T*his is probably a huge mistake, isn't it?" She took lens after lens from Sarah and tucked them neatly into her camera bag in preparation for the weekend in Petoskey.

"It's a job, and you need it right now."

"Right. I do." She tugged the zipper closed and lifted the bag upright on its wheels.

"Just don't forget that he is an engaged man."

Maggie still hadn't mentioned the engagement to Simon, but she would have all weekend to ask him about it.

"And have fun." Sarah gave her a hug goodbye. "But not too much fun," she said with a wink.

Maggie walked down the street to Walker's Photography, where she was to meet Simon for their drive north. She was greeted by Pete, who was as sweet as always.

"Have a seat, Maggie. Simon should be here any minute."

"Thanks. How are you doing?"

"Oh, I'm doing pretty well. And yourself?"

"I can't complain." She grinned.

"I heard everything worked out for you with the governor's daughter."

"Yes, it did." She couldn't contain her smile.

He tapped his forehead. "Didn't I tell you everything would work out?"

"You did."

Maggie took a look around. It was actually the first time she'd stepped foot in the studio since they opened in March. Large portraits were displayed all along one wall, mostly families and a few senior pictures. Just inside the door were several large cushioned chairs around a table covered in album samples. There was a reception desk, a meeting room, and a hallway, which led to offices and the portrait studio.

"This place looks great," she gushed. "You really improved it."

"Thank you," Pete replied. "Simon did pretty much everything. He's got much better taste than I do for this sort of thing."

She nodded. "Well, I like it."

The automatic doorbell sounded as Simon entered the building.

"Ready to go?" Simon walked over and grabbed the camera bag and suitcase from her.

"Yep. Thanks."

She followed him out to the car and there, sitting shotgun, was Anna Klein.

"Hi, Maggie."

"Hi, Anna." She had assumed the reason Simon needed help was that Anna couldn't work this wedding, but maybe it was a bigger affair than she thought. That would explain the need for another shooter. She had been so excited at the idea of getting out of town for a wedding that she hadn't stopped to question him about the details.

She climbed into the back seat behind Anna, while Simon loaded her things into the trunk.

Anna rotated in her seat. "How are you? Busy with weddings this summer?"

Maggie nodded. *Except for all the cancellations.* "How do you like working with Simon?"

"I love it. He's teaching me so much about photography. I couldn't imagine a better boss." Anna flipped her long blonde hair over her shoulder and smiled at Simon as he took his seat behind the wheel.

Simon smiled at Anna, which annoyed Maggie. She rolled her eyes and leaned back into her seat.

The majority of the four hour drive, Simon and Anna talked about weddings they had worked and laughed about funny situations that were only humorous to the people who had been there. Maggie wasn't really a part of their conversation, but she understood the camaraderie between photographer and assistant. She wished Sarah was there with her.

She stared out the window at the passing scenery. The woods seemed to grow thicker and more lush the further north they drove. She turned up the volume on her iPod to drown out the conversation in the front seat, the classic rock station Simon had the radio tuned to, and the constant incoming text notifications on Anna's cell phone.

She had never known anyone who texted as often as Anna. It was especially annoying while trying to converse with her. Even so, it was easy to like Anna. She was young and lovely with a vibrant personality. There was something so hopeful about her. She was fresh out of college with so much going for her and a world of endless possibilities. Maggie envied her and wished she could feel a glimmer of that again in her own life.

She glanced over at Simon. He was dressed casually in a dark t-shirt and jeans. His hair was tousled, like he had run his fingers through it before he rushed out the door, but still looked perfect. She could still remember how soft his hair felt that night in Vegas.

The music in her ears drowned out all other sounds, but she watched Simon's mouth as he spoke to Anna. Her mind wandered back to their Vegas kiss and her cheeks suddenly warmed. She closed her eyes and tried to concentrate on the music, but soon felt pressure on her leg. Startled, her eyes popped open to see Simon's arm draped back between the seats, his hand resting on her thigh.

He glanced back at her, and his lips formed words she could not hear.

She pulled the earbuds out. "What?"

"Do you need me to stop at the next rest area?"

She shook her head. "I'm good."

He turned his attention back to the road, but kept his hand on her knee a moment longer, squeezing a little before he removed it.

She put the earbuds back in, closed her eyes, and leaned her head back against the seat. As she drifted off, thoughts of kissing Simon filled her mind, and she didn't even try to stop them.

The sun was sinking low in the sky by the time they arrived at the Perry Hotel in downtown Petoskey. After settling into their rooms and grabbing a quick bite to eat, they stopped by the Rose Garden

Veranda, the site for the next day's wedding. It was a beautiful location overlooking the Little Traverse Bay, but Maggie was confused when she counted chairs set up for less than a hundred people. Clearly, Simon and Anna would have been sufficient to cover a wedding of this size.

When Simon and Anna retired to the hotel for the night, Maggie didn't follow. She walked toward Bayfront Park instead. Things felt so much lighter since the news about Lacey and George's wedding. She practically skipped down the steps and through the tunnel that led under the road to the park. There were quite a few people out and about on this warm summer evening, running around in the grass, tossing frisbees, and kicking soccer balls.

Maggie walked the long sidewalk with its row of trees leading to the marina. Children were climbing and sliding on the playground while their parents sat on nearby benches to watch. A couple sat on the rocks along the shore watching the sunset. She stopped at the base of the tall clock tower and looked up.

"That's a big clock." Simon's voice startled her.

Her hand flew to her heart.

"I didn't mean to scare you," he apologized with a smile.

She glanced over her shoulder. "Where's Anna?"

"Back at the room." He tilted his head toward the hotel. "She was really worn out from all that texting earlier."

"Poor girl." Maggie walked further out to look at the rows of docked boats. She leaned against the rail.

Simon leaned against the railing next to her, his arm resting against hers.

The sun was nearing the horizon, leaving everything blanketed in a golden glow. Maggie glanced over at Simon, his eyes sparkled at her in the evening light. *I will not give in to those eyes. Must think about Michelle.* She looked again toward the sun, and they stood together in silence watching it disappear below the line where sky met water.

The light breeze off the bay along with Simon's proximity made her shiver. "Well, I think I'm gonna call it a night."

As she turned to go, Simon stepped in front of her and grabbed the railing on either side of her waist.

"What are you doing?" she asked, not making eye contact with him.

"What I've wanted to do for a really long time." He leaned in and pressed his lips to her forehead.

"Simon, this isn't right. We have to think about Michelle."

He brushed his fingers along her jawline and lifted her chin.

She looked up at him nervously. *Oh, this is very bad.* She grabbed onto the lower railing behind her to keep from touching him.

He leaned in close. "Michelle and I broke up."

Maggie was shocked at his reply. "You broke up with Michelle?" The thoughts flew through her mind at a mile a minute. "I thought you were engaged."

"What?" His response came out as a laugh. "Engaged? Who told you that?"

"Cindy ... er, Billy." She was confused and flustered.

"Who?"

"From the coffee shop in town."

"Well, they were misinformed."

"Then you're not marrying Michelle?"

"No." He brushed his thumb softly against her cheek.

He was single. No more Michelle. Why had Bill told her they were engaged? Her mind returned to the ceremony site they'd seen earlier and the small number of chairs that were set up. Was this wedding an excuse to get her here? What was Simon thinking?

"Simon." She could barely find her voice. "This is a really small wedding."

He grinned. "Yes, it is."

"Not something you need an extra shooter for." She stared at him with an accusatory look.

He shrugged and flashed an amused grin.

Just as she thought.

She immediately tensed up as he pushed the hair back from her face and leaned in closer.

"We should talk about this," she stated.

His fingertips floated softly across the straps of her tank top and over her bare shoulders.

Maggie's eyelids closed as she concentrated on the sensations flowing over her. She squeezed the railing and braced herself for what was next.

He touched his nose to hers, and she opened her eyes to look at him.

"Let's talk later." He tilted his head to the side and his lower lip brushed hers.

Ring!

Her cell phone went off, causing her to jerk her head to the side.

"Ignore it," he whispered.

She reached to her hip for her phone. "I can't."

His lips brushed against her ear sending an electric shock all the way to her toes.

She yanked her phone out to see who was calling. "It's Sarah."

His right hand brushed the hair back over her shoulder. "Call her back." His breath was warm against her throat, and he planted a row of kisses up her neck.

Maggie felt like she was floating.

Ring!

She suddenly experienced a wave of panic. There was nothing in their way now, nothing to keep them apart. It had been different when he was with Michelle. She could flirt with him without the worry of getting hurt. But now, they could be together. She knew it's what he wanted, but she wasn't sure she felt the same. She wasn't sure she was ready.

Even after all this time, it felt like some kind of betrayal to Ben, which was absolutely ridiculous given his indiscretions. But she had given her whole heart to him, deep down to the core of her being, and imagining a future with someone else still seemed unfathomable.

And what kind of future could she have with Simon anyway? He was just another guy who was unable to be faithful, and she would never let herself be in that situation again.

A tightness in her chest made it increasingly difficult for her to breathe. If Simon continued this way, she was sure she would suffocate.

Ring!

"Simon," she managed to whisper.

He misinterpreted the tone in her voice. His hand, which had been resting softly on her shoulder, slipped down her back sending little shivers up her spine as he pulled her closer to him, moving his kisses to the other side of her neck.

The tears were imminent, every muscle in her body tense. Her heart beat rapidly in her chest, and she shook from the paralyzing fear that had overcome her. She suddenly twisted her body and shoved him away.

"Simon! Stop!"

She took several slow breaths in and out before looking him in the eyes.

The same wounded expression he'd worn in Vegas was back again.

Ring!

She looked away as a tear slipped down her cheek and answered her phone. "This is Maggie." Her voice cracked.

Simon walked quickly away along the promenade toward the hotel.

"How's it goin'?" asked Sarah.

"You were right. I'm in a lot of trouble."

She watched as Simon grew smaller and smaller and disappeared into the tunnel.

August 15, 2009

True Colors

Maggie stood in the breakfast buffet line waiting to grab a muffin and some juice. She scanned the dining room and saw Simon seated by the window alone. He was reading the paper and drinking a cup of coffee. For a moment, she thought about sitting elsewhere, as far across the room from him as possible, but she found herself walking right to his table. Maybe he'd had enough time to calm down about last night.

"Good morning," she spoke timidly as she took the seat across the table from him.

"If you say so." He was not over it.

She tried to get him to look at her, but he stared at his newspaper.

"I'm sorry about last night," she began. She hadn't meant to hurt him.

"Don't worry about it. Won't happen again." He was very short with her.

"Simon." She leaned her head forward, trying to get him to look up.

When he did, she was taken aback by the coldness behind his eyes and forgot everything she had planned to say to him.

He looked at the table briefly then straight into her eyes. "Ben hurt you. I understand that. What I don't understand is why you still let him. I know you've been dealing with a lot lately, and I've tried to be a good friend to you. But I can't keep doing this." He paused for a moment. "You're not ready to move on. I get it. But I'm not gonna wait around until you are." The muscles in his jaw tightened as he clenched his teeth together. He turned his attention back to his newspaper as Anna joined them.

"Good morning." Anna was cheerfully oblivious.

The tears stung Maggie's eyes. "Excuse me." She fled the table leaving her breakfast behind.

Maggie moved through the day as if on auto-pilot, barely paying attention to what she was doing. She tried to avoid Simon as much as possible and do what she was there to do. But she couldn't stop thinking about his comments at breakfast. It wasn't her plan to push him away and hurt him the way she had. The news of his breakup with Michelle had surprised her. And it was rather presumptuous of him to think she would instantly fall into his arms. After everything she had been through with Ben, she thought Simon would have been a little more sensitive and given her a little time to process everything.

And then there was the issue of faithfulness. If he was so willing to leave Michelle for her, what would stop him from leaving her for someone else. This was her greatest fear, and it was this fear that had completely paralyzed her.

She spotted Simon across the room shooting the couple's first dance. The more she thought about it, the more upset she became. *What right did he have to be angry with me anyway? If anyone should be upset, it should be me.*

When the reception dances were through, Anna approached Maggie. "Simon said you can go back to your room if you want. All the main events are pretty much over, and he can handle the rest on his own."

"Whatever." Maggie rolled her eyes and walked away from the party. She was too upset to find the bride and groom and congratulate them as she normally would.

Back in her room, she threw herself on the bed and hugged her pillow. Her mind replayed everything once again. She touched her neck, and her stomach flipped at the thought of his lips there. Rolling onto her back, she closed her eyes. It wasn't that she didn't want Simon to kiss her, but there was still a part of her that remembered what it felt like to be dumped. And that fearful, overly cautious portion of her heart was afraid it would happen again, which was part of the reason she was still alone five years later. That and her irrational feelings of unfaithfulness to Ben. If she continued on this way and let the fear control her, she would be alone forever.

As she sat up, the muscles in her body screamed from carrying her equipment around all day. She filled the bathtub and soaked for a long time, replaying every moment from the night before as well as the events of the past several months. By the time she climbed out, her fingers and toes were shriveled up like prunes, and her annoyance with Simon had drained away with the bath water. She slipped on a tank top and pajama bottoms and plopped onto the bed while she combed her hair. She closed her eyes. Simon's words *had* gotten through to her, and he was right. She still allowed Ben to hurt her after all this time. And she wasn't ready to move on. Or was she?

Lord, I don't know what to do. I do care about Simon. He's the first guy I've had any real feelings for since Ben. I'm just so afraid of being hurt again. Please show me if he's the right guy for me.

The sound of Simon's hotel room door slamming caught her attention. Or maybe it was the door across the hall. She wasn't certain, so she stuck her ear against the wall separating their rooms. There was definite movement within.

She paced back and forth for a while, unsure of herself, worried that if she went over there, he might slam the door in her face. But she needed to talk to him, to apologize again. She had to make him understand why she had pushed him away. It wasn't because she didn't want him, but because she was scared to open her heart and trust someone again. He needed to know she might finally be ready to try … with him.

When her nerves were gathered, she pulled her hair up in a loose wet bun, grabbed her key, and headed next door in her pajamas.

Am I really doing this?

The "do not disturb" sign was hanging on the door, but she didn't care. She raised her hand up to knock. Her stomach was all nerved up again.

What do I say? Hi, Simon. You're wrong. I am ready for you.

She lowered her hand and took a deep breath. Then, before she had a chance to back out, she knocked three times.

There was a rustling sound of movement behind the door. The deadbolt clicked, and the door opened.

Maggie's jaw almost dropped to the floor.

"Hi, Maggie." Anna greeted her with a smile, wrapped up in only a bath towel.

"I ..." She didn't have words.

"Do you need Simon?" Anna glanced back over her shoulder toward the sound of the water running in the bathroom.

"No. Sorry." She was completely flustered.

"Do you want me to order up some room service?" Simon called from within.

"Goodnight," Maggie blurted and hurried back to her room, slamming the door behind her.

Maggie sat on the end of her bed shaking, tears streaming down her cheeks. She could hear Anna and Simon talking and laughing. Oh, how she wished she could switch rooms. She quickly searched her bag for her iPod and headphones and raised the volume as loud as she could stand.

I can't believe it. I am such an idiot. Thank you, Lord, for giving me an answer so quickly. He is so not the one for me.

On Sunday morning, Maggie sat at the same table by the window and watched the boats floating around in the bay. The sun was shining and puffy white clouds drifted across a bright blue sky, but her mood was more suitable to a grey, rainy day. She took a sip of her coffee. The muffin sitting in front of her remained untouched.

"Good morning, Maggie." Anna was as perky as ever. She had no clue what she had done.

Maggie barely acknowledged she was there. She rubbed her eyes, puffy from last night's tears.

"Were you OK last night?" Anna asked, not really paying attention, but texting someone as she spoke.

"Fine." Maggie wanted to throw Anna's stupid phone into the bay. She understood the need to stay connected, but this girl was ridiculous.

Maggie took another sip of coffee.

"Morning, ladies." Simon sat across from Maggie. He gave her a quick once over. "Everything OK?"

She peered over the edge of her coffee cup at him, then returned it to the table with a loud clink.

"Maggie?" He stared at her.

Her eyes narrowed. It annoyed her to hear him call her by her name. She didn't answer him.

He looked at her with honest concern. "Mags? What's wrong?" He waited for a response.

She glared at him. He had never called her that before. It infuriated her so much that she grabbed the muffin from her plate and tossed it at his head.

"*Ow!*" Simon grabbed his head. "What the?"

Anna covered her mouth to keep from laughing.

"You are a jerk!" Maggie knocked her chair over backwards as she stood and rushed out of the room toward the elevator. She couldn't wait to get back to her room and pack so she could get out of there. If only she didn't have to spend four hours in the car with *them*.

"*Whoa! Whoa! Whoa!*" Simon ran toward her as the elevator doors began to close.

"No!" Maggie entered the elevator and pressed the "close doors" button over and over.

He stuck his arm in between the doors to stop them and climbed in next to her.

She tried to step out, but he grabbed her arm and pulled her back as the doors closed. She poked the button for their floor, and the elevator began to move.

"Let go of me, Simon," she demanded.

"What is going on?" He did not loosen his grip on her arm. "Is this about breakfast yesterday?"

Maggie twisted her arm out of his grasp as the doors opened. She sped out into the hall to the door of her room.

He was right on her heels.

She fiddled with her room key, trying to unlock the door, but her anger and his presence caused her to drop it numerous times. She groaned in frustration.

"Maggie, calm down." He bent and picked up her key.

"Don't tell me what to do," she snarled as she grabbed for it.

He held it above her head, just out of her reach. "I'll give you this key when you tell me what's wrong."

She leaned back against her door with a *thud*.

"Look, I'm sorry about what I said at breakfast yesterday. I really am. I was just upset. But I'm over it now, and I am truly sorry for the way I spoke to you."

Maggie shook her head. Of course he was over it. He had already moved on to his next conquest. "This isn't about the other night."

"No?" he asked. "Then what?"

"It's about last night."

"What? The wedding? Did you want to stay until the end of the reception?" He looked at her searchingly. "I thought you worked pretty hard all day and you might need some rest."

She rolled her eyes. "That's not it."

He grabbed her arms and looked into her eyes. "You're gonna have to give me a little more of the story here. What did I do?"

"Anna," she replied pointedly.

"You're mad at Anna?"

"Just you." She stared at him smugly.

Simon groaned. "Again, Mags. I need more."

"Stop calling me Mags," she spoke through gritted teeth.

"What?" Simon let go of her arms and walked a few steps down the hall, running his fingers through his hair in frustration. He spun around and returned to her. "Maggie, please."

"I went to your room last night." She was embarrassed to admit it.

Simon raised an eyebrow and grinned. "You came to my room?" But a sudden look of realization crossed his face, and his expression turned serious. "And you saw Anna."

Maggie did her best to stop the tears from falling.

Simon took her arms once more. "I can explain."

She shook them off. "No need." She glared. "You sure move quickly."

He nodded as if in agreement. "That's what you think?"

"It's what I know."

He shrugged his shoulders. "Well, what did you expect?"

"Not that. But I guess I shouldn't be surprised. You're still the same Simon you were in college. The same Simon who broke Emma's heart."

"Emma?" He looked completely bewildered. "Why are you bringing that up? That was years ago."

"And she was devastated. You were the first guy she ever had real feelings for, and you just blew her off and paraded every other girl in our dorm in front of her."

"That's not exactly how it went down."

"Yes, it is. I should have known this would always be a pattern with you."

His mouth dropped open, and his eyes widened. "Are you kidding me? We were eighteen years old. We were just kids."

Her eyes narrowed. "And you haven't changed a bit."

He shook his head furiously and tossed the key at her. "Be down at the car in an hour."

"Forget it! I'll rent a car," she declared bitterly.

"Fine!" he yelled over his shoulder as he stormed away.

"Fine!"

October 31, 2009

Happy Anniversary

A few weeks after the horrible Petoskey trip, a bit of happiness arrived in Maggie's mail in the form of an invitation to Vi and Dave's anniversary party at Pete's on Halloween. Maggie was overjoyed when she opened the envelope and saw their names together. Some people were meant to be together in good times and bad. Things hadn't been the same when they were apart. Seeing them come together over the summer and rekindle their relationship gave her a glimpse of what it takes to make real love work. They had weathered the storm and come out on the other side stronger and more in love than they were before.

On Halloween night, Maggie and Sarah spent the evening passing out candy and taking pictures of all the little ghosts and goblins that stopped by her shop. Maggie loved this annual tradition. The photos were developed a few days after Halloween and strung across the room with clips and a wire. Parents would stop by the following week for a print of their child along with a discount coupon for more prints or a photo session. It was a fun way for her to connect with the community and, hopefully, help her to book more sessions.

When the trick-or-treating was through, Maggie left her car at work and rode with Sarah to Uncle Pete's. They drove slowly through town to avoid all the little kids crossing the streets.

Sarah parked her car next to Simon's and got out.

Maggie stared at his car for a minute. After all that had happened up north, she really didn't want see him.

Sarah turned around when she realized Maggie wasn't following her. She walked over to the passenger side and opened the door. "What's the matter?"

"Nothing." She shook her head as she climbed out.

"Are you sure?"

"Yep!" She tried to sound chipper.

Sarah gave her a look. "I need to go find Tom."

"Go ahead." Maggie waved her away.

Sarah hesitantly left her side.

The yard was decorated with orange Chinese lanterns and white lights strung between the trees. The bonfire was already burning strong, and there was a table with cider, donuts and cookies, as well as a pumpkin shaped anniversary cake.

The invitation had read "costumes optional", so Maggie opted not to dress up. She glanced around and noticed about half of the guests were in costume. The guests of honor were dressed as the King and Queen of Hearts, which seemed appropriate.

Sarah and Tom suddenly emerged from the house.

"*Argh!*" Tom called out. He was dressed as a pirate with a black eye patch and wielded a "dangerous" looking plastic sword. Sarah, the pirate's wench, was on his arm.

"Cool costume, Tommy."

"*Argh!*" he repeated.

"Is that the only thing you know how to say?"

He seemed deep in thought for a moment. "Uh ... shiver me timbers?"

"Nice, Tom." Maggie chuckled.

"That's Cap'n Tom to you." He resumed the pirate speak.

Maggie shook her head. Out of the corner of her eye, she noticed Simon approaching.

"Hey," he greeted them.

Maggie looked him over. He was wearing a trench coat and carrying a flashlight and a stuffed alien toy under his arm. "Who are you supposed to be?"

He held up an FBI badge. "Fox Mulder. FBI."

She laughed at that. "The X-Files are closed, Mulder." Simon had been at their apartment nearly every week during college watching that television show with Michelle. She never understood their fascination with it, but they watched it religiously. Michelle even had a big "I Want To Believe" poster—a gift from Simon—on the wall of her bedroom.

"You didn't dress up," he stated.

She held up the camera that was hanging over her shoulder. "I'm a photographer."

He shook his head, reached into his pocket, and tossed a red wig at her. "Let's go, Scully. The truth is out there."

Tom grabbed the wig from Maggie's hands and pushed it onto her head.

She rolled her eyes, adjusted the wig, and followed them across the yard to the bonfire.

Maggie sat alone roasting a marshmallow. She watched Vi and Dave on the other side of the fire. They were so sweet and attentive to each other, and it made her smile to herself. All they had gone through and here they were back together again.

Her thoughts turned to Petoskey and sadness washed over her. She had been so close, standing at Simon's door, ready to tell him she wanted to try with him, and then everything had gone so horribly wrong.

But God *had* answered her prayer. Maybe not in the way she thought it would be answered, but she was thankful to be reminded of the kind of guy Simon really was. She would rather be single for the rest of her life than go through that kind of pain again. *Bullet dodged.*

While she was lost in her thoughts, the marshmallow she had been roasting was lost to the fire. She pulled the empty stick out of the flames, leaned it against the hay bale she'd been sitting on, and walked to the end of the dock. It seemed a lifetime ago since she and Simon had been in that very spot. She stared out at the lake, trying not to think about them splashing and laughing and holding each other that night. Things felt very different now.

Footsteps against the wood planks made her heart skip a beat. She turned to see Pete approaching her.

"Hello there, Maggie."

"Hi, Pete."

"Can I talk with you?"

"Sure."

Pete took a seat and patted the dock next to him.

She nodded and took a seat.

"I'd like this conversation to be just between us if that's all right with you."

Maggie looked confused. She and Pete had never talked much before this, at least not about anything serious.

"Of course," she replied.

"I've been watching my nephew this year, and I've seen a change in him since he started coming to town." He paused for a moment. "I'm not so sure I like what I see."

"What do you mean?"

"I see too much of myself in him."

"And that's a bad thing?" asked Maggie.

"Just between us, right?" He looked her in the eye for confirmation.

She nodded again. "Absolutely."

"I love Vi. I always have, and I always will."

Maggie was shocked at his confession and surprised he was trusting her with such personal information.

"I loved her all those years ago, and I waited for her for a long time." He sighed. "And she chose Dave."

She could see the pain in his eyes now. Much like her, he was very good at hiding his true emotions. When they were all together playing cards, everything seemed fine. But he had opened himself up for her to see a deep love and even deeper hurt, which he normally tucked far down inside.

"I never knew." Maggie had a strong urge to comfort him. "If you love her so much, how can you spend so much time with them? How can you host their anniversary party?"

"It's hard to be around 'em sometimes, but I *am* thankful for their friendship."

They sat in silence for a few moments. She wasn't sure what this had to do with Simon.

"This is the life I chose. I'm alone because I waited too long for a woman who never really loved me."

"It's not too late," Maggie encouraged him. "You could still find someone to share your life with."

"*Nah.*" he shook his head. "I'm fine with being alone. But I don't want that for Simon."

"Simon?" She cocked her head to the side, confused.

"I love my nephew. He's the son I never had." Pete looked her in the eye again. "If you care for him at all, you need to let him know." He paused and looked out at the lake then back at Maggie. "But if you don't, then please tell him now, so he can move on with his life. I don't want Simon to end up like me."

"Simon's not waiting around for me, Pete."

Pete reached over and squeezed her hand. "I think he is."

A lump suddenly formed in her throat, and she couldn't speak.

Pete looked at her searchingly.

She nodded to let him know she understood.

He patted her on the back as he got up, then walked back to the fire.

Maggie sat for a long time thinking about Pete's words. He obviously didn't know his nephew as well as he thought. Simon had no trouble getting women. He would never have to be alone if he didn't want to.

She closed her eyes and tried to make some sense of her thoughts. There *was* a part of her that cared for Simon. She had admitted as much in her prayers that night in Petoskey. But all she had to do was think about Anna standing in his hotel room to know that he was not the man for her.

As much as she respected Pete, there was really no need to have such a conversation with Simon, because he wasn't pining away for her. He had already moved on.

Maggie and Sarah sat by the fire roasting marshmallows. This time, Maggie's marshmallow survived and came out a golden brown. She popped it into her mouth and glanced across the fire to see Simon staring at her.

He grinned, and her stomach suddenly tied up in knots.

She hoped he would stay on his side of the fire. *Nope.*

He walked over and took a seat on the hay bale next to her. "I need to tell you something very important."

She swallowed hard.

Simon hugged the stuffed alien toy. "My sister was abducted by aliens," he stated dramatically and faked crying.

"Give up the chase, Mulder," she replied with a laugh.

He grinned at her.

"Tom and I are leaving soon, Maggie," announced Sarah. "Are you ready? Or maybe someone could give you a ride back to town to get your car." Sarah directed her words at Simon.

Maggie gave Sarah a disapproving look.

"Yeah, I'll take her," Simon eagerly offered. "If that's OK with you." He gazed at Maggie with soft hazel eyes reflecting the blazing fire.

Oh, boy. Maggie managed a nod. Maybe they would need to have a conversation after all.

At the end of the night, Simon drove Maggie back into town. They were silent for most of the drive, but she could feel his eyes on her, and it made her extra nervous.

He pulled into the parking space next to her car, jumped out, and opened the door for her.

"Thanks for the ride." Maggie climbed out and fished her keys from her purse. She unlocked her car door and dropped her purse and keys on the seat.

Something across the street caught her eye, and she thought she saw movement within the coffee shop. They weren't open this late, and she wondered if maybe she should check it out. She would hate for her friends' shop to get robbed with her standing right across the street.

"I'm really sorry about my behavior in Petoskey," Simon interrupted her thoughts.

"Oh, Simon." She let out an exasperated breath as she pushed the car door shut and turned to face him. "I don't wanna talk about Petoskey. It happened. Let's just forget about it."

A pained expression crossed his face. She couldn't stand that look. It was the same look he'd had in Vegas and Petoskey, and it broke her heart that she was the one who put it there.

With a sudden urge to comfort him, she stepped forward and hugged him. "I really think we're just better off as friends." She pulled back and leaned in to give him a quick kiss on the cheek, but he turned his head at the last second and their lips met briefly.

Maggie took a step back, and they looked at each other with surprise.

His glance went from her eyes to her lips and back to her eyes again. And then he leaned in and touched his lips to hers—again and again and again. Slow and sweet, they sank into the kiss. It had been months since they first kissed in Vegas, but it had been nothing like this.

Maggie leaned back against the door of her car and pulled him with her. *Must stop.* Her brain kept telling her this, but she couldn't make herself push him away. She couldn't remember ever being kissed like this.

Simon held her face softly with one hand and wrapped his other arm around her back. His fingertips landed just under the bottom edge of her sweater and rested against her lower back. The heat from his touch nearly burned her.

She let the kiss continue, knowing they needed to have that conversation for sure now.

Relief overcame her when he pulled away first, because she didn't have the clarity of mind to tell him to stop. She looked up at him, his lips moist from their kisses, slightly out of breath. He looked incredibly handsome, and Maggie wanted nothing more than to kiss him.

"I want to kiss you again." Simon seemed to read her mind. He leaned in again and brushed his lips so softly against hers that they were barely touching. "But I need to tell you something first."

Maggie didn't speak and neither did Simon. She moved her hands from where they rested on his hips around to his lower back, moving further into his arms, even though she knew she shouldn't.

He let out a slow breath and his fingers drifted down her cheek, his thumb brushing over her lower lip.

"Forget it," he breathed, and he kissed her again, deeper this time and with more urgency. His hand pressed flat against her back, holding her firmly against him.

Must. Stop. Kissing.

A bright light suddenly flashed at them, and they jumped apart.

"Everything OK here, Maggie?" It was Sheriff Hank Sanders. "I got a call."

"Of course, officer," Simon mumbled.

"We were just heading home, Hank," she explained. Her cheeks were on fire. *Thank God for Hank.*

"See that you do." Hank snickered as he lowered his flashlight.

"Wait! You got a call about us? From who?" she asked.

Hank shrugged as he climbed back into the patrol car.

Simon started laughing.

Maggie didn't think it was funny at all. She glanced across the street at State Grounds again.

"Aren't we a little too old to get caught making out by the cops?"

She looked over at him. She was disappointed in herself for being so weak and letting the kissing happen. Her hands covered her face for a few seconds.

Simon took a step closer.

She rotated a little to subtly block his advance. She needed some distance to organize her thoughts. "I'm sorry, Simon. I did *not* intend for that to happen."

"Well, I don't think either of us did." He had a cocky grin on his face. "But I'm not sorry, and I'm ready for things to get *really* intentional." He was flirting with her now in that way of his.

Maggie's throat tightened, and she had trouble forming words. "I ... I meant what I said, Simon. Just friends."

Simon stepped closer, and she held her hand out to stop him.

He looked at her questioningly.

"Look, tonight was fun. And this was ..." She glanced at his mouth for a second, and her resolve began to weaken. "... really nice."

He pushed her hand aside and moved closer.

She straightened up and took a deep breath. "Can't we just let things be the way they are?"

"What fun is that?" He spoke in a whisper and took her hand in his.

She looked at the ground and squeezed his hand. She had to get a grip and stick to her guns.

"Simon." She could barely get his name out.

"Maggie," he whispered and moved again. He was now standing against her, his hand sliding around her waist again. His breathing was shallow, and his lips brushed against her forehead.

Here we go. Please God, give me the strength to do this. As nice as it was to feel wanted, she knew it was wrong to lead him on when she knew he wasn't right for her. She owed it to Pete after he had opened up so much to her. She grabbed Simon's hand, pushing it down away from her waist as she took a step backwards.

"What's wrong?"

She wasn't sure where to begin.

Simon looked exasperated. "You have to stop doing this to me."

Her eyes met his.

"I kiss you and it feels like you want me to. It feels like you've changed your mind. And then you pull the rug out from under me and knock me down all over again."

"I'm sorry. I don't mean to."

"But you do. And every time, I wish I could understand. I wish I knew what you wanted. It's enough to drive a guy crazy."

Even though she didn't want to, Maggie knew it was time to be very clear with him.

"I want someone who will do anything to make me happy. Someone who will always be honest with me and never hurt me. I need someone I can rely on." She let go of his hand.

He looked perplexed. "And you don't think I'd make you happy?"

"Never again will I be with someone who can't be faithful to me."

"Is this about Petoskey?" There was a sudden desperation in his voice.

"It doesn't matter what happened in Petoskey. You were with Michelle when we kissed in Vegas and when we were under the dock on the Fourth of July. I can't trust someone who would cheat on their girlfriend with me. And that's the thing—I *don't* trust you."

Simon looked at the ground and shook his head. "That's kind of a big thing."

"After everything I've been through, I need a relationship built on honesty and trust." Maggie could see the pained expression on his face again. "I'm sorry if this isn't what you want to hear, but it's how I feel."

"So that's it?" He looked into her eyes. "This isn't happening?"

She hated the way he was looking at her, knowing she was the reason he was hurting.

"What can I do to prove that you can trust me?"

"Oh, Simon, please don't make this more difficult than it already is."

He stepped closer again and took her face in his hands. He spoke in an intimate whisper. "What I said that morning in Petoskey ... I didn't mean it. I would wait for you forever."

Pete was right. Maggie took a step back toward her car, and Simon's hands slipped from her face.

"Please don't," she begged.

He nodded sadly without another plea and opened the car door for her. "Goodnight, Maggie." He looked anywhere but at her face.

Maggie climbed into the car, and he shut the door behind her. A single tear slid down her cheek as she watched him walk back around his car with head hung low. He put his car into gear, backed out, and took off fast enough to squeal his tires on the pavement.

She had done it. She had told Simon the truth. This was the right decision for her and for him—she believed that. So why did she feel as if she might throw up? And why did her heart ache so much?

December 19, 2009

Sarah & Tom

$\mathcal{A}$ light snow fell overnight leaving a beautiful dusting over everything. It was picture perfect for Sarah and Tom's Christmas wedding. The girls started the morning together at a lovely breakfast prepared by Patty and Vi, while the guys woke late and had brunch at Mill's Landing, another favorite local restaurant.

"I wish I didn't have to walk down the aisle with goatee guy," Gina announced through a bite of chocolate chip pancakes. Sarah's teenaged cousin was a pretty, petite brunette, who was more interested in talking about guys than anything else. She was less than enthused that she had to link arms with Bill from State Grounds. "Why can't I walk with the hot one?"

"The hot one? Which one is that again?" Maggie knew exactly who she was referring to.

Sarah shook her head. "Be nice, Gina."

Leslie, Sarah's best friend from high school, chuckled. She was the complete opposite of Gina, with long blonde hair and a more reserved demeanor.

"I'd take Leslie's guy if I had to," Gina replied.

Leslie's guy was Derek, a friend of Tom's from work, who wasn't bad to look at either. He was a buzz cut blond with a stocky build.

Sarah's patience was wearing thin. "We already went over this. You're walking with Bill."

Gina pouted and picked at her bacon.

Maggie was thankful to be past those high school years. She nearly laughed aloud remembering herself pouting on many occasions when she didn't get her way. It never worked with her parents. It almost always worked with Ben.

The salon was up next for hair and makeup, then on to the church, where Patty, Vi, and Sarah's mother, Marie, were waiting with the dresses and a light lunch. After lunch, the bridesmaids got dressed, laughing and chatting the day away.

It wasn't until Shannon and Jamie arrived for pictures, that the day kicked into high gear. They split up. Shannon stayed with the girls, while Jamie went to photograph the guys.

Once Sarah slipped into her dress and her mother affixed her veil, it all became very real.

Maggie was overcome with love and pride at the sight of Sarah as a bride. It seemed surreal to be standing in that room with Sarah in her wedding gown about to walk the aisle and become Tom's wife. She quickly retrieved her camera from her bag and snapped a few pictures.

"Hey! Put that thing away," Sarah ordered. "You're the maid of honor today."

"I know. I can't help it." She tucked the camera away as ordered and walked over to her almost sister-in-law. "You're the most beautiful bride I've ever seen. And you know I've seen a few."

Sarah laughed as she hugged Maggie tightly. "I love you, Mags."

"I love you, too."

Leslie brought them tissues to blot their tears and made sure Sarah's makeup was still perfect.

Maggie snuck out to the room where the guys were getting ready and knocked on the door.

"Everyone decent in here?"

"Come on in," Tom called.

She walked in and spotted her brother dressed in his tuxedo with a red rose boutonniere attached to the lapel. She laid her hand over her heart.

"Oh, Tommy." She fought back tears as she embraced her brother.

"I'm really doing this, Mags."

"I know," she sniffled.

"How's Sarah doin'?"

Maggie noticed the affection that oozed from Tom's voice when he mentioned his beloved's name.

"She's amazing. And she looks like an angel. Most beautiful bride I've ever seen."

He smiled, then clapped his hands together once. "OK, let's get this show on the road."

"Sounds good to me," Simon interjected.

Maggie hadn't noticed him standing there to the side of the room. Her eyes met his.

He gave her a once over. "Wow!"

She felt herself blush. "Well, uh," she stuttered. "I'll see you guys out there." And she quickly exited the room.

Maggie took a deep breath in and let it out as she walked back toward the girls' room. Despite the fact she had rejected him, there was still an attraction there. She wished there wasn't because it would make her decision a lot easier to follow through with.

She stopped to look into the church sanctuary. Jamie was there with camera in hand photographing the room and all the lovely decorations. It was glowing from the Christmas trees all draped in white lights and the candles lining the aisles. *Perfect.* It reminded her of the Christmas wedding they had photographed a year ago. Had it only been a year? So much had happened since then.

Never would she have imagined that Sarah would marry her brother or that Tom would marry before she did. But it was the way things were meant to be. If things had gone on as planned with Ben and she had married first, life might have turned out very differently. She might never have hired Sarah and then where would they be today?

She often wondered how long that marriage would have lasted, how much more devastated she would have been if she would have had to suffer through a divorce. And when she thought about it now, she felt relieved. There was a peace about the situation that had never been there before. God had protected her. He had saved her. All that had happened over the past year had taught her that. If she had jumped into something with Simon without asking God to show her whether he was the right one, she might have been right back in the same situation again.

She suddenly sensed someone watching her and turned to find Simon standing in the hallway behind her, looking incredibly handsome in his tuxedo. He walked slowly toward her, holding something behind his back.

"Can you help me with this?" He held out his boutonniere.

"Can't DeDe help you? I really should get back to Sarah."

"She's busy helping the other guys. I thought I should go straight to the expert." He grinned at her.

"And what makes you think I'm an expert?"

"I saw you helping the groomsmen in Petoskey."

She flinched at the mention.

"Please." He gave her his best puppy dog eyes and pouty lip.

She rolled her eyes and reluctantly took the flower from him.

"Don't stick yourself," he warned.

She raised an eyebrow at him. "I'm an expert, remember?"

With the pins clamped between her lips, she held the flower against his lapel to find the right spot. Her hands began to tremble as she felt him watching. If only he didn't have this effect on her.

She pulled the pins from her mouth one by one and stuck them through the jacket and flower in opposite directions to hold it firmly in place.

"There you go." She patted his chest.

"Not even one drop of blood," he replied with a grin.

"I can't stop shaking." Sarah held her hands out to show everyone.

Maggie took her hands and squeezed. "You've got this."

"It's go time," DeDe interrupted. She expertly arranged everyone in the order they were to enter as they had practiced at the rehearsal the night before. The prelude music was playing in the sanctuary as they moved through the foyer of the church to the doors. A few late stragglers were corralled to some side entrance doors and seated toward the back. The music changed to the processional and DeDe directed Leslie and Derek down the aisle, followed by Gina and Bill.

Simon held his arm out to Maggie. "Here we go."

Maggie took a deep breath and slid her arm through his.

She glanced back at Sarah, who was waiting in the hallway behind them with her father, trying to stay hidden from view.

Sarah smiled and blew her a kiss.

She blew a kiss back at Sarah, then headed into the sanctuary with Simon. It felt so strange to walk the aisle with him. *If things were different, maybe it would have been us.* She immediately shoved that insane thought aside.

The doors closed behind them in preparation for Sarah's grand entrance.

As they reached the front of the church, the "Bridal March" began, and the doors opened. Sarah was breathtaking. She beamed as she floated down the aisle to Tom.

Maggie glanced over at her brother just then. He wore the biggest smile she had ever seen, and tears filled his bright green eyes.

The familiar click of a camera shutter caught her attention, and she noticed Shannon crouched down at the front of the aisle capturing Tom's reaction. She was grateful for such talented friends, who were as committed to capturing every minute of the wedding as she would have been.

The ceremony was a beautiful reflection of their love. Sarah and Tom even wrote their own vows.

"Tom, when I started working for your sister, I never would have dreamed that it would lead me to you. My whole life I was waiting. Praying for the one. And I always hoped it would be an instant connection and that, somehow, I would just know. That first day you came into the shop ..." She paused as emotion overwhelmed her. "... I knew it was you. The one God had for me. You became my best friend, my confidante, my other half, more than I ever hoped for. I commit myself to you today, forever and always, faithfully yours."

Maggie wiped a tear from her cheek. She glanced over at Simon, who was smiling at her.

"Sarah." Tom brushed away a tear of his own. "From the moment I met you, I knew I couldn't go another day without having you in my life. There you were, this beautiful, sweet, caring woman. And for some reason—God only knows—you wanted me in your life, too. God made us for each other. You're my best friend, my other half, more than I ever *dreamed* of. I commit myself to you today, forever and always, faithfully yours."

Maggie thought about the last line of their vows—faithfully yours. That's what she wanted. Someone truly faithful to only her. She longed for that person so much, the one who would be hers forever and always. She prayed it wouldn't be too much longer before God showed her who he was.

When Tom and Sarah had exchanged rings as a symbol of their love and faithfulness, the pastor announced, "By the power vested in me by the state of Michigan, I now pronounce you husband and wife."

They looked into each others eyes with smiles bright enough to light the room.

"Tom, you may kiss your bride."

"Yes!" Tom replied as he took her in his arms and kissed her for the first time as his wife.

Everyone applauded, and Maggie felt her heart bursting with happiness.

The ballroom above the Walldorff Brewpub & Bistro was decorated with more Christmas trees, white twinkly lights, and candles everywhere. The Christmas theme coordinated well with the two-toned burgundy striped wall covering. The main table was set up along a wall with six floor-to-ceiling, narrow, arched-top windows, original to the century old building.

Once the bridal party was announced and seated, it was the moment Maggie had been dreading all day—her maid of honor speech. With microphone in hand, she took a deep breath to steady herself and glanced over at Sarah, who gave her a thumbs up for support.

"Hello, everyone. I'm Maggie, Tom's big sister. Let me start by saying that I am a horrible public speaker. I'm much better staying behind the camera where I belong."

Her family and friends got a kick out of at that.

"But today, I will be brave and stand up here in front of all of you. Today is one of those days full of moments that will stay with me forever. I was so honored to stand next to my best friend and my baby brother as they pledged their lives to each other. I don't know why I didn't think of setting them up years ago."

Laughter and knowing glances came from the crowd.

"But these things work out when the timing is right, when it's God's timing, and it was most definitely that." Maggie directed her words at her new sister. "Sarah, over the past four years, having you as my assistant has been so wonderful. You've become one of the most important people in my life. You know, I always wanted to have a sister and you've become that to me, and now you're *officially* my sister, so that worked out really well."

Sarah smiled at her.

"Tommy, I couldn't be happier for you right now, little brother. I only hope that I'm half as happy one day." Maggie raised her glass. "To Tom and Sarah. I love you guys."

The room filled with the sound of clinking glasses, and some guests repeated, "To Tom and Sarah."

Tom and Sarah stood and hugged Maggie. The girls laughed as they wiped each others tears for what seemed like the hundredth time that day.

Maggie handed the microphone to Simon.

"Where do I begin?" he spoke. "First of all, Sarah, I need you to lay your hand on the table in front of Tom."

Sarah gave him a confused look and placed her hand on the table.

"Now, Tom, please lay your hand on top of Sarah's."

"Are we playing 'Simon says'?" Tom joked.

The room exploded with laughter.

Tom did as he was asked.

"Tom, it has been a privilege getting to know you over the past year, and I'm so honored you asked me to be your best man. Sarah, since you and Tom have been together, I've seen his whole outlook on life change. He went from kind of a miserable single guy ..."

"Hey!" Tom interrupted.

"Sorry, Tom. I call 'em like I see 'em."

Simon paused for the laughter to subside before continuing. "As I was saying, he went from a sad single guy to completely smitten and in love. Seeing you two together gives me something to aspire to."

He glanced in Maggie's direction for a brief moment.

"So, Tom. I asked you to lay your hand on Sarah's. Are you enjoying that?"

"Um ... sure." Tom raised a quizzical brow at his friend.

"Good, 'cause it's the last time you'll ever have the upper hand."

Some laughed, while others groaned at Simon's joke, but everyone enjoyed his antics.

He raised his glass. "To the happy couple."

Clink. Clink. Clink.

Sarah and Tom hugged him, then he walked straight to Maggie and clinked his glass against hers.

The newlyweds held each other close as they danced to "Better Together" by Jack Johnson. They leaned their foreheads together, then shared a kiss. Maggie's heart ached a little as she watched from the side of the dance floor. She wondered if she would ever have that kind of love. It's what she wanted. She was more than ready now, but maybe the time had passed for her. Each birthday brought her closer and closer to the big 4-0. Who would want someone her age? Maybe she would end up an old maid. But could she be happy living a single existence like Pete? He seemed content, but she knew that was a facade, that deep down he was sad and regretful of his past. That wasn't the life she wanted.

The bridal party joined the couple for the second dance of the night. Simon took Maggie's hand and led her out onto the floor. He pulled her close and wrapped his arms around her back, leaving her arms resting against his chest. He let go for a moment, but only to lift her arms up around his neck.

"Nice speech," was all she could think to say.

He smiled at her and brushed a curl out of her face. His fingertips traced her cheek as they had done on Halloween night.

She tensed up. Her cheek tingled from his touch. This was not what she expected of him tonight.

He lowered his hand to the small of her back, and they danced.

Maggie looked over at Tom and Sarah. "They look really happy."

Simon leaned in so his lips were touching her ear. "We could be that happy."

"Simon." She let out an exasperated sigh and wished he would accept her decision.

"I can't change what's already happened. I can't take things back.

But I also can't help how I feel about you. And you can keep pushing me away as many times as you want, but I'm not going anywhere." He kissed her cheek and hugged her tightly.

She didn't know what to say. Every instinct told her to bolt out of there as fast as she could. But she kept dancing with him, her arms loosely wrapped around his neck, wondering if this song would ever end.

His lips pressed against her neck, and his fingers softly tangled in her hair.

She had never felt so conflicted in her life. In his arms were things she longed for—comfort, intimacy, friendship—but there was still the matter of trust, or lack thereof. This could only end badly.

He lifted his head and leaned his forehead against hers. His breath was soft against her face, his lips mere inches away.

Maggie felt lightheaded, partly from his closeness, but also from frustration and anger welling up inside. He was pushing the issue again. Why wouldn't he respect her enough to let her be? She lifted her head and tried to lean away to put some space between them, but he held her closer.

At the last note of the song, relief washed over her.

Simon loosened his grip as Sarah and Tom danced over to them.

"Hey, Mags." Tom put an arm around his sister. "Will you dance with me?"

"Gladly." She didn't look at Simon as she danced away with her brother.

Late into the reception, Maggie returned to the table to rest her aching feet. Dancing for hours in high heels was rough. She watched the rest of the bridal party, who seemed to have an endless amount of energy. Bill stepped away from the group and joined her at the table.

"Had enough dancing already, huh?"

Maggie nodded and sighed, completely exhausted. She watched Simon and Gina dancing to a fast song.

"His girlfriend wouldn't like him doing that."

She looked at Bill in confusion. "What girlfriend?"

"That blonde girl I always see him with," Bill replied.

"Oh, you mean Anna?" Maggie shook her head. "No, she's just his assistant."

"That's not what I heard." He was staring in Simon's direction. "They always look pretty cozy to me."

She was concerned by Bill's expression.

"She probably wouldn't like how he was dancing with you earlier either."

"What's your problem with Simon?" she asked.

Bill looked her straight in the eye. "You're too good for him, Maggie." He leaned in closer. "You can do so much better."

The meaning behind his not-so-subtle comments was obvious, which made her very uncomfortable, and she had a sudden realization.

"It was you, wasn't it? On Halloween night. You called the cops on us."

He shrugged his shoulders. The guilt was written all over his face.

She was appalled. "I knew I saw someone. Why did you do that?"

"He was taking advantage of you."

"I can take care of myself, Bill."

Bill scooted his chair closer to hers. "I was just trying to protect you from guys like him, guys like Ben."

She winced at the mention of Ben's name.

Bill laid his hand on top of hers. "I like you, Maggie. I always have."

She yanked her hand out from under his as fast as she possibly could, completely flabbergasted. "I'm sorry, Bill. I just don't feel that way about you."

He shook his head disappointedly. "But maybe you could someday. I'm a good guy. You know that. We have the same friends, we like the same things."

"How do you know what I like?"

"You like my coffee, and that great band at your birthday party."

"The band? That was you, too?" She thought back to her birthday and the news he had given them that night. "Hey, why did you say Simon was engaged when he wasn't?"

"I may have stretched the truth a little bit there," he admitted. "But I did it for us."

Unbelievable.

She took a deep breath and let it out before she spoke, trying to collect her thoughts.

"Bill, I understand what you were trying to do … or what you thought you were doing, and I'm … flattered." *And very creeped out.* "But …"

"But you love Simon," he interrupted.

"What? No, I don't!" she snapped.

Bill didn't look convinced.

"But you and I," she continued. "We're not right for each other."

"You never know unless you try." He raised an eyebrow at her.

She knew deep down that Bill was a good guy, but he had gone about things in the worst possible way.

He attempted one final plea. "I might just be the best offer you ever get."

Worst possible way.

She promptly stood. "I'm sorry, Bill." Her feet couldn't take her away from the table fast enough.

Maggie walked to the far side of the dance floor to escape. Bill had always been nice to her, but she never took it as more than friendship. This turn of events was both unexpected and unfortunate.

Sarah suddenly slid across the floor in her direction followed by Tom.

"Mags, we saw you talking to Bill, and we have to warn you. Bill has a huge crush on you."

"You're too late," Maggie replied. "He already professed his like for me."

"I'm sorry I didn't say something sooner. He's been acting kind of strange lately," Tom admitted. "Asking about you and stuff."

"We were just talking to Cindy, and she confirmed our suspicions," Sarah added.

"It's fine. I feel kind of sorry for him."

"You do?" Sarah asked.

"Well, I'm annoyed he tried to meddle in my life, but it's kind of sad that he thought he could lie to manipulate me into a relationship with him."

Tom shook his head. "You are way too nice, Maggie."

She glanced across the room at Bill, who was right where she left him. "I guess I just understand what it feels like to love someone who doesn't love you back."

When Tom and Sarah had departed the reception with a sparkler send off, Maggie joined the rest of the bridal party downstairs at the bar for one last drink. Bill kept his distance from Maggie and took the seat next to Leslie instead.

She hoped this wouldn't affect her friendship with Cindy or make things awkward at State Grounds.

Simon sat next to her and ordered them each a beer, as he had the first night he came to town.

"I don't drink beer," she stated.

He looked at her like she was an alien. "I didn't know."

"You never asked." She grinned at him.

"More for me then," he replied with a chuckle.

One last drink turned into many as the group talked and laughed late into the night. When Maggie's eyes began to droop, she knew it was time for this wonderful day to end. Simon insisted on walking her to her car. She could tell he'd had a few too many drinks and was in no shape to drive home, so she guided him next door to her shop instead.

"It's too late for work, Canon," he slurred.

She quietly led him to the sofa, and he flopped down, pulling her along with him.

He leaned his head against her shoulder and wound his fingers through hers. "I like that."

"What?"

"Holding your hand."

She grinned. Tipsy Simon was cute.

He lifted his head and gazed into her eyes.

"I'm so in love with you."

Her jaw dropped a little at his confession.

He grinned and laid his head back on her shoulder, and his eyes slid closed as sleep took over.

This was unexpected. She knew he cared about her, but love. Love was a whole different thing.

December 25, 2009
Christmas Day

As Maggie stepped inside her parents house, she was overwhelmed with the familiar sights and smells of the holidays. But there was an underlying nervousness that she couldn't shake. Simon's car was in the driveway, so she knew he and Pete were there for Christmas dinner again this year.

Her father greeted her and took her coat. "Magpie!" He lifted her up in a bear hug, spinning her around.

"Daddy, put me down," she cried.

He chuckled and guided her into the kitchen, where everyone was hanging out.

Tom and Sarah were playing cards with Simon and Pete.

"Merry Christmas, newlyweds."

"Merry Christmas, my sister," cried Tom.

"Hey, Mags," Sarah replied with a smile.

Simon immediately stood and walked across the room to greet her. "Merry Christmas, Maggie." He wrapped his arms around her and squeezed her tight, pressing his lips softly to her cheek.

"You, too, Simon."

She caught Pete's eye, and he gave her a concerned look.

"I have something for you." Simon pulled a key from his pocket.

"Oh, thanks." She hadn't seen him since he passed out on her office sofa after the wedding. His unexpected declaration of love had been more than she could handle. Unsure of what she would say to him when he awoke, she left a note along with her spare office key and went home.

She didn't know if he remembered saying it, but it was out there. And it was all she had thought about for the past week. He loved her. But did it make a difference? Love is fleeting, and his love might just as quickly transfer to someone else—like Anna.

The doorbell rang, and she opened the door for Vi and Dave, who came bearing casseroles and a bag of gifts.

"Merry Christmas, Maggie." Vi hugged her.

"Magnificent Maggie!" Dave exclaimed.

"Oh, that's a good one." Maggie hugged him. "I might use that."

They walked together into the kitchen. Vi immediately began helping Patty with dinner while Dave joined the group at the table, who were telling funny stories from the wedding day.

Maggie glanced around the room. Maybe they weren't all blood related, but they had become an important part of each other's lives over the past year, and they were her family—even Simon. Last Christmas, they were fighting on the front porch, and she couldn't stand the sight of him. Now, he was ... a friend.

She walked over and put her arm around her mother. "Love you, Mom." She grabbed the bowl of potatoes and started mashing.

Patty gave her a sweet, motherly smile and a kiss on the cheek.

The group at the table suddenly exploded with laughter over an unfortunate incident at the reception when Great Aunt Lois had lost her skirt.

"Stop that!" Patty scolded them. "Aunt Lois couldn't help it when that little boy pulled her skirt down."

"Yeah!" Tom tried to speak through his laughter. "But she just kept dancing."

"She didn't even try to pull it back up," Dave added, his shoulders shaking uncontrollably.

Everyone had tears in their eyes from laughing so hard.

Maggie walked over and dropped a box of tissue in the middle of the table.

Once the delicious meal was eaten and the table cleared, everyone gathered in the living room for a very special presentation.

Maggie plopped down in her favorite recliner and tucked her legs underneath her.

Tom walked up to the television, turned on the DVD player, and popped in a disc.

"What are we watching?" Maggie was very curious. They had been so secretive all day.

"It's our wedding," Sarah happily replied.

"Seriously?" She clapped her hands excitedly.

"My uncle took some video, and he burned it onto a disc for us this week." She curled up next to Tom on the couch.

Simon walked into the room and sat in front of Maggie's chair, leaning against it sideways with his arm draped across her lap.

"Excuse me." She poked at his arm.

He looked up at her with a grin, ignored her protest, and pointed toward the TV.

Tom's face popped up on the screen. He stood at the end of the aisle waiting for Sarah, wiping his tears as she walked toward him.

Everyone aww'd in unison.

As they watched the ceremony and listened to the vows, Maggie got tears in her eyes again.

Simon gave her hand a squeeze and didn't release it.

Maggie looked over at her new sister-in-law, who was also crying and holding her husband's hand. She watched Tom wipe a tear from her cheek and kiss her on the nose. Sarah laughed a little as she wiped her tears.

The video then went on to the reception and the speeches.

"Oh no!" Maggie covered her face with a pillow. "Is that really what I sound like?"

When it came to Simon's speech, he and Tom pointed across the room at each other.

Everyone either laughed or groaned again at Simon's upper hand joke.

"Yeah, I found that one online," he admitted.

"Cheater!" cried Tom.

"Guilty as charged."

Sarah and Tom's dance was next. They looked so happy and in love as they spun around the dance floor together.

When it was time for the bridal party dance, butterflies floated around in the pit of Maggie's stomach. There they were—she and Simon dancing.

Simon squeezed her hand again, and she removed it from his grip and hid behind the pillow again.

Sarah's uncle had moved around and among the group to get video of everyone as they danced. Maggie couldn't remember seeing him at all, and she hoped he had missed her and Simon's interaction. There was Gina dancing with Bill and Derek dancing with Leslie. Then the camera rotated around just as Simon whispered in her ear and kissed her cheek.

Simon looked up at her with a smile, trying to hold back his laughter as everyone said, "*Oooh!*"

"Dude, that's my sister," Tom cried jokingly.

Maggie blushed and kept her face hidden. She couldn't believe that was captured on the video, and in front of her whole family.

"What did he say?" asked Vi with a wink.

Simon answered so Maggie didn't have to. "I told her how beautiful she looked."

The *aww's* filled the room again.

"Fast forward," Maggie cried. She pushed Simon's arm from her lap and fled to the kitchen.

Sarah jumped up and followed. "What was that?" She spoke softly. "What did he say?"

Maggie looked into the living room to make sure everyone was still watching the video. She pulled Sarah further into the kitchen with her. "He said he can't help the way he feels about me, and I can keep pushing him away, but he's not going anywhere."

"Oh, Maggie." Sarah grinned at her.

"Then after the reception, he was kind of drunk, so I took him to my office to let him sleep it off, and he told me he's in love with me." It was the first time she had spoken the words aloud, and they sounded strange and foreign. No one had been in love with her for a very long time.

"Now what? Are you two getting together now? I saw how cozy you were in there."

"No, we're not getting together."

"What's going on in that head of yours, Maggie?" Sarah gave her a look that called for complete honesty.

"He was drunk when he said it."

"Not the first part. And drunk people tend to tell the truth."

"It's just his way of trying to get me to change my mind about him, even though I told him we're just friends, and that's all we'll ever be."

"Are you sure this is what you want?"

"I am. But even if I wasn't, it would never work out. He says he's not going anywhere, but he will."

Sarah shook her head sadly. "Why do you say that?"

"Because someone will come along—like Anna or some other random girl—and it'll be the same thing all over again."

"You can't know that," Sarah replied.

"But I do." She got louder as she spoke. "Because I know *him*. I was engaged to *him*, and *his* name was Ben."

"Maggie." Sarah's voice was filled with concern.

"Ben left me brokenhearted with a whole lot of empty promises." She took a deep breath and let it out, fighting back the tears.

Sarah took her hands. "Maggie, Simon is nothing like Ben."

"That's not true. If you recall, he wasn't faithful to Michelle when we almost made out under Pete's dock. And that night in Petoskey, I was going to tell him that I had feelings for him and that I was actually ready to move on—or at least try—with him, but he was already with somebody else. We weren't even together, and he broke my heart."

Sarah handed Maggie a tissue from the box left on the kitchen table.

She dabbed the tears from her eyes. "So that's how I know. Because no matter what he says, I'll just end up betrayed and alone. Again."

A sudden shuffle in the kitchen doorway caused the girls to stop talking. Maggie turned slowly and cringed.

Simon stood in the doorway staring blankly at them.

She wondered how long he had been standing there, but gathered from his expression that he had heard the majority of their conversation. Maggie didn't know what to say.

His eyes revealed his level of pain and disappointment.

"I'm not Ben," he declared coldly and walked out of the house.

THE GOVERNOR OF MICHIGAN AND MRS. HARTMAN

ALONG WITH

SENATOR AND MRS. SUMMERS

REQUEST THE HONOR OF YOUR PRESENCE

AT THE MARRIAGE OF THEIR CHILDREN

Lacey Eleanor Hartman

AND

George Thomas Summers

ON SATURDAY, THE NINETEENTH OF JUNE

TWO THOUSAND TEN

AT FOUR O'CLOCK IN THE AFTERNOON

The Grand Hotel

MACKINAC ISLAND, MICHIGAN

COCKTAILS IMMEDIATELY FOLLOWING ON THE PORCH

RECEPTION AT SIX O'CLOCK

THE THEATRE AT THE GRAND HOTEL

June 18, 2010

Journey to the Island

The next six months leading up to the Mackinac Island wedding went by in a blur. Maggie kept busy with work and tried not to think about what had happened with Simon at Christmas. He left that day and never came back. He disappeared, just as she predicted he would.

With Simon gone, her life should have gone back to normal, but something was different. Something inside her had shifted.

While sorting through some boxes at her parents' house after the holidays, she came across a few of her old photo albums from high school youth group. There were so many memories on those pages—hayrides, winter retreats, summer camp, and trips to Cedar Point. Youth group was the place where she first discovered her love for photography and capturing real, unposed moments. Fran, Pastor Jon's wife, had affectionately dubbed her the "youth group photographer", and her photo albums held the proof.

Looking through the hundreds of pictures, she came across one of her and Ben from camp the summer she turned sixteen, and she was reminded of a low point in their friendship. Finally aware of Maggie's feelings for him, he began to pull away. This left her overly emotional and filled with teenaged angst. The summer was ruined, or so she thought. She had pictured hanging out at the beach, getting ice cream, spending lots of time together, but the only time she saw him was at church. He gave any number of excuses why he couldn't hang out, and Maggie had been miserable. Not exactly the sweet sixteen summer she had imagined.

Staring at the photo, she recalled a moment from camp that difficult summer. Kneeling in the empty camp chapel, she had given her feelings for Ben to God. The worry over that relationship had been replaced with a sense of peace, and she knew in that moment that she could fully trust God with her heart and her future. God was enough for her.

Maggie was thankful that memory had resurfaced, and she had been clinging to it for months. It had led her back to a place she thought she'd never go again, a place that held so many memories of Ben—First Baptist Church. It was difficult to walk through those doors at first and not grieve for the past, for the years spent within those walls with Ben, but it got easier as the weeks went by. She was welcomed back with open arms by so many she had loved and missed. And now, like that day in the camp chapel, she felt peace. It had been a long time since she had felt so peaceful and so sure God would take care of her.

In the months since Christmas, Maggie began to pray for her business as she had in the beginning. Somewhere along the line, she started to trust in herself rather than God to succeed and that had gotten her nowhere. As her faith renewed more day by day, her fear over all the cancelled weddings faded and new bookings came.

She had also started praying for Simon. Maybe there was no future there, but she did care about him, and she wanted him to be happy.

Tom told her Simon had thrown himself into his work. "He's probably trying to become a better man for you," he had teased.

Maggie wondered what Simon was really doing. She knew he was staying away to avoid seeing her, and part of her felt bad for tearing apart their little family dynamic.

Pete once mentioned that Simon had been doing quite a bit of traveling. She wondered where to. Was he traveling for weddings? Was he on vacation with someone? Had he found someone new? She spent a lot of time replaying the events of the past year and second guessing her decisions, but in the end, she believed it was right for her.

Whatever the reason for Simon's disappearing act, she would have to face him when she and Sarah rode up to Mackinac with him and Anna for the wedding.

Maggie was nervous and excited. She couldn't hide it. She was practically bouncing off the walls of her shop.

183

"Settle, girl," Sarah ordered. "You're good. We've got all the equipment cleaned, charged and ready. No worries."

"I just want them to get here so we can go. I'm too excited to sit still."

She checked her email to pass the time. There was a short message from DeDe saying, "See you on the island," and some junk mail. She powered down her computer.

"Mags," Sarah called from her desk.

"Yeah?" she replied as she locked the door of her office behind her. She turned around to find Simon standing just inside the door.

"Hi," he spoke sweetly with a little grin.

"Hi." She was surprised when her stomach flipped at the sight of him, and she realized in that moment how much she had actually missed him. It felt surreal to have him standing in front of her again.

"Hi," Sarah repeated them. "OK, let's blow this joint."

Simon helped with the bags, holding the door for Sarah, then Maggie.

Maggie stopped just outside the door. He continued to hold it open for her.

"I have to lock up," she told him.

"Right." He seemed nervous. He let go of the door and followed Sarah down the sidewalk, where Anna was waiting in the car.

Maggie looked back at her shop. "Magnolia Photography" was painted on the glass with the white magnolia logo above it. *Look how far I've come. My little business is finally making a name for itself.*

She hopped in the back seat of Simon's car with Sarah, and they took off for the northern lower peninsula of Michigan.

Maggie and Sarah amused themselves on the four-hour drive by sending Twitter updates via their cell phones.

@magnoliaphotog: heading north with @sarahlovestom
@simonwalkerfoto and @annakleinphoto
for the wedding of the year!

@sarahlovestom: @simonwalkerfoto's taste in music sucks!

Maggie laughed at that. Simon's love of classic rock was completely annoying.

@magnoliaphotog: @sarahlovestom - totally agree! LOL!

@sarahlovestom: @magnoliaphotog - Maggie is the greatest sister/best friend/boss EVER!

@magnoliaphotog: @simonwalkerfoto is driving like a grandma.

@sarahlovestom: @annakleinphoto just fell asleep on our drive to Mackinaw City and snorted.

@magnoliaphotog: @sarahlovestom - ROFLMBO! Can't believe she's not texting in her sleep.

They were laughing out loud at their updates so much so that they had themselves in tears.

"What are you two doing back there?" asked Simon.

"Nothing, Grandma," replied Sarah.

Maggie burst out laughing. This was much better than the last ride north she'd made with Simon and Anna.

Simon adjusted the rear view mirror until he was looking at her. "Why do I have the feeling this laughter is at my expense?"

This just made them laugh more.

And when Anna snorted in her sleep again, they all started laughing.

As they neared their destination and rounded a bend in the highway, the Mighty Mac came into view. The Mackinac Bridge was the largest suspension bridge in the Western Hemisphere at five miles long and was an awesome sight to behold. Just before the bridge was Mackinaw City, where they hopped a ride to the island on a Star Line Hydro-Jet Ferry. They decided to sit below deck in the covered part of the boat rather than up top in the wind.

Maggie sat alone on a bench toward the front of the boat and pulled one of her cameras out to document the boat ride. She turned her camera on the others, who were sitting on the bench behind her.

They gave her their best cheesy grins.

Simon hopped up onto the bench with her and snatched the camera. He took a picture of the three girls, then sat next to Maggie, put his arm around her, and held the camera out in front of them for a little self-portrait action. He pulled her against his side and leaned his head against hers so they would both fit into the shot.

"Thanks." She retrieved the camera from him.

He kept his arm around her. "I still don't get the Canon fascination. Nikon is so much better."

She rolled her eyes. "Not this again."

"Yes, this again. Haven't I convinced you yet?"

"I actually think both are fine cameras, Simon. I just happened to pick up a Canon first, and I stuck with it. That's really all there is to it."

He tapped her on the nose. "Fine. You win."

She looked at him in shock. "I win? Wow!"

"What's that look?"

"I never thought you'd give up this fight so easily."

"Well, I'm a new man," he revealed with a grin.

Maggie didn't respond to that, but he did seem different somehow.

She settled in for the half hour ride with the slight bouncing of the boat and the warmth of Simon's arm draped comfortably against her back. Every now and then she'd snap a picture out the window.

When they approached the island, she took a few photos of The Grand Hotel through the glass. The hotel was so large, it could be seen clearly from far out in the water.

Once the boat docked, they gathered their belongings and boarded the carriage, which waited to take them to the hotel. No automobiles were allowed on Mackinac Island, the only forms of transportation were by foot, bicycle, or horse drawn carriage.

The horses pulling their carriage were Hackneys named Buck and Leo. The driver, Joshua, was a friendly man, who was quick to share the history of the island and all about the care of the horses.

"This your first time to the island?" Joshua asked.

"I've been here before," replied Maggie. "But it's been a long time."

"You have?" asked Sarah. "I didn't know that."

"Yeah, we vacationed here a few times growing up."

"Me, too," Anna interjected. "Maybe we were here at the same time when we were kids."

Maggie shook her head. "I doubt it, since you probably weren't even born when I was here."

Anna laughed, but it sounded fake and forced. "Oh, I forgot you're much older than me."

Maggie looked at Sarah, then back at Anna. "I'm not *that* much older than you."

"Well, forty is a lot older than me," Anna declared.

A laugh escaped from Simon before he could catch it.

"Hey!" Maggie slapped him. "I'm *thirty-two*, Anna."

"Oh my gosh, Maggie. I'm so sorry." Anna was messing with her stupid cell phone again. "I'm so bad at guessing people's ages."

Simon looked back at Maggie and mouthed, "Sorry."

She rolled her eyes at him.

As the carriage rounded the corner and headed up Grand Avenue with it's long row of trees and old fashioned street lights, the majestic white porch of the hotel peeked through the trees.

"Oh my goodness." Sarah's mouth fell open.

The carriage turned to the left and pulled up to the front of the hotel.

"The Grand Hotel," the driver announced.

"Wow!" Simon exclaimed.

"Double wow!" agreed Maggie. She had seen the hotel before, but it never ceased to amaze her.

The porch was huge—longer than two football fields—with a hundred white rocking chairs spread along its length for the guests to relax and enjoy the view of the Straits of Mackinac. Thousands of red geraniums, the hotel's signature flower, decorated the porch, and American flags flew proudly along its expanse.

"This is really impressive," Simon gushed as they climbed the stairs.

When they arrived on the porch, they took in the view of the straits, the gardens below, and the famous Esther Williams swimming pool.

"I could get used to this," Maggie said with a sigh.

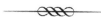

Once they were settled in their rooms and rested from their journey, Maggie and Sarah returned to the porch to await DeDe's instructions for the rehearsal. She arrived within minutes along with a very familiar face.

"Hello, team!" DeDe greeted them. "Simon and Anna are already with the couple. We're about to get started, but let me make some introductions. Governor, I'd like you to meet Maggie James and her assistant, Sarah James."

"James and James," the governor stated as he extended his hand to Maggie. "Are you two related?"

"By marriage, sir. Sarah recently married my brother."

"Well, congratulations, young lady." He reached out to shake Sarah's hand as well.

"Thank you so much," Sarah replied.

"I hope you'll enjoy your time here with us and take lots of pictures for my little girl."

"Oh, we will," Maggie promised. "It's so lovely to meet you."

"And both of you as well." He left them then to join his family for the rehearsal.

DeDe gave Maggie a squeeze. "You look great, by the way. That dress is killer."

"Thanks!" She felt beautiful in her tea length pink sundress with the flowing skirt.

"Are you ready for this?"

Maggie nodded. "Absolutely."

"Then go do your thing."

The bridal party and family gathered in the Tea Garden around the fountain, where the ceremony would take place. DeDe's planning and efficiency got the rehearsal done in record time, and every moment, every detail of the rehearsal and dinner, was thoroughly documented by Maggie and Simon.

When dinner was over, Lacey and George went with Simon to the west end of the porch for pictures at sunset with the straits in the background. Maggie followed, leaning against one of the pillars to watch from a distance.

Unlike that day back in college when he had made her feel so uncomfortable in front of the camera, he was very good at getting his couples to relax and be themselves. He had a way of getting them to interact with each other and with him so they were comfortable enough to do some of the more fashion inspired poses that he was known for. She was a little envious of his talent at that moment.

When Lacey and George left, Simon walked over to the edge of the porch and looked out at the water. He stood there for several minutes and seemed deep in thought.

The click of her heels against the porch floor turned his head.

"You are amazing at this job," she complimented him.

He gave her a once over, really looking at her for the first time all night. "Miss James," he spoke in that flirtatious way of his. "*That* is a dancin' dress."

She spun around and the dress lifted a bit, then flowed around her legs as she stopped.

He stepped forward and took her hand, spinning her around, then pulling her backwards into his arms.

"Hi," he whispered, then spun her out again making her skirt twirl even more.

Maggie laughed happily.

He spun her around once more, then pulled her in. This time, he placed one hand on her back and held her hand against his chest with the other, and he started to sway.

"Simon, there's no music."

"Who needs music," he whispered into her ear.

She smiled and relaxed into his arms. "I meant what I said. You're very talented."

"Thank you." He looked at her seriously for a moment. "You're pretty good, too."

"Pretty good, huh?"

"Well ..." He pretended to question himself. "Pretty anyway."

She playfully punched his chest.

"*Ow!*"

Maggie looked back as she heard some people walk out onto the porch. She felt a little funny dancing with no music, and Simon sensed it.

"Will you walk with me?" he asked.

"I should probably get some rest for tomorrow," she replied.

"But you'd rather take a walk." He confidently took her hand and led her down the steps, along the drive, and off of the Grand Hotel property. He weaved his fingers through hers as they walked Grand Avenue toward town.

She squeezed his hand and let go. She didn't want to give him the wrong idea. Although, showing up in this dress and dancing with him on the porch probably weren't the best decisions she had ever made. And walking together in the moonlight in this romantic setting made her feel weak around him.

"So, what happened to you?" She broke the silence first.

"What do you mean?"

"You disappeared." *I knew you would.*

"Miss me?" he asked with a little twinkle in his eye.

She glanced over at him, the street lights glowing on his face, his eyes on the sidewalk ahead.

"Yes." Even she was surprised by her answer.

He looked over at her. "Really?"

"Don't get all flattered," she commanded. "I should be really ticked off at you right now."

"Should you?"

"Stop responding with a question."

"Why?"

She groaned in frustration. "Simon."

"Sorry."

"So, where have you been?" she asked curiously.

"Around."

She was fed up. "Single word answers won't work either. Can we go back now?"

"Can we?" He grinned mischievously.

Maggie groaned again. He wasn't taking her seriously at all.

"I'm kidding." He held up his hands to block any attacks. "Just walk with me a little longer, OK?"

They walked in silence through the town. It was quiet except for the *clop clop clop* of the horses' hooves on the street. He took her hand again and wound his fingers through hers. She didn't let go this time.

He led her past the shops and hotels to the boardwalk. They passed the library and several cottages and came to a little bench just before the boardwalk ended. It was dark there, with only the subtle lights from the boardwalk path, the faint glow of the houses, and a light from the elementary school across the street.

Simon sat on the bench and gently pulled Maggie down beside him. They sat for a few minutes listening to the water rushing in and out along the shore. He held tightly to her hand.

Maggie was the first to speak. "What is with you? You seem different somehow."

"I've been doing a lot of soul searching the past few months," he admitted.

This surprised her.

"I've made a lot of mistakes," he continued. "I know that. And I'm sorry. I'm so sorry, Maggie. I knew you didn't want to be with me, but I pushed the issue anyway, and I feel really bad about that."

Maggie gulped. She didn't know what to say.

"I haven't made the greatest choices in my life, and that's because my focus was in the wrong places. I see that now."

"What do you mean?"

"I mean if I had actually paid attention in chapel back in college, maybe I would have figured out sooner that God's plans are better than mine."

She was surprised to hear him speak of God. Though they had attended a Christian college, Simon had always seemed much more interested in girls than in his spiritual life.

"I've been looking for happiness everywhere but where I should've been. I've been trying to find it on my own, and that hasn't really worked out very well."

"Well, it sounds like your soul searching has been a good thing," she managed.

He replied with a squeeze of her hand.

"I'm thinking of leaving Michigan," he confessed.

"You're what?" Maggie felt completely blindsided.

"Uncle Pete's doin' fine with his studio now. We talked about it, and he doesn't really need me to help him anymore. I've actually been thinking of moving since before he asked for my help, so I think it's time."

"What about the wedding part of his business?" Surely Simon needed to stick around for that.

"Oh, Pete's been referring all his wedding calls and emails to you for months now."

"He ... he has?" Maggie barely got the words out.

Simon nodded. "Yeah, I told him to."

She hadn't questioned why there was a sudden pickup in inquiries over the past few months. That's how things went sometimes. There would be a lot of emails all at once and then very few for weeks, so she had thought nothing of it.

Her mind raced. She was shocked by this turn of events. "Where will you go?"

"California," he answered without hesitation.

Maggie swallowed hard. *So far?*

"There's just nothin' keeping me here anymore." He avoided looking her in the eye. "I've been spending a lot of time out there at my parents' house, looking for a place to live, getting things ready to transition my business out there."

Maggie let go of his hand. She couldn't concentrate with his thumb rubbing against hers, and she had things she wanted to say. "So, you're not just thinking about this then? You've already made your plans. You're leaving."

Simon was silent.

Maggie stood. "Why am I not surprised?" She fled down the boardwalk.

"Maggie, wait!" He had to speed walk to catch up with her.

She spun around to face him. "What was that all about at the wedding then, if you were already planning on leaving?"

Simon looked out at the dark waters, avoiding eye contact once more. "I wasn't planning to leave then."

"Right." Maggie nodded knowingly. "So this is about what I said at Christmas."

He looked at her again. "I'm glad I heard that, otherwise I never would have known that's how you really felt."

"I knew this was gonna happen." Her anger boiled up. "You can't tell someone you're not going anywhere then totally disappear from their life."

He was flabbergasted. "You didn't believe me when I said that anyway."

"Yeah, well ... I wanted you to prove me wrong." Maggie blurted the words without thinking, and she was as surprised as Simon by this sudden, unexpected truth.

It hung in the air between them.

Sudden tears sprung to the surface. She tried unsuccessfully to hold them in.

Simon stepped closer and took her face in his hands, gazing tenderly into her eyes.

"Then tell me to stay." His voice was soft and filled with affection.

Maggie couldn't say anything. She wanted to, but she couldn't seem to reconcile the changes in him with the untrustworthy man she thought he was. And fear of another broken heart was still holding her back from telling him what she really wanted to, from asking him into her life, from finally moving on.

She looked down.

He let go and sighed. "Then I'm going."

She watched him walk briskly across the yard of the elementary school, back over to Grand Avenue, and up the hill toward the hotel. She couldn't bring herself to follow.

Sadness washed over her, and then a sudden panic that she might never see Simon again after Sunday. Tears spilled over her cheeks, and all the reasons she'd been holding onto for not being with him seemed insignificant in that moment. She cared more for him than she ever realized. Now, all she could do was pray.

Oh, Lord, I thought he wasn't the one for me, but my heart is breaking right now. I think I've made a huge mistake. Was I wrong about him? Has he really changed? Show me what to do. Please, help me to see the big picture.

June 19, 2010

Lacey Hartman & George Summers

*M*aggie awoke on the wedding day with puffy eyes from crying herself to sleep. Sarah had been asleep when she returned to the room, so she shut herself in the bathroom and let the tears flow.

She sat up in bed thinking almost all night. For all those months, Simon had stayed away, avoided vendor gatherings, and this year's convention in Vegas. He stopped coming to her parents' house to play cards with Tom and the guys. She no longer saw him around Hastings. He really had disappeared.

But could she blame him? After he overheard her conversation with Sarah, she understood. She had hurt him deeply with her words. But she thought he would eventually come back. She thought at some point there would be a conversation and all would be well again. Because he always came back.

Only he didn't. And now he would be thousands of miles away. He was leaving for good.

As the morning light filled the room, Sarah stirred. She rolled over and saw Maggie's sad expression.

"Mags, what's wrong?" Sarah climbed over onto the bed with her and held her while she cried.

"Simon's moving to California," she mumbled.

"California? Wow! I can't believe that."

"It's because he heard us talking at Christmas."

Sarah shook her head. "I'm sure that's not why he's moving."

"It is. He's leaving because of what I said."

Sarah put her arm around Maggie. "Did he say that?"

She nodded in reply. "He wanted me to tell him to stay, but I don't think I can."

"Why not?" Sarah hugged her. "Oh, Maggie, why do you think you're so upset about him leaving?"

Maggie had no reply.

"It's because you love him, and you don't want him to go." Sarah shifted until they were facing each other. "Look, I know you've been hurt before, and I know you're really scared, but you have to let that go. You have to finally take this chance or you're never going to find out if Simon's the right guy for you. You have to be willing to open your heart again, even at the risk of it being broken. Otherwise, you're not allowing God to bring you the one he's been preparing for you all this time. Maybe that's Simon. Maybe it's not. But you have to try."

Maggie wrapped her arms around Sarah and hugged her tight.

Sarah grabbed a tissue and wiped the tears from Maggie's face. She then scurried about the room, grabbed a wet washcloth for Maggie to wash up with, brewed a pot of coffee, and laid their clothing out on the bed. She really was an amazing assistant and sister.

Maggie walked over to look at her reflection in the mirror. "I can't go to the wedding looking like this."

"I'll take care of you." Sarah called the front desk and had some cucumbers sent up to help take away the puffiness.

Maggie laid back on her bed with the cucumbers over her eyes, trying not to cry again. But every time she thought about her conversation with Simon, the tears threatened to fall. *Get control of your emotions. You have a job to do.*

"Here's coffee."

Maggie heard her set it on the stand next to the bed.

"You're the best," Maggie declared. "Thank you." She peeled the cucumbers from her eyes.

"Now, if Simon's leaving, then he might as well see what he'll be missing." Sarah held up Maggie's little black dress. "Let's make you look stunning."

Maggie looked at her dress and smiled. "Let's."

Sarah worked magic on Maggie's hair, giving her soft curls all over her head. She normally pulled her hair into a bun or ponytail to keep it out of her face while she worked, but on this day she left it down.

Her long loose curls flowed over her shoulders and tickled her back, half of which was revealed by the low cut back of her dress.

There before her in the mirror was the reflection of a beautiful girl, with no evidence of puffy eyes. She smiled at Sarah.

Sarah smiled back confidently. "He's an idiot if he leaves."

The girls gathered their equipment and headed to the salon, where Lacey and her bridesmaids were getting their hair and makeup done. Maggie was relieved that Simon was spending the morning with the guys on the golf course. She would be able to work much better without him around, at least until the wedding.

"Good morning, Maggie," Lacey greeted her with a hug. "Hi, Sarah."

"Are you ready for this?" asked Maggie with a smile.

"More than ready to marry the man of my dreams," Lacey gushed.

The salon was alive with commotion as the bride, her eight bridesmaids, and two flower girls were worked on by several hair stylists and makeup artists that Lacey had hired for the occasion.

Maggie photographed every step of Lacey's hair being styled and each stage of her makeup. Lacey was a beautiful girl, but when they were through, she looked breathtaking.

When the rest of the girls were ready, carriages took them to the Governor's Summer Residence, situated on the bluff above town. It was such an honor to be invited into this home, which had been used as the summer residence for every governor of Michigan since the mid-1940's.

As soon as she entered the house, Maggie walked over to the windows and looked out at the view of the straits and the little town below. She was very grateful that her job had brought her to this beautiful place.

She listened as the bridesmaids chatted and waited on Lacey hand and foot. They made sure she was comfortable and had something to eat so she wouldn't pass out at the ceremony. The maid of honor poured several glasses of champagne and a couple tiny cups of juice for the flower girls.

"To Lacey and George." She held her glass in the air.

Maggie smiled to herself as she snapped a few shots of the flower girls tapping their cups together and then against Lacey's glass.

"I think it's time you put on your dress," Lacey's mother announced.

The house was suddenly a flurry of activity as the girls headed up to the getting ready room. Lacey's elegant Vera Wang wedding gown hung near the window with the light cascading onto it. Maggie photographed the dress and Lacey's pink peep-toe Jimmy Choo heels.

The bridesmaids helped Lacey carefully climb into her dress and her mother fastened her up. The room grew quiet as they all stepped back to take a look at the bride.

Lacey glanced over at her reflection in the mirror and fanned at her eyes with her hands as she started to tear up. "Now it feels real."

Her mother walked over and gave her a hug and a kiss on the cheek. "Your father and I are so proud of you."

"Thanks, Mom," Lacey replied.

The carriages returned to the residence fifteen minutes before the ceremony was to begin. Maggie rode in the first carriage with the bride and some of the bridesmaids, while Sarah rode in the second. The carriages made their way down the hill to the hotel and turned right into the hotel drive. They drove past the security guards set up to keep out uninvited guests and press, and pulled up to the front steps. The timing was perfect.

The guests had all arrived and were seated in the Tea Garden with the groom and his groomsmen in place.

Sarah climbed out and headed down to the garden, while Maggie captured the girls exiting the carriages. She then quickly made her way to the bottom of the hill and captured Lacey's grand entrance down the staircase, where her father was waiting to offer her his arm. He leaned over and kissed her on the cheek, and she smiled at him endearingly. They walked together across the lawn and down the aisle of rose petals.

George was beaming as Lacey approached.

Maggie spotted Simon at the front of the aisle shooting the

groom's reaction. She felt a little twinge of panic at the sight of him, but pushed it aside.

The governor lifted Lacey's veil and gave her a kiss.

Click. Click. Click.

She smiled as she captured the moment and remembered how important this job of hers was. These photos were the very things that would help keep these moments fresh in their minds for many years to come.

The ceremony was beautiful with traditional vows exchanged. Maggie was standing in the center of the aisle about halfway down, clicking away, when a sudden hand on her shoulder startled her.

"Excuse me, miss."

A gentleman squeezed around her on the right and walked to the front of the aisle. It wasn't until he turned around that she realized who it was.

"I wrote a special song for Lacey," George announced.

This was not a surprise to Maggie as it had been discussed during the planning meetings with DeDe.

"And since I knew I would be a little too nervous to sing it myself, I found someone who could do a much better job of it. So here to perform my song is Mr. Michael Bublé."

This was a surprise.

The guests applauded as Michael began to sing of George's love for Lacey.

Maggie could hardly believe their choice of artist, and she wondered if Simon had anything to do with it. She smiled to herself as she photographed Michael performing the song.

Lacey and George weren't watching Michael at all. They were looking deep into each other's eyes, and Lacey was crying tears of joy.

At ceremony's end, the guests made their way to the porch for cocktails while the portraits were taken. Simon and Anna handled the formals, while Maggie and Sarah photographed the guests at the cocktail hour. Maggie was once again relieved that she and Simon were working separately.

"There you are," Anna called after her. "Simon needs you."

Maggie took a deep breath. *Be professional. Don't think about last night. Don't you dare cry in front of him again.*

Lacey greeted her as she approached. "Maggie, I know we asked Simon to do the formals, but we love your casual style of portraits, and we'd love to do some with you, too."

Maggie glanced over at Simon.

He nodded at her and bowed out without a word, heading for the cocktail hour.

She took Lacey and George onto the steps and had them sit together and cuddle and kiss. Then they walked out onto the property, and she asked them to walk hand in hand along the woodsy path. She even had them sit on a couple of chaise lounges by the pool. They had a fun time laughing and talking with Maggie, and she got some relaxed shots of them enjoying their first hour of marriage.

"Thank you, Maggie. We can't wait to see these." Lacey gave her a hug.

"You're welcome. George, the song you wrote was just beautiful."

"Thanks, Maggie."

"And Michael Bublé." She gave him a thumbs up. "Great choice."

"We had a little help with that." George winked at Lacey.

Maggie wondered if her suspicions were correct.

DeDe had not exaggerated when she gushed about the reception. The Theatre was decorated in the most luxurious way possible. The ceiling was covered in beautiful draped silk and the room had been professionally lit for a dramatic look. The floral arrangements stood high above the tables, all of which were surrounded by Chiavari chairs and covered in exquisite linens with letterpress menus neatly tucked in the folds of the napkins.

"Wowsa!" Sarah exclaimed when they walked through the doors.

Maggie stood in awe at the sight. They had been waiting all day to see this room. Simon and Anna were the ones to photograph the room earlier in the day, while they were with the ladies at the residence.

"So?" DeDe walked up beside them. "Didn't I tell ya?"

"Yes!" Maggie took off to photograph everything she could. Though Simon had taken pictures of the room earlier, Lacey and George had told her they loved her detail shots. It was one of her favorite things about weddings, and she did not want to disappoint them.

As she worked her way around the room, she noticed an old fashioned photo booth in the corner, the kind you would find in shopping malls or carnivals. Some of the guests were standing near it, waiting to have their pictures taken. She thought of the photo booth in Vegas and smiled.

By the time she returned to the entrance, the bridal party was lined up. Once they were announced and seated, Governor Hartman took the microphone and stepped up to the head table. Maggie moved to get a better shot as he began to speak.

"Welcome, everyone. My wife and I would like to thank all of you for joining us here on Mackinac Island this weekend. We appreciate you all taking time out of your summer to travel here for Lacey and George's big day."

Maggie snapped away as he continued on with his speech. She noticed Simon out of the corner of her eye, shooting from the other side of the room. She turned on her heel and took some pictures of the guests laughing at something funny the governor said, but she wasn't really paying attention to his speech anymore. She was very aware of Simon and the fact that the end of the reception meant the end of everything for them. When the wedding was over, they would go home—her to Hastings and him to his new home in California.

After the meal, Michael Bublé took the Theatre stage and began his wonderful crooning. George led Lacey onto the dance floor for their first dance as husband and wife.

Maggie watched them dance. Her heart ached as it had the night she watched Tom and Sarah's wedding dance. But this time it wasn't that she was afraid of never finding love again, it was because she was afraid she may have already found it and was about to lose it forever.

The newlyweds had taken dance lessons before the wedding, and they wowed the crowd with a choreographed number. When he dipped her back and kissed her, Maggie smiled through her camera viewfinder.

Click. Click. Click.

Sometimes, in the middle of a wedding, there were moments—true and pure—so full of love that you could almost see it flow from one person to the other. It always took Maggie by surprise, this overwhelming feeling of joy. This dance was one of those moments. She was also keenly aware of the huge responsibility photographing a wedding was and how much couples trusted her to capture their day.

Michael performed a few more slow songs for the traditional dances then exited the stage, and another band took over for the rest of the evening. The music shifted to something a little more upbeat, and the dance floor filled quickly.

Maggie wished she had half the energy the guests had at that moment. She was physically exhausted from the long weekend and emotionally exhausted from Simon. She began shooting again and tried to will herself to get a second wind, but she was spent. *Need coffee.*

She walked over to the coffee bar and grabbed a cup of caffeinated goodness. As she stirred in some cream and sugar, Anna joined her and got a cup for herself.

"Hey, Maggie."

"Hi," she replied.

"Isn't this the most gorgeous wedding you've ever seen?" Anna took a sip of coffee. "*Ow!* That's hot. I burned my tongue."

Maggie rolled her eyes at Anna's ditziness.

"This has been so fun working with you again," Anna declared. "If you ever need an assistant to fill in when Sarah can't, you let me know."

"Yeah. I'll do that," she lied.

"Hey, Simon has another wedding booked for next summer in Petoskey. Maybe we can work together there again."

Maggie wished this conversation was over.

"That would be fun, right?" Anna asked.

"Yeah," she answered sarcastically. "Only next time, maybe Simon can save some money, and you two can just share a room."

Anna looked at her with a strange expression. "Why would we share a room?"

"You shared a room last time," she replied with annoyance and an edge of anger.

"No, we didn't!" Anna looked shocked and disgusted at the same time.

"What?" Maggie wasn't sure she had heard her right.

"Are you talking about that night when you stopped by the room? Oh my gosh, you thought ..." Anna chuckled. "No! I complained that my back hurt from carrying the cameras all day. He had that big jacuzzi tub in his room, so we swapped. He was just being nice."

Maggie thought she might be sick. "You swapped rooms with Simon?"

"Yeah."

"But you were in a towel."

"Oh, I couldn't figure out how to get those darn jets to work. Simon came over and fixed it for me." She looked at Maggie again with a screwed up face. "I can't believe you thought I spent the night with Simon. He's my boss. That's *way* inappropriate."

"Right," Maggie mumbled.

Anna shook her head and walked away.

Maggie couldn't move. She was frozen in place. She stood holding her coffee cup and stirring. Her mind raced. *He didn't sleep with her. He didn't.*

When she saw Sarah across the room with DeDe, she forced her legs to move, walking slowly—as if in a trance—through the crowd of dancing guests. She didn't notice any of them.

"Hey, Mags." Sarah noticed her strange behavior. "What's wrong? You look pale. Are you sick?"

Maggie was shaking now. The coffee spilled over the edge of her cup and ran down her arm, but she didn't notice.

"He didn't sleep with her." She finally spoke the words aloud.

DeDe pried the coffee cup out of her hand. "Who didn't sleep with whom?"

Maggie looked Sarah in the eyes. "He didn't sleep with Anna."

Sarah's eyes widened. "He didn't?"

All Maggie could do was shake her head *no* over and over.

"Sit down, Maggie." DeDe helped her over to a nearby chair, cleaned the coffee from her arm, and went to get her some water.

"What do I do?" she repeated over and over. Tears filled her eyes. "All these months, I pushed him away, because I thought he couldn't be trusted. Because I thought he slept with her."

"Just relax." Sarah put an arm around Maggie and rubbed her back. "You're gonna give yourself a heart attack."

She felt dizzy, her breath coming in bursts. "I think I'm having a panic attack. I can't breathe."

DeDe returned and pulled a bag out of her emergency kit. "Here! Breathe into this."

Maggie took a few slow, deep breaths until she had calmed down. She took a sip of water, then looked over at Sarah. "I blew it. I'm such an idiot. I ruined this. And now he's going away."

"Just go talk to him," Sarah pleaded.

"I can't. I've made a mess of everything."

DeDe took the seat next to her. "I think it's time I told you a little story."

June 19, 2010

The Plan

$\mathcal{A}$s DeDe spoke, the wedding and all the guests seemed to disappear around them.

"Last year, after Lacey and George were through all their vendor meetings, I sat down with them to go over things. As you know, part of my job was to help them along with their decisions. Even though I praised you and your work, they decided to go another direction and hire Simon as their wedding photographer."

Maggie gave her a confused look.

"It was actually decided before your birthday party, but I didn't have the heart to tell you when you asked me that night."

"But they hired both of us." She didn't understand what DeDe was saying.

DeDe laid her hand on Maggie's arm. "I'm getting to that."

"Sorry." She took a sip of water.

"They called Simon first thing that next week, and he was very excited to get the news. Only, the next day, he called me and asked if I could set up a special meeting with the couple as soon as possible. We were able to work in a conference call later that day."

Maggie listened intently.

"In this meeting, Simon asked them if they would reconsider hiring you for the wedding instead."

"What?" Maggie was shocked and confused.

"He really talked you up, told them how talented you were, what an amazing style you have, and how well you work with your couples. And since they already loved you and your work, they were happy to go along with his plan."

"I don't get it. What plan?" She wasn't sure whether she would like this story or not.

"If they hired you for the wedding, Simon would shoot for free. They would get two photographers they loved for the price of one."

"Simon didn't get paid for this wedding?" Sarah interrupted.

Maggie's mouth hung open as she stared at DeDe.

"His only stipulation was that we let you believe they hired both of you."

"Wh ... Why would he do that?"

"I guess his uncle told him how upset you were about all the cancelled weddings."

Maggie's mind raced through all the details. "So, he gave up this commission ... and he had to pay out of his own pocket to come here. Paying Anna, paying for travel, and for the rooms." She sat still for a minute letting it all sink in.

"He was very adamant that I kept this to myself." DeDe smirked. "He didn't want you to think that he did this because he felt sorry for you."

"Then why did he do it?"

DeDe looked at her with raised eyebrow. "Why do *you* think?"

Maggie walked outside for a breath of fresh air and sat on the nearest bench. *He gave me this wedding. Gave it to me.*

She stared at the camera sitting in her lap. *And he didn't sleep with Anna.*

Her mind replayed the weekend in Petoskey again. She had made a huge assumption. But if he hadn't slept with Anna, why had he let her go on believing that he had?

Her thoughts were all jumbled. She couldn't make sense of anything. And did any of it really matter anymore? He was going to California anyway.

What do I do? Do I tell him that I know about Anna? Do I tell him I know about the wedding when DeDe wasn't supposed to tell me?

Sarah came outside looking for her. "There you are. Are you OK?"

"I don't know," she replied. "I'm not sure where to go from here."

"Do you want to be with him?" Sarah got straight to the point.

Maggie closed her eyes and nodded. "What do I say to him?"

"Just say what's in your heart."

"I wish I knew how to put it into words. I feel like such an idiot right now."

Sarah took her hands and started praying aloud. "Lord, please give Maggie guidance right now as she makes this decision. Give her the right words to say to Simon and the strength to say them. Thank you for healing old wounds and giving us tender hearts capable of loving again. Amen."

"Amen," Maggie repeated.

Sarah squeezed her hands. "Maybe when you go back inside, you'll see him and just know what to say."

Maggie raised an eyebrow.

"Or maybe not," Sarah shrugged.

"That's so reassuring."

"We need to go back in anyway, because the governor would like a picture of the photographers with their family."

"Oh, goody." Maggie was so much more comfortable behind the lens. She took a deep breath and let it out.

Sarah hugged her before they went back in. "Everything will work out. I believe that."

Maggie opened the door and stepped inside the Theatre again. The band was still going strong, and the dance floor was as lively as it had been an hour before. This party was sure to go late into the night. She watched Lacey and George dancing in the middle of the floor and, suddenly, there he was. Simon stood in the middle of the dance floor, shooting from the center of the action.

Her heart began to flutter, and she felt weak in the knees as she watched him work. She didn't know what she was going to say, but she knew she had to speak to him. He moved around to the other side of the dance floor and disappeared into the sea of people.

Maggie lifted her camera and shot several photos of the dancing. She moved up by the stage to get pictures of the band and some details shots of their instruments and music. She climbed up on the stage and got a few shots from behind with the dancing guests in the background. Then, she shot over their shoulders as they played. The drummer looked back at her and made a crazy face, which made her laugh.

She sat on the edge of the stage and took some more pictures of the dance crowd. Someone suddenly grabbed her leg and tugged. When she looked up from behind her camera, her mouth went dry.

"Hey!" Simon climbed up on the stage next to her. "How's it going?"

"Fine," she replied. Her palms began to sweat like a nervous teenaged girl sitting next to the boy she liked.

He sat with her for a few minutes watching people dance.

"Are you as wiped as I am?" he asked.

She nodded, but couldn't find her words.

"Only a couple more hours. Tops." He gave her a cute grin and hopped down.

She watched him move into the crowd of guests and raise his camera once again. It took everything within her to gather the courage to jump off the stage and go after him. She came up behind him on the dance floor and gently grabbed his arm.

"I need to talk to you," she declared, still not quite sure what to say.

"Sure." He led her through the crowd to the coffee bar, where it was a little quieter.

She tried to come up with the right words. Her lips opened several times, but nothing came out. She bit her bottom lip softly.

"Maggie, what?" He seemed slightly annoyed that she wasn't speaking. "I need to get back to work. What did you want to talk about?"

"I know what you did for me," she blurted.

"And what did I do?"

Tears stung her eyes. "I know you gave me this wedding."

His expression changed with the sudden realization of what she meant. "Oh." He looked down at his camera. "You weren't supposed to find out about that."

She tried hard to keep from crying in front of him. "Why not?" Her chin quivered.

He looked her in the eyes. "I didn't want you to feel like you didn't earn this, because you did. You deserved this wedding."

"So did you."

"I wanted you to have it," he declared.

"Why?" she asked as the tears spilled over.

He gently brushed a tear from her cheek. "I just wanted you to be happy." He smiled tenderly.

Maggie knew now. She had been wrong about him for months—probably years. He wasn't like Ben at all. He would do anything to make her happy and he had.

She suddenly gained a boost of confidence. "I *am* happy," she spoke through tears.

"Good." He smiled at her.

"I'm happy for another reason."

He had a slightly confused expression.

"I'm happy you didn't sleep with Anna."

He closed his eyes for a second and smiled. "No, I didn't."

"I'm so sorry I jumped to conclusions and made such ridiculous assumptions."

He shook his head. "I should be the one apologizing for that. I was upset, so I let you think it happened. It was stupid and immature, and I should have told you the truth a long time ago." He paused. "I tried to tell you at Halloween, but I got a little distracted." He grinned at her.

Suddenly overcome by a strong urge to be near him, she moved forward and wrapped her arms tightly around his waist.

He held her awkwardly with their cameras hanging in between them. Their lenses banged together, and they laughed.

Maggie pulled back and looked up into his eyes. It was her turn to make the first move. She suddenly realized they were standing very near the dancing guests, and this didn't look very professional.

Out of the corner of her eye, she spotted the photo booth, and it appeared to be empty. She grinned up at Simon. "Come with me."

He didn't have much choice but to follow her as she led him across the room by his tie, both of them smiling all the way.

"Where are we going?" he asked.

She pulled back the curtain to the booth and pushed him inside. "Sit," she commanded. She removed the camera from around her neck and set it on the floor at their feet.

"I'm not a dog," he replied with a grin, echoing her own words from long ago.

She pushed on his shoulders until he sat on the bench and tugged the curtain closed behind her. Simon set his camera on the floor next to Maggie's. The booth was tiny, and Maggie bumped the photo button as she seated herself on Simon's lap.

He had that look again. The one he got when he was amused by something.

"Simon," she said as she slid her arms around his neck.

"Maggie," he wrapped his arms around her, softly caressing the bare back her dress revealed.

She looked him in the eyes. "Please don't go to California."

His mouth fell open a bit at her statement.

Maggie slid her fingers through his hair as she leaned in and touched her lips to his.

A little moan escaped from his throat, and he kissed her back with everything he'd held inside for the past six months.

They breathed into each kiss, his hands gliding softly up her back and into her hair.

There was a sudden flash. Then another. Then another. They started laughing as they kissed, both realizing that the photo booth was going off.

Flash!

"I'm sorry, Simon," she whispered against his lips. "For pushing you away, for hurting you over and over, for everything."

His fingers traced her cheek as they had done several times before. "I just want to be with you. But if you're not ready, I can wait."

Maggie leaned in and planted a soft kiss on his lips. "No more waiting," she whispered.

They laughed and smiled as they kissed again, almost giddy from their declarations.

Outside the booth, there was a rustling sound, and they froze with their lips touching. But the rustling stopped, so Maggie reached up and loosened Simon's tie, leaning in to plant kisses on his neck.

Simon let go of her long enough to gently lead her lips back to his as he kissed her slowly this time, like their Halloween kiss, only this time with so much more meaning behind it. They were together now, and he kissed her without reservation.

Suddenly, the curtain of the photo booth flew open causing them to jump.

"I found them." Lacey held a strip of black and white photos of them in her hand. "Aw, look at you guys. Simon, was this part of your plan?"

"Absolutely." He smiled proudly.

George and DeDe stood off to the side laughing at Lacey's discovery.

Maggie blushed as she climbed off of Simon's lap. "We're so sorry." She was mortified. "This was totally unprofessional."

Lacey put an arm around her. "No apology necessary. I had a feeling about you two." She led Maggie across the room, followed by Simon and George. "My dad would like a picture of our family with you and Simon."

Anna was waiting with camera in hand to take the picture.

"Well, did you enjoy the day, young lady?" asked the governor.

Maggie, still blushing, looked over at Simon and smiled. "Yes, sir, I did."

George punched Simon in the arm. "Yeah, she did," he joked.

Those who had been witness to the photo booth laughed.

The governor looked at them strangely, wondering what their laughter was about. "I guess I missed something." He smiled and put an arm around his wife.

Maggie and Simon stood in the middle of the group with Governor Hartman and his wife on one side and Lacey and George on the other. Simon took her hand, which made her smile from ear to ear. She hoped she didn't look like a smiling fool because she couldn't stop.

After the picture with the governor, Michael Bublé graciously agreed to a few photos with the group. Maggie was starstruck when Simon introduced the two of them and when Michael put his arm around her for the picture.

"Simon!" Michael approached with hand extended. "Hey, thanks for setting this up."

"No, thank you for coming out." Simon shook his hand and pulled him in for a quick bro hug. "And congrats on your recent engagement. I'm happy for you, man."

"Thank you," Michael said. "Hey, tell your parents I said hello."

"Will do." Simon waved goodbye to his friend.

Maggie stared up at him in confusion. "What is happening right now?"

Simon chuckled. "I've known him for a few years now. We met out in L.A. I'll tell you about it sometime."

She had a feeling life with Simon was going to be an adventure.

He kissed the back of her hand and went back to work.

Maggie felt like she was floating above the floor.

Sarah came running up and almost knocked her over. "What happened? DeDe told me there was an incident with you two in the photo booth."

"Wow! Word travels fast around here."

"Well, it's DeDe. What do you expect?"

Maggie laughed at that.

"So?" Sarah was dying for information.

"I told him not to go." Her smile had grown bigger since their picture with the governor.

"Oh, Maggie." Sarah gave her a hug. "So, does this mean what I think it means?"

Maggie nodded happily as she watched Simon across the room working as hard as he had all day long.

"This is awesome." Sarah clapped her hands. "I knew it. Didn't I tell you it would work out?"

She nodded again.

Simon looked over at her then with a smile so full of love she thought she might burst. Every time he looked over she was watching him, until he eventually came over to where they were standing.

"You can't do that," he stated.

"What am I doing?" she feigned innocence.

"You can't keep watching me."

"Do I make you nervous?" she asked.

He leaned in and kissed her firmly.

Sarah watched them, thoroughly amused.

Simon went back to work and left Maggie with a goofy grin on her face for the rest of the night.

When the happy couple had departed in their carriage for an evening ride around the island and all the guests had gone to their hotel rooms, Maggie found a table near the door to pack up her gear. She tucked her cameras and each lens into the correct slot in her camera bag. Her memory cards were all zipped up and secure, ready to load the images and back them up on the laptop in her room.

"Hey." Simon joined her and started packing up his own gear.

"Where's your assistant to help you with your bags?" she asked.

"Oh, I let her go about an hour ago. She had some texting to do," he joked.

Maggie smiled at that.

"Where's Sarah?" he asked.

"She's somewhere with DeDe."

She lifted her bag from the table and over her shoulder.

"Let me." Simon relieved her of the camera bag. "Where to?" he asked with a slightly raised eyebrow.

"Let's go to the porch," she replied with a grin.

He took her hand, and they walked through the hotel and out onto the porch.

Holding Simon's hand felt incredibly comfortable, like it was the most natural thing in the world, like she'd been doing it forever.

He set their bags next to the closest rocking chair and took a seat. "Come here." He tugged on her arm, and she climbed into his lap for the second time that night.

"Hey." She still couldn't wipe the smile from her face.

"Hey." He wrapped his arms around her waist and kissed her softly on the lips. A shiver shook his shoulders.

"Are you cold?" Maggie leaned into him more.

"*Mmmm.*" He shook his head. A light breeze blew in from the lake, but he was far from cold. He pressed his lips to hers again. "I can't believe I'm allowed to do that now," he whispered.

She grinned and laid her head against his chest as he rocked the chair back and forth. They sat like that for a while, enjoying the feeling of holding each other, finally able to do that just because they wanted to.

"Do you remember that day in Wilkins' photography class?" Simon suddenly asked.

Maggie lifted her head and looked at him. "What day?"

Simon looked thoughtful. "The first time we met, when we had to take pictures of each other for that assignment."

"Oh my word." Maggie was amazed. "I can't believe you remember that."

He nodded. "Oh, it's ingrained in my memory."

"Really?" She raised an eyebrow at him.

"Well, yeah. You told me I sucked at making people comfortable in front of my camera. I couldn't very well forget that."

She started laughing. "Well, I *was* very uncomfortable."

Simon squeezed his arms tighter around her. "That was the day I knew."

"You knew what?"

"I knew we'd end up together someday."

Maggie smiled and shook her head in disbelief. "You did not."

"Well, I haven't been able to get you out of my head since that day."

"Simon." She looked at him with uncertainty. "You're teasing me, right?"

He shook his head. "I'm completely serious. No matter what I did, you were always there in the back of my mind. And it drove me crazy that you always avoided me."

She laughed again. "Well, it drove *me* crazy that you were always around."

He made a funny face at her, and she leaned in and kissed his cheek.

Simon shifted and retrieved his wallet from his back pocket. He opened it and rifled through the contents, sliding an old, worn photograph from within. Hesitantly, he turned it around to face her.

Maggie's mouth fell open. "Simon!"

He grinned shyly as he held a copy of the picture he had taken of her in the library that Halloween day over fifteen years before.

"I ... I can't believe you have that."

"I told you. I knew."

Her eyes began to tear up a little.

"And here we are. Was I right or was I right?" Now there was the Simon she remembered from all those years ago, still a know-it-all.

213

She kissed his cheek and looked him in the eyes. "It just took us a while to get here."

He pulled her closer and pressed his lips gently against hers again. His fingertips moved in a shiver-inducing path down her back, and she softly sighed.

"You two are incredible," DeDe announced as she walked through the door onto the porch.

They pulled apart and looked over at her.

"Thank you so much for all your hard work this weekend. Lacey and George wanted me to tell you they had a great time today."

"Thanks, De," Simon replied. "We wouldn't be here right now if it wasn't for you."

She winked.

"De, thank you for everything." Maggie reached out and squeezed her hand.

"They also wanted me to give you this." She held the photo booth pictures of Simon and Maggie from earlier in the night.

Maggie snatched them from DeDe's hand. There they were, their first moments together—really together.

"Thank you," she called after DeDe, who walked away with a wave.

Maggie held the pictures up for Simon to see.

A large grin spread across his face. "We're gonna have to frame that and put it in our office."

"Our office?" She looked at him curiously.

"Oh, yes," he replied. "I've got big plans for us, Miss James."

"Have you now?"

"Yes, I have. And my first plan is to convert you to Nikon cameras."

Maggie laughed and kissed him again. "Never gonna happen."

He looked into her eyes and grinned in that Simon way.

"Never say never."

May 9, 2011
A New Beginning

As they drove along main street Hastings, Maggie could see a small crowd gathered on the sidewalk outside. Butterflies floated around in her stomach. She wasn't sure why she was nervous, because she was more than ready. It was more the excitement and anticipation than anything else.

Simon pulled the car into a parking place in front of State Grounds. Bill and Cindy were standing on the sidewalk outside, as was Leslie, Sarah's bridesmaid. She and Bill had kept in touch after Sarah and Tom's wedding and had been seen together often in recent months. Maggie was happy he had found someone else to turn his attention to.

She and Simon walked hand in hand across the street to join the waiting group of family and friends in front of Maggie's shop.

Among the crowd were the mayor of Hastings, several local business owners, and a reporter and photographer from the local newspaper, The Reminder. Maggie's family was all there, as were Vi, Dave and Uncle Pete.

The mayor shook both Maggie and Simon's hands. "Nice to see you."

"You, too," she replied. "Thank you for doing this."

"Well, you're welcome," the mayor said. "We always support our local businesses."

Maggie spotted Sarah and Tom standing with her parents and excused herself, leaving Simon to talk with the mayor.

"Hey, you guys made it." She greeted Sarah with a hug.

"Of course," Sarah declared. "You think we would miss this?"

"Well, I know you have your hands full these day." She turned to Tom and reached for the little thirteen pound bundle of joy in his arms. "Let me hold my niece."

Tom handed her the baby.

Maggie touched her soft baby cheeks. "Hey, baby girl." She leaned in and kissed the top of her head, inhaling the sweet baby scent. "Claire, you are the most beautiful baby in the world."

Tom nodded. "We think so."

Claire pushed the pacifier out of her mouth accidentally and began to cry. Maggie grabbed it and popped it back into her mouth.

"Is this a vision of things to come?" Simon asked as he approached them.

Tom and Sarah laughed.

Maggie grinned up at him. She couldn't imagine being any happier than she already was, but the thought of a baby with Simon made her feel all warm inside.

"The mayor wants to get started."

Maggie sighed and reluctantly handed the baby back to Tom.

Simon took her hand, and she followed him back to where the mayor stood.

"Good morning, everybody," the mayor began. "Thank you for coming out today to welcome a new, yet familiar, business to our town."

Maggie squeezed Simon's hand and, as had become her habit, she rubbed her thumb against the gold wedding band on his left ring finger.

"Simon's uncle, Pete Walker, would like to say a few words," the mayor announced.

Maggie looked at Simon. "Did you know he was going to say something?"

He shrugged. "No."

Pete stepped up next to the mayor. "Thank you, mayor. If someone had told me a few years ago that we would all be standing here together now, I never would have believed it. Maggie and Simon's relationship didn't exactly get off to the smoothest start, but I have to officially take credit for everything."

Maggie smiled. It was true. Had it not been for Pete asking for Simon's help with the studio, things might have been very different.

"My nephew Simon has been such a joy in my life and a big part of my business for a long time now. And I need to thank him. For being there for me and for helping to bring my studio back to life after all these years. Thank you, Simon."

Simon walked over and hugged his uncle.

Pete held a hand out to Maggie. She joined them and took his hand as he continued.

"Now, Simon lived many years as a bachelor and, honestly, I worried about him. I couldn't let him end up like me, of course."

That brought a little laughter to the audience.

"But Maggie was different. I knew it from the moment Simon told me this feisty girl had turned him down."

Maggie and Simon both laughed at that.

"And I was right. There was something special between them. I have had the privilege of watching them work together on several occasions now, and they are the perfect team. They're photography styles are quite different, but they compliment each other in every way. So when they came to me last fall and told me they were not only joining their lives, but also combining their wedding photography businesses into one, I knew it was the right decision. And I was also a little relieved Simon wasn't going to end up a bachelor forever."

The laughter erupted again.

Simon put his arm around Pete and squeezed.

"So congratulations to Simon and Maggie. I'm very happy for you, and I wish you much success."

Maggie glanced up at the new sign above the shop that read, "Walker Wedding Photography". It felt good to finally have their last name up there, to say goodbye to her old business name and all its baggage.

The mayor approached the red ribbon that was fastened across the front of the shop. He held out the scissors. "Here you go, Maggie."

Maggie glanced over at Simon and smiled. "I love you."

He squeezed her hand. "And I love you."

They took the handle of the scissors and cut through the ribbon, officially marking the grand opening of their new studio and the beginning of a very bright future. Together.

She looked at her family and friends surrounding them, then at the man she adored standing next to her.

The big picture. I see it now.

Acknowledgments

*F*irst and foremost, I thank God above all else for giving me this creative mind and guiding my writing journey. Also for the life He has given me and all I've experienced to get to this point. There would be no book if not for that.

I must thank my wonderful Launch Team ladies. These girls helped in so many ways—from reading the manuscript and giving feedback to sharing on social media to knocking down the doors of local coffee shops and libraries and passing out bookmarks—to get the word out about this sweet little book, and I couldn't be more grateful to them. Special thanks to Anita, Blanche, Carrie, Dianne, Heather, Jen, Kay, Kim, Laura and Nicole.

Thanks to my beautiful cousin, Sarah, who so graciously allowed me to use one of her wedding photos for the cover of my book.

To the many amazing couples I worked with during my wedding photography days. Your beautiful weddings inspired me and helped bring the weddings in this book to life.

Huge thanks to Heidi for being the "Sarah" to my "Maggie". I couldn't have gotten through all those years of shooting weddings without you.

To my Mom, for being my biggest fan. She let me ramble on and on about the book and was just as giddy as I was about it.

My family has been so supportive, letting me read portions of the book to them, giving me such great suggestions. They are quick to tell me when something I've written doesn't sound right. If not for their suggestions, Simon would have fist bumped Michael Bublé instead of giving him a bro hug. We had a good laugh over that one.

This is the book that started it all for me and it never would have happened without the support and love of my husband, Jacob, who introduced me to NaNoWriMo and let me type away in front of my computer for a month to finish that first draft. Over the years, as I doubted myself and so often procrastinated, he encouraged me to finish. I'm so glad I finally listened to him.

And to you, my readers. Thank you from the bottom of my heart.

Krista

An excerpt from *Hello, Forever*
(the sequel to Goodbye, Magnolia)

Prologue

It all happened so fast.

Maggie had never actually seen someone get punched or witnessed up close the cracking sound knuckles make on impact. She stood on the sidewalk in front of her apartment in complete and utter shock. How had it come to this?

Simon shook off the obvious pain in his hand as he spun around and marched toward his car.

"Simon!" Maggie cried.

He kept moving.

"Simon Walker, you better stop walking right now!"

His steps slowed.

"Please don't leave like this."

He turned to look at her. His hands were still balled up in fists, his jaw was set from gritting his teeth, and the hurt in his eyes was unmistakable.

"Please don't leave me."

His shoulders sank, and a look of sheer sadness swept over his face.

Her heart raced as he took one step toward her then turned toward his car again. "You promised we would always talk to each other," she cried desperately.

He glanced back over his shoulder at her. "I can't right now."

Maggie watched Simon climb into his car and drive away. She couldn't breathe. She thought nothing could be more painful than the day Ben broke her heart, but she was wrong. It hurt so badly that she couldn't even cry. She felt paralyzed, in complete shock. Had she lost him? Was it really over?

Maggie whipped around to face Ben, who was holding his cheek, in pain. "This is all your fault."

"My fault? *He* punched *me*."

"Why did you have to come here, Ben? After all this time, why couldn't you just let me be?"

He opened his mouth to speak, but she didn't give him a chance.

"I was finally happy. Do you know how long it took me to feel that way again? And you ruined it. You ruined everything."

Manufactured by Amazon.ca
Bolton, ON

27051017R00127